DR. MICHAEL FRIEDRICHS

Eidolon's Wager

Eidolon's Wager

For information about this title or to order other books and/or electronic media, contact the publisher:
Zala Press, A Division of New Leaves Clinic
1500 N.W. Bethany Blvd., Suite 200, Beaverton, OR 97006
www.NewLeavesClinic.com

ISBN: 978-0-9831386-0-0

Printed in the United States of America

FIRST EDITION

Interior Design by 1106 Design
Jacket Design by Matt Haley
Cover Model is Priya Chaison

To my wife, Cynthia, who taught me
that love shouldn't hurt.

"I would give you some violets,
but they withered all when my father died."
SHAKESPEARE: *HAMLET*

Chapter

1

I COULD LIKE THIS TOWN, Victor thought, resting his chin on the steering wheel. The crisp September air brought a smile to his face despite the farmer's market congestion. When traffic moved again, a rich canopy of elm trees cast shadows onto the windshield. In the park, equestrian statues towered over flowerbeds bursting with color. And in the shifting sunlight, Victor saw children bobble to the strains of a bluegrass band.

As he pulled to the curb, Victor heard a bicycle clatter against the pavement. Fearing the worst, he sprang from his car. He found no rider—just an odd, black bike, decorated with skulls and armored with furniture tacks. Happy not to meet its owner, Victor cautiously laid the pedaled deathtrap against the curb. He drew blood and, dappling his jeans with a crimson finger, dug for change to feed the parking meter.

The Sentient Bean café was dark and jazzy, save for a lit confections cabinet. Victor bent to inspect the scones, only to see a face behind the glass. Both men popped up, startled.

The baristo spoke with an English accent, his fingers dancing at the ends of lacy cuffs. "Good day, my Lord! How might I be of assistance?"

"I'm feeling like something dark," Victor said, pointing to the chocolate torte with blackberries.

"You've come to the right man. Might I interest you in some tea? We have a wonderful mint spice from our colonies." The man blinked at Victor with a pair of eyes like crab apples. Victor suspected that the stranger had a thyroid condition.

"Um, no … thanks. I'll have bottled water," Victor said. He gestured toward the refrigerator. "Give me the *Evian*."

"No you don't! The torte needs an *astringent*," the man insisted with his index finger raised.

"An astringent?"

"*Evian* spelled backward is '*naïve*,' which you'd have to be to BUY water in a town noted for its abundance of drinking fountains. Trust me. You want coffee with that."

Victor laughed, his interest piqued. "I've only been in Portland for a week. I don't even have an umbrella yet."

"Good heavens! You're not from California, are you?"

"Tucson. Arjona University."

"Did you like it?"

"School is a great place to hide from life. Arizona, however, sucks."

"Oh?"

"Where to begin … my apartment had more *la cucaracha* than a taco stand, it's hotter than Africa, and the sapless plant life is suited to make a crown for Christ. What else do you want to know?"

Rubin's eyes became slits. "So you're a poet?"

Victor chuckled. "No. A refugee. Tell me about those drinking fountains."

"In the same year of the Titanic's sinking, God bless their souls, a socialite grew tired of seeing drunk people everywhere. He donated drinking fountains to the city. Benson Bubblers, they're called … and they're on every corner."

"You've convinced me. Make it a medium soy latte."

"Large is only a dollar more, and comes with free advice."

Victor sharpened his gaze. "So be it."

"As you wish. There are things you need to know in order to survive in Portland."

"Do tell."

"The Columbia River Gorge is not an eating contest. Also, locals don't carry umbrellas. Umbrellas are for pussies and people from Vancouver."

"Good to know." Victor felt that the human tongue was designed for the Queen's English. But coming from the baristo's mouth, it sounded like a speech impediment. "Pardon for asking, but are you from New Zealand?"

The man dropped the brogue like a rag doll. "Nah. Los Angeles."

"So why do you…?"

"I'm enriching your café experience. Aesthetics are everything." The baristo lodged a filter into the espresso maker. The luxurious aroma of fresh organic coffee permeated the air.

Victor looked at the man's nametag. "I appreciate your sartorial taste … um, Rubin. But aesthetics are *far* from being everything. In fact they're quite meaningless."

"Oh? So where do you find meaning?"

Victor could scarcely hear his own words over the shrieking of steam. In the spirit of the game he brought his thumb to his chest. "From titles. Schooling. As an educated person I have a responsibility to mankind, and it gives me a sense of purpose."

Rubin slid the coffee across the bar. "Wormwood."

"What's wormwood?" Victor asked, blowing the steam from his coffee. He pondered Rubin's pencil-thin Errol Flynn moustache, concluding that it must have been drawn with eyeliner.

The English accent reappeared, this time from London's East end. "A her-bal ingredient in *absinthe*. It's bitter, and has 'alucinigenic effects—not that different, mind you, from your delusions about responsibilities!"

Victor crossed his arms. "Alright then, so what gives YOUR life meaning?"

A line of customers had formed, but Rubin just stared at the ceiling. Pulling on his weird facial hair, he finally answered, "We find meaning through *love*."

"Ah! You're a Victorian," Victor said. "You're the kind of guy who wishes you had a dead wife, so that you could pine away at the foot of her sarcophagus."

"Precisely."

An elderly woman was now waiting at the register. Ignoring her, Victor added, "Love is biology, Rubin. It's nothing but pheromones talking."

The silver-haired woman finally set her purse on the counter. "I'd like a bear claw and a low fat Americano, if you boys don't mind!" Then she turned to Victor with a face like a prune. "And you, young man, sound like my dead husband."

Rubin jumped to Victor's defense. "Excuse me, madam. You have miserable taste in coffee, so your opinion is worthless to us."

"WELL! In all my days I've NEVER…" She snapped her purse shut and gathered her things to leave.

"I'm not surprised. You smell like soap. And if you want drip coffee you should go to a gas station!"

Victor stepped back so that she could storm off. The bell above the door jingled. The next customer, a kid with a skateboard, asked if Rubin knew how to do chai tea.

"What does this look like, a fucking martial arts studio?"

Again, the bell jingled as the customer left.

"You sure do have a way with people," Victor said, smiling. "Where were we?"

"We were talking about love." Wiping down the espresso machine, Rubin's eyes glazed over. As if in a dream, he mumbled, "It isn't biological. Love is magical."

"That's bull crap."

"Bull crap is fertilizer, and my grass is greener because of it. Having betrothed my heart to the most amazing woman alive, I'm a living monument to my ideals."

"As I am to mine," Victor insisted, his chin thrust upward. He enjoyed the fact that Rubin overspent his budget with twenty dollar words like 'betrothed.'

"So … man of titles and responsibilities, what do you do for a living?" Rubin asked.

There it was. The most tedious question people ask a psychologist, mostly because it leads to a SECOND, even more tedious question. Hating himself for not being prepared, Victor answered stupidly, "I'm a psychologist, like Dr. Phil."

"You're a doctor?"

"A Ph.D. I'm in Portland to do my residency."

"So you're not a *real* doctor."

Victor grit his teeth. "More like a witch doctor, Rubin. Our tradition is older than theirs."

"So doc, have you figured me out yet?"

There it was. The *second* most tedious question. Victor was certain that no one ever asked a dentist on the street to comment on their halitosis.

"I haven't collected enough data, Rubin, but you have some kind of mental illness to be sure."

"Nice going doc. I left the Navy on a medical discharge. They said I was a 'clinical narcissist.'"

Victor closed his eyes. "I'm sorry. That was reckless of me."

"Think nothing of it. Truth is I was *too good* to be in the Navy. There's no such thing as mental illness. People used to have person-alities—like Captain Ahab, Heathcliff, or Scrooge. Now all we have are personality disorders."

Victor scratched his head. "And depression."

"Thank God! There'd be no art without depression."

"There'd be no *drug industry* without depression. One in ten people are on Prozac." Victor lifted his coffee.

"YOU'RE NOT ACTUALLY GOING TO DRINK THAT ARE YOU?" Rubin jabbed at Victor with his finger.

"That's the point of a coffee shop, isn't it?" Victor asked, frozen, with the cup on his lip.

"Coffee goes bad after ten minutes. The oil that gives it flavor escapes on the steam." Rubin packed the funnel with fresh grounds. "Let me make you another."

For the first time in recent memory Victor found himself enjoying the company of another human being. He reached across the counter. "My name's Victor. We really should be friends."

Rubin shook his hand. "Pleased to meet you, Victor. Although I must warn you. Like a river, a person's life can be either harnessed or left to meander to the ocean," he said, making waves with his fingers. "As such, I'm a trickle in an abandoned lot. Drawn by the gravitas of life, my powers drain into the earth, to places that don't oft see the light of day. It's a burden, really."

"So I've gathered."

"What's your burden? Daddy not approve of you?"

Victor pinched his chin. "Well done, sir, although that could be said about most graduate students. The cross I bare is a never resting mind."

"Oh?"

"Let's just say that I carry a certain memory like a pallbearer. The skeleton in that closet is so heavy that at times I can barely breathe…"

"There are things in my closet as well. Go on."

"…I've spent my days wondering why life can't be a movie with a tidy ending and an editing room heaped with poorly acted moments. In pursuit of this question I've commended my soul to gods of psychology."

Rubin rose to his toes. "How utterly Steampunk! You're a moralist! You simply must meet my friends!" Rubin wrote his telephone number on a java jacket. "Beware … we're goth as fuck!"

"You'll have to tell me what that means later. I just remembered the parking meter," Victor said. He looked at his watch and headed for the door. "Thanks for the organic coffee. You'll be hearing from me!"

"By the way, that was *my* bike you ran over," Rubin shouted.

"Of course it was!"

"Don't sweat it," Rubin said, bragging like a father at a softball game. "I park him there just to annoy people!"

Victor paused to register the comment. He sipped his coffee and pushed the door. Stepping into the sunlight he realized that his smile, too, was organic.

Chapter
2

THE LEAVES IN WASHINGTON PARK wore cinnamon hues before Victor found time to relax. With his briefcase full of work each night, he'd been too busy to pursue friendships. So when his boss, Dr. Lindsey, pushed for a neglected staff 'meet and greet,' he jumped at the chance. The doctors all agreed to meet at a metrosexual martini bar in the gentrified Pearl District.

Dr. Hammon was nice enough, Victor thought, with a brain addled by gin and vermouth. With long gray hair and a kind smile, she was the kind of hard working person Plato called the ideal citizen. Sadly, her vanilla persona was not mere subterfuge. She actually became *more* boring with alcohol.

Dr. Clifton, the senior resident, had a handlebar *molest*-ache and an endless stream of glad-handy fluff at the tip of his tongue. Victor pictured him running for office—bemoaning morality's decline while snorting cocaine off a hooker's ass. There was little hope that they would become friends.

So Victor got home early, and had all but resigned himself to a lonely year when he found Rubin's telephone number in the junk drawer. He dialed, only to reach an answering machine. With strains of *Vivaldi* playing in the background, Rubin's effeminate voice announced that he was indisposed. Two days later, Victor threw down his keys to find his answering machine blinking.

"Hello Victor, this is Rubin. So glad you called. You must come to the coffee shop at once! I have the most dreadful news. It seems my time on earth is short." There was a pause. Then Rubin quoted King Lear, *"As flies to wanton boys are we to the gods. They kill us for their sport."*

It was eleven o'clock, too late to return the call, so Victor resolved to telephone Rubin on the following day. As he reached for the phone at work, cheese sandwich in hand, Dr. Lindsey called and demanded a meeting "at once."

As Victor would come to learn, when it comes to the treatment of crazy people, it takes one to know one. In this regard, Dr. Lindsey was overqualified. A moldering wreck of a woman with boyish black-dyed hair, at forty-nine she'd abandoned her family for a graduate career. Since that time she'd taken on more water than the Bismarck.

Bland on the inside, she curtained her windows with sky-blue eye shadow. Like many women her age, she wore bright scarves to create the appearance of a chin, and sported red fingernails that—like a frog in the Amazon—warned predators that she was disagreeable to the stomach. These efforts neither hid her age, nor rendered her pleasing to the senses.

She had no sense of humor, a map of which was recorded in the lines around her mouth, and was possessed of a work ethic that could motivate the Amish to unionize. She had reached a place in life where she had no choice but to keep working, for to admit now that she was replaceable would surely have killed her.

So she labored like a dwarf beneath her mountain of paper work, finding reprieve in cigarettes and booze. She expected employees to share her insanity and, like a tenured professor who can't teach, was lauded by Pioneer Community Hospital as an example for all to follow.

Despite these idiosyncrasies, Victor found things to like. She was predictable, and like a bird that picks meat from a crocodile's teeth, their relationship was mutually exploitive. Victor was meeting his licensing requirement, and she was milking him for fifty billable hours of work each week. Best of all, because most of what she knew was outdated, she kept their meetings mercifully succinct.

Victor knocked twice.

"Come," she crowed.

"You wanted to see me?"

Dr. Lindsey was perched behind her desk as if it were a dead deer. Without speaking, she began to leaf through papers. Victor gathered a pile of medical charts from a chair and placed them on the floor.

"First of all, thanks for skipping lunch," she said at last. "If it's okay I'd like to squeeze in our supervision at noon on Wednesdays. I've been working with Dr. Hammon on a new contract with Whispering Pines Nursing Home, and I'll need to be in Beaverton."

"Wednesdays work just fine. I can eat trail mix."

"So. You seem comfortable with your new job. People are saying good things about you," she added.

"They are?"

Victor examined a quilted jack-o'-lantern on her desk. It was the kind of thing that renders good luck at BINGO.

She continued, "I can't remember the last time I had a resident who created such a stir with the ladies."

Victor straightened his tie. That kind of talk made him uncomfortable, especially from her.

"The ladies?" he asked.

"Oh, you know, the nurses. People keep asking if you're single, but I never know what to tell them."

Victor wondered if it was SHE who wanted to know. His saliva dried up.

"So what should I tell them?" she pressed.

Victor noticed a picture of her daughter tipped over on the desk. Somehow the battleaxe had trapped someone's sperm a hundred years ago. His face soured. "Um, you can tell them I'm single."

She nodded, then frowned the way she always frowned when she didn't know what else to do with her face.

Victor ran his fingers through his hair. She had called this meeting for *some* reason, and it likely had nothing to do with his love life.

"So, did you find an apartment?" she asked, still rummaging through her papers.

"Yes, I did, about two weeks ago. Things have been kinda hectic but I'm finally settling in. I found a great place on Southwest Park Avenue. It has a cobblestone courtyard, a pool on the roof, and its right across the park from a great coffee shop."

"Isn't that expensive?" she interrupted, in her usual sarcastic tone.

"Yeah, but aesthetics are everything." Victor smiled.

"I think you're getting ripped off. It's crazy what they charge downtown."

Just as a dog barks and a bird tweets, the woman has to say something negative, Victor thought.

"Anyway, I noticed that your case load has been too light. How many patients do you have?"

Victor opened his briefcase. Cradling a black notebook with brass embellishments, he scanned his notes. The list didn't look 'light' to him. "I have twenty clients. No, make that nineteen. Do you remember Mr. Bellioti, that co-dependent guy?"

"No."

"His wife lit his truck on fire, remember?"

Dr. Lindsey looked at the ceiling, which is apparently where she kept her memories. "Oh yeah, they were getting a divorce, right?"

"Yeah. I got a call from him saying they were back together. He was all happy and stuff."

"You're disappointed?" Dr. Lindsey put her arms behind her head. The chair creaked like a cemetery gate.

Victor smelled perfume and brimstone. "Yeah, I think she tricked him somehow."

"Victor, when I was a girl, my Romanian mother taught me an old Gypsy curse…"

With her pig eyes and leathery face, Victor pictured her sticking razor blades inside apples.

"…she used to say 'I curse you to be yourself.' You have to let people make their own mistakes."

"I know. It's just that…"

"Any time you find yourself fantasizing about what a patient should do you're making a mistake."

"I know. We're mental midwives. We help people give birth to their own ideas."

"That's right! I bet your patient's wife caught on that he was getting ready to leave her."

"That's possible."

"A family is a mobile in a baby crib. Tip one side and the whole thing shifts." She dangled her claws in demonstration. "Anything else?"

"No. Not really." There were plenty of things worth discussing, but Victor was done with it.

"Let's talk scheduling. With the holidays looming you should plan on having more in-patient cases from the locked psychiatric unit."

"Looming?"

"Fortunately, because of the suicides, we get more business in the fall. It's the overcast weather, I suppose."

Victor failed to suppress his distaste for her.

"Victor, if a person is still alive, they're undecided. Our job is to talk 'em out of it." She paused for a moment of deep reflection. "You can't watch someone twenty-four hours a day."

She was hiding something, perhaps that one in six psychologists have a patient commit suicide. Like a good therapist, Victor finished the conversation so that she would not have to.

"I'm clear."

She exploited the opening. "I was looking at your resume and you have no experience with teenagers."

"That's true. I've worked mostly with adults and brain damaged people," Victor said.

"Well, this should be good because a lot of the critical care patients are kids. Have you ever worked with Borderline persons before?"

"Does my mother count?"

Dr. Lindsey rolled her eyes, knowing that Victor could not possibly be *that* transparent. "I'll give you the first case that comes across my desk," she snapped, closing her notebook.

"Thanks!"

Suddenly, there came a knock at the door. Dr. Lindsey made a show of being overworked and underpaid, her head flopping with exasperation.

"I'm sorry to interrupt you, Debra," came a voice from the hall. "It's Randy. Have you gone to lunch yet?"

Licking her paws, Dr. Lindsey fixed her hair. "Oh, Dr. Schramek! Please come in. I want you to meet our new resident, Dr. Albrecht."

Victor rose from his chair as a short man with cream hedgerows entered the office. He was well dressed with a silk bowtie and a physician's coat. His stethoscope dangled as he shook Victor's hand.

"Victor, this is Dr. Schramek. He's the chief pathologist at Pioneer. He has a Ph.D., *and* an M.D.," she bragged.

M.D.? Minor Deity, Victor thought to himself. "It's my pleasure," he said aloud.

Dr. Lindsey spoke. "We've been thinking about expanding our training program. We want you to sit in with the neurology residents when they do brain cuttings."

"Brain cuttings?" Victor swallowed hard. He felt the polished physician's steely eyes.

"Yes, we examine different brains in varied states of pathology. I dissect them and describe things as we go. I'll cut it up like a ham." Dr. Schramek made a knife with his right hand as he minced the left.

Victor felt excitement and mortification. "I'd love to see that!"

"Good then. What are you doing at two o'clock tomorrow?"

"Um, Thursday? Charting probably. It's the end of the month so I'll be doing productivity reports."

"I want you to come and see me at the morgue. We'll glove you and throw you into the ring."

This was precisely the kind of thing that Victor, the ambulance chaser, lived for. It had been a while since he'd stoked his beloved sense of dread. He held a calendar on his leg while his pen trembled. "That would be October 31st, Halloween, right?"

"Yep," Dr. Schramek said, rubbing his stomach. "So Debra, I'm thinking sushi."

As the two made their lunch arrangements, Victor gathered his things. He felt like a third wheel. When a pause finally arose, Victor spoke. "I have a question."

"Ask away," said Dr. Schramek.

"If you're a pathologist, why do you wear a stethoscope?"

"It's my job to make certain that we don't dissect living people by accident."

Victor looked at him with eyes like saucers.

"Can't you take a joke, lad? Pathology isn't the only thing I do here."

Victor let out a sigh of relief.

By five o'clock, Victor found himself performing a learning disability assessment on an unemployed obese woman with six children. She'd arrived half-an-hour late, sipping a chocolate shake and complaining of fibromyalgia. Watching her stare at a pile of blocks, all Victor could think about was how her brain might look if cut up like a ham.

When at last the shadows grew long on the Ross Island Bridge, Victor hurried home. It was a short stroll across wet leaves to Rubin's coffee shop, and he took pleasure in the smells of fall.

The door jingled, interrupting the cool ambiance of the café. Portland State University students lounged about with glowing laptops and shoeless feet hiked into their chairs. Victor was about to speak when interrupted by the scream of foaming milk. Rubin acknowledged him, nodding while spooning a dollop of cream into a mug.

"Medium caramel no fat latte with whipped cream! Medium chai with biscotti!" he shouted. Then he stepped behind the register.

"Welcome to *The Sentient Bean*, sir. Would you like to try our new *Pumpkin Spice Frothaccino?*"

"Sure. Sounds great," Victor answered. Then he changed his mind. He knew more about bulimia than he'd learned in school. "Wait. On second thought make it a soy latte."

Rubin winked. "The usual, then?"

"Yeah," Victor said, retrieving his wallet. Rubin assumed his post behind the espresso machine, and Victor could see that he was limping.

"I must confess. I had no idea how complicated making coffee could be," Victor said, making small talk.

"Oh, yeah. It depends on the bean, the grind, the pressure of the tamp, duration of the draw..."

"Sounds like rocket science. Say, Rubin. I got your message last night…" *Rubin shows no hint of sadness. He must be a very strong man to bare such news courageously,* Victor thought.

Rubin set Victor's coffee on the bar and shouted, "Large soy latte!" Then, in a whisper added, "I can't talk. See that raver chick over there?"

Victor spied a hard-bodied, freckled girl with low cut jeans busy rearranging packs of sugar. She wore a serious look, which seemed silly considering that she had a lollypop in her mouth.

"That's my boss, Jenn," Rubin said.

"What makes her a 'raver chick'?"

"Duh! She wears bell-bottoms in the twenty-first century."

"That means she's a raver?"

"She sucks blow pops and never knows the names of her favorite songs. Look at her shoes, you can tell from how they're worn down. Plus, her name's Jenn for fuck sake."

"Wow." Victor felt like he was in the presence of a Zen master.

"You're talking to a fucking Jedi when it comes to women. I'm a member of Oprah's book club."

Victor marveled that Rubin could be so lively despite having a terminal illness. When Jenn finally went to the stockroom Victor seized the opportunity.

Hoping to soften the discussion, he blurted, "You're not gonna believe what I get to do tomorrow!"

"What?" Rubin asked, wiping the espresso machine.

"I'm gonna dissect a brain."

"On Halloween?" Rubin bellowed, causing patrons to look up from their books. "That's awesome! Could you snag me a chunk?"

"Of brain? Of course not!" Victor narrowed his eyes. "You seem to be doing well, considering your illness."

"It's my own dumb fault. That's what I get for not getting enough fresh air," Rubin said, nonchalantly. Then he grumbled, as a customer walked into the café. "This would be the perfect job if people weren't constantly asking for coffee."

Rubin seemed nonplussed by his impending death. Victor mulled this over until the customer left, then asked, "Have you made plans? I mean, how much longer do you have?"

"The doctor told me two weeks at most."

"Two weeks? Holy shit!"

"Yeah, then I won't need to wear this brace anymore."

"Brace?" Victor asked, his head askew.

"I had surgery on my knee. I tore the ligaments."

Victor was taken aback. "You mean you're not dying?"

"Of course I'm dying. So are you."

"But you said on the message that you were dying!" Victor said, incredulously.

"Oh, THAT. Well, I just read Yalom's book on existentialism. He says that the inevitability of death makes life richer."

"Go on."

"We're all terminal, if you think about it."

"That's true, Rubin, 'cause when you get off work tonight I'm gonna kill you."

Rubin glanced over Victor's shoulder. "Jenn's pissed again. She's cleaning tables, which is supposed to be my job. Can you meet me at my house tonight? I get off work at eight. You can kill me then."

"I don't know your address."

Rubin hurriedly wrote it down. "If I'm not there my *fiancé* will let you in."

"Okay," Victor exhaled.

"Be sure you come, 'cause there's gonna be a slaughter tonight," Rubin whispered. "I can't tell you more right now. Just be there."

Chapter

3

$\mathcal{N}$ORTHWEST PORTLAND WAS A DENSE suburban forest. Ideal
for trick-or-treating, its craftsman-style homes had lattice
porches, rose-lined sidewalks and short, leaf-covered driveways.
Victor rolled down the window to read the house numbers. Nearly
all had pumpkins on their peeling steps, carved and flickering in the
encroaching dark. The last house on the street boasted a scarecrow
in an obscene position. Two pumpkins had been wedged into a pair
of overalls to create the effect of a straw man exposing his ass. Victor
confirmed the address.

Climbing the steps, he noticed the blue light of a television. He
was about to knock when a shadow moved behind the curtains. Above
the yapping of a dog, he heard several locks turn. The door cracked
open to reveal a svelte woman. She was wearing an oversized t-shirt,
and from what he could tell, precious little else. Crossing her tanned
legs, she self-consciously pulled the shirt toward her knees.

"Can I help you?" she asked.

"Hi. Does Rubin live here?"

"Yeah."

"Great. I'm a friend of his. He told me to meet him here after work."

The woman craned her neck to look at the clock. "He won't be home for another twenty minutes." Then she fell silent, staring with a tilted head. "Do I know you?"

"I can't imagine you would. I just moved here from Tucson." Then he automatically said the same dumb thing as always. "It's really hot there."

She didn't seem keen on discussing the weather, so Victor slung a thumb over his shoulder. "I can wait in my car."

The woman shook her head. "I'm sorry. I was napping. Why don't you wait on the porch? That rocking chair *kicks serious ass*. It's made of entombed wood."

A tiny black dog with ears like Anubis looked up at Victor from behind her ankle.

"What's your friend's name?"

"Oh, this is Cerberus." Pressing her knees together, she picked up the dog and kissed the valley between its ears. "She's all bark and no bite."

The woman had brilliant brown eyes, the irises ringed with yellow. The effect was startling.

"Adorable..." Victor mumbled, sleepily.

She blushed.

Victor petted the animal, and Cerberus licked his hand.

"She likes you," the woman proclaimed. "She hates Rubin with a passion, but that could be 'cause she's female."

Victor collected his thoughts. This incredible woman was surely Rubin's fiancé. He felt a tinge of guilt, knowing that thoughts are the seeds of actions. "I'm gonna sit down in that 'kick ass' rocking chair and wait for Rubin, if it's all the same. I don't wanna bother you."

"You're no bother," she insisted. "Do you mind if I come out for a cigarette?"

"Are you kidding?" he asked against his better judgment. "I'd love it."

Eventually she returned with a pack of *Virginia Slims,* a bottle of wine and a pair of long-necked glasses. She curled up in a high-backed wicker chair and placed a cigarette on her lip. Victor smelled peaches.

"Do you smoke?" she asked.

"Yes, of course..." He didn't really smoke, which made him wonder why he lied. To Victor, smoking was a psychological indicator of how much abuse a person is willing to tolerate. "May I have one?"

The woman's hair fell into her eyes as she set the glasses on the uneven slat floor. Balancing too many things, she placed the lighter on the porch rail. "Care for some Brazilian Pinot?"

"Brazilian?"

"The Portuguese have been making wine in Sao Paulo since the fifteen hundreds." She paused, then added, "I grew up in South America. We have a summer home in Venezuela, near Caracas."

She held the bottle between her feet and without breaking eye-contact drove the corkscrew in. She had a ring on the middle toe and her manicured nails shined like raspberries. Victor was glad that she was doing all the talking.

"We stopped using the house after my parents divorced. It's quite nice—a gorgeous villa overlooking the Caribbean."

Victor smirked over his preternatural insight. Indeed, she was emotionally scarred. "That sucks ... about your parents, I mean. Care to talk about it?"

"There isn't much to tell. It happened a long time ago."

The cork popped.

"Do you know what? I don't think I've introduced myself, and here I am asking about your life. My name is Victor."

"My name is Angelita."

"Tell me more, Angelita."

She looked down and smiled. "Like many a hurricane I was born on the gulf coast. Raised in a family of physicians unable to heal themselves, I never wanted but for those things important to the soul. My dad was a Cuban psychiatrist in political exile, and when I was very young we moved to Santa Cruz…"

Victor listened intently. Angelita seemed frazzled and vulnerable.

"I have a knight-in-shining-armor complex," Victor said at last, swirling his wine before burying his nose in the cherry bouquet. "That's why I became a psychologist. There's something gratifying about walking hand-in-hand with a stranger to a place they've never been."

"I can imagine," Angelita sighed, breathing smoke out of her nostrils. "So you have a Ph.D.?"

"Yeah, I work at Pioneer."

"It must be fun to give advice all day," Angelita said, swallowing a mouth full of wine.

"We don't give advice. I listen to stories, and then I tell them the truth as I know it." The cigarette in his hand dropped a column of ash, which he brushed from his pants.

"I imagine a person would feel comfortable telling you anything," Angelita cooed, blinking slowly.

"Perhaps the wine is feeding your imagination."

"Hardly. I think it's romantic what you do—a man who helps people. A hero."

"Not so glamorous. I help people clean out their refrigerators. Every bad thing that ever happened to you is like a pot of leftovers. The more pots you stick in there, the dimmer it gets." Victor strained to reach the bottle.

She pushed it toward him with her foot, training her sultry eyes. "Insults *are* a lot like stinky leftovers, especially when it's your mom's cooking."

"Words have power. That's why the Egyptians drew circles around them. They can help or hurt."

"Sounds like you have eccentric interests."

"Interests or issues?" Victor joked. "I have a lot of *those*."

"That's certainly Rubin's opinion. He says only fucked-up people study psychology."

"I'm not surprised. Rubin had a bad experience with a Navy shrink."

"Yeah. But what's your opinion? You of all people would know." Pinching the filter, she inhaled the rest of her cigarette.

"I think it's true to a point. Most grad students are obsessive and self-absorbed; chasing grades, titles and degrees. I promise you that a sane person would never go to school for twenty-two years."

Angelita snickered. "I can believe that."

"I'd also argue that it's a good thing to *want* to know yourself. Remember the Oracle of Delphi?"

"Of course, 'know thyself,' but I don't think it would be helpful to tell my problems to a doctor. When I get depressed I know it's just anger without enthusiasm." She crushed her cigarette in a beer can.

"*Of course* you need other people," Victor argued. "We're myopic when it comes to our own faults. Like an iceberg, what you can't see will sink you."

"True enough."

"Take relationships. You have to admit that the one common denominator of all of your disastrous affairs is the fact that YOU were there."

"Ouch," Angelita vocalized, her interest piqued. She tapped the pack of cigarettes against her palm, pulled another, and laid it upon her lip. Her eyes darted about the porch—her lighter was missing.

"Therapy works because you can't see your own face. The lighter is on the ledge behind you."

"*Touché*," she admitted. "It seems I'm lost without you, Victor. But maybe that's what you want."

"I should be so fortunate…"

An uncomfortable silence fell on both of them.

"So. What do *you* do for a living?" Victor asked.

"I work in a nursing home."

Victor coughed. "Doing what?"

"Activities and recreation. I'm putting myself through art school."

"Art? No kidding. I think aesthetics are everything!"

"You and Rubin have a lot in common, then. I love men who love art!"

Victor was feeling lecherous. He finished his wine then traced the curve of the glass. "To the Romans, Bacchus was both the god of inspiration and chaos. It's best that I stop while inspired."

"Yes it is," Angelita agreed, looking past Victor and into the yard. "Rubin's back."

"Speak of the devil and who doth appear?" Rubin exclaimed, hobbling up the steps. Tapping his cane, he bowed with such zeal that he nearly lost balance. "*Old Scratch* at your service!"

Victor was privately relieved. "So what happened to your leg, anyway?"

With the aplomb of a sideshow barker he explained, "'Tis an embarrassing tale that I should rather not impart, but with adequate remuneration I would happily bend your ear."

Angelita rolled her eyes.

"Yes, my love. You know it well." Rubin walked behind the wicker chair and caressed her neck.

"I need a back rub! P-l-e-a-s-e!" she moaned.

"With delight, my precious," Rubin answered, his silly British accent reappearing. "Victor, would you be so kind as to trade seats?"

With surfeit emotionality, Rubin expounded on his injured leg, saying, "I went to the hospital with knee pain and they asked all these stupid questions like, 'are you a night watchman?' and crap like that..."

As he spoke, Victor fiddled with Rubin's cane. The handle, a brass rabbit head, came loose. He unscrewed it as Rubin spun his yarn.

"...the doctor can't figure it out, which isn't surprising since they haven't cured anything since polio. Then it dawns on me that when I play my online vampire game I wedge my feet against the back of the computer desk. I tore my ligaments! Can you believe it?"

Angelita spoke into her lap, "He's on the Internet for hours." Her head hung flaccidly, jostled by Rubin's skilled massage.

"Let it not be said that video games are harmless," Rubin said, finishing.

"You wouldn't catch me saying that," Victor reported as the handle came off the cane. A glass cylinder of rum slipped into his hand.

Rubin smiled. "You've discovered how I get around the high cost of drinks—which brings me to my next point. You're cordially invited to a Halloween party at the goth club. It's called *Demonic Submission*."

"Gee, that's not pretentious," Victor said incisively. He felt jealous that Rubin was touching Angelita, and found it difficult to be agreeable.

"It's a bondage and submission event put on by the Portland sex industry." Rubin gave a sinister laugh. "The last time I was there I saw a guy with a horse whip in his ass. The cops almost shut it down."

"Sounds enchanting. Angelita, are you going?"

"Nah, I got spanked enough as a kid."

Victor felt dispirited, and this sudden convergence of emotions puzzled him. Until now his hope with Rubin had been to eviscerate the dark underbelly of Portland. Now there was a curious change in focus.

"Just wait till you see the VIP room," Rubin said, enticingly. He drove his thumbs between Angelita's shoulder blades. "Serious shit goes on up there—orgies, threesomes, anal…"

Angelita winced. "Rubin, you're gross!"

Victor remembered that he had not been with a woman in months. He stood up, adjusting his pants. "Can I use the restroom?"

"I don't know. You need my help?" Rubin teased. "It's at the top of the stairs."

Victor excused himself, taking due note of Rubin's influence on the home's ramshackle décor. A barbarian sword hung on the wall, and across the fireplace an army of hand-painted lead miniatures besieged a toy castle. The room was a virtual comic shop with stacks of graphic novels blocking the stairwell. When Victor finally ascended to the throne room, he found it in no better condition.

Honestly fascinated by the bohemian lifestyle of his friends, Victor explored the upstairs. Rubin's bedroom featured a meticulously made bed with Jacobean posts. A row of leather-bound tomes graced the shelves. Perfectly aligned as if a ruler had been used, the stack was held in place by a stone gargoyle. A copy of *Wuthering Heights* with a satin ribbon lay on the nightstand.

The closet door at the end of the hall was off its hinges, revealing an assortment of black garments which hung like bats. Another room was lit by a string of Christmas lights. Inside, a futon with a lump of sheets served as a bed for someone, and the smell of peaches revealed it to be Angelita's chamber.

Irresistibly curious, Victor spied a pair of brocade panties on the floor. Paintings leaned against the walls, mostly of gaunt faces. Some were framed, others were not. A small easel in the corner was covered with cloth, but it was too dark to tell what was being realized there. Backing from the room he stepped on Cerberus' tail…

"Yipe!"

A bundle of sheets on the futon stirred. They opened like a rose, revealing a black haired woman. She was naked but for the comforter which she clutched to her bosom.

"I'm sorry. I didn't know you were here," Victor said backing toward the door, apologizing profusely. He found his way back to the front porch.

"I met your roommate," he confessed once there.

"Which one?" Angelita asked. "There's a whole menagerie here."

Victor was disheveled. "I don't know. I must admit, I was looking at your artwork. Please accept my apology, but it really was exquisite."

"No biggy. Everyone goes in my room. Persephone sleeps there when her allergies act up," Angelita said, nonplussed. "Fuckin' Rubin's in there all the time."

Thus Victor discovered that, for a young person trying to make it in Portland, renting a house in large groups was the only way. They cared for each other, provided warmth and a sense of support. As annoying as it surely must be, Victor was envious of what they shared. They were a family—a tribe.

Rubin snatched the wine bottle. "We're on rat patrol tonight," he blurted between swallows.

"That's disgusting! I don't know why you guys do that." Angelita made a sour face, which is hard for women like her to do. "I'm calling PETA on you dirt bags."

"Women bring life into the world, but men bring justice," Rubin said ostentatiously, placing one hand upon his heart. "I love you Angelita, but what you don't understand, being a product of Catholic school, is that there's a time when killing is the right thing to do."

"We're gonna kill people?" Victor's mouth was agape.

Angelita became caustic. "No. Rubin and his gang of rabble-rousers torture innocent mice and call it virtue."

"Notice, Victor, yon damsel did not complain when my gifted hands plied her neck."

"I noticed," he said, wondering how such different people could be in a relationship.

Rubin continued. "Unlike us, Angelita has two X chromosomes. This leaves her perpetually imbalanced, and prone to extremist views."

"I'm not *that* liberal," she protested, tucking both knees beneath her shirt to fend off the chill.

"My love, you have never so much as flown in an airplane that had a right wing," Rubin retorted.

"Well you suffer from testosterone poisoning!" she countered.

"Any more Sapphic clichés? Perhaps, a woman needs a man like a fish needs a bicycle?"

"I've always been a lesbian trapped in a man's body," Victor joked, hoping to end the dispute.

Angelita made a show of pouting. "I like you more than Rubin."

They all laughed, but Victor knew that sometimes people laugh out of fear.

Rubin warned, "She's not your type. She marches in every Earth Day parade. If there's a protest at Pioneer Square, and there are plenty, you'll find her in her *Birkenstocks*."

"Rubin's just mad that I'm a vegetarian." Angelita looked at her housemate, who was sticking his tongue out. "He cooks the most extraordinary gourmet meals, but I pass because they have meat in them."

Rubin hissed, "Do you know how hard it was to get bull testicles? And all you ate was the mushrooms polonaise."

"I'm vegetarian also," Victor revealed. "Years ago I made a pact with God to give up meat for serenity. God hasn't kept his part of the bargain."

"Veg-e-tarian is Indian for 'bad hunter,'" Rubin said, crossing his arms.

Victor was not prepared for what happened next. Angelita rose from her chair, crossed the porch, and sat on his lap.

She was hard bodied, yet soft in all the right places. Victor smelled her skin as he roped his arm around her waist. There was no other place to put his hand, except to let it dangle on her thigh. This was turning out to be a pretty good night.

"Now it's two against one, Rubin," Angelita teased.

"Hitler was a vegetarian, so you two are in good company."

Angelita stayed on Victor's knee longer than she had to, and even placed her hand upon his. Whatever she said from that point he didn't hear. Intoxicated by desire, he hugged her more tightly.

"Hitler was a deutschbag. Speaking of fascism," Angelita asked, "when is your pack of gothtards coming over? Red owes me for that half-pint of vodka he stole."

"Excuse me, my dear. Never utter that vile word 'rat' in the same sentence as my esteemed associates. We're meeting at Pioneer Square tonight."

"Then you can remind him," Angelita said, finally rising from Victor's lap. Again, he had to conceal his enthusiasm. Surely she'd felt it.

The two exchanged mundane words about overdue rent before Rubin excused himself to change clothes. Once again, Victor and Angelita stood on the porch alone. Victor wanted to say something cool but came up empty handed. Finally, she smiled.

"Hermoso desconocido," she said, moving a tendril of hair from his eye. "Dios permita nos encontremos otra ves."

"I'm sorry. I don't speak Spanish."

"You don't have to. We share the language of compassion. Let's do lunch sometime."

"That would be great."

Angelita smiled and climbed the stairs. Victor watched her legs as she ascended, then stumbled into the yard to get some air. He was all but ready to call it quits for the night when Rubin emerged wearing combat boots and a ridiculous camouflage uniform. He also carried a tool box, a fishing rod and a baseball bat.

"You ready to go?"

"It's time you explained what we're doing tonight," Victor said, briskly.

Rubin flashed a sinister grin and handed him a baseball bat.

Chapter

4

ICTOR DROVE RUBIN TO HIS APARTMENT. From there, they ambled through the lush forest arcade in the dark. Like all organisms, the city of Portland was not without parasites. But as Rubin explained, its alleys were free of any hazard that couldn't be resolved with a stern voice. As they walked, Victor listened without judgment, which he'd learned was the key to experiencing anything.

"A cockroach can live nine days without its head," Rubin blurted.

Victor looked him over. "What is it with you?"

"What do you mean?" Rubin asked, stopping at a crosswalk. As he punched the chrome button, a flock of bicycles rushed past like sparrows. "Fucking Zoobombers."

"I mean all those funny things you say—About platypus venom, or butterflies having taste buds on their feet. Why do you do that?"

"Maybe I want you to like me."

In the heart of Portland, Pioneer Courthouse Square was a blend of urban stadium and public park. Rising from the rubble of a demolished hotel, it was conceived to bring the citizens together, possessing both artistic form and function. Roman columns surrounded the square—some toppled to create tables for playing chess. As such, it was dubbed 'Portland's Living Room.'

Three million visitors annually enjoyed a host of cultural affairs in its embrace, including the bombastic Rose Festival, when eight magnificent Clydesdale horses were stabled there. But if the red bricked plaza was the city's living room, hundreds of its adolescents were still lying on the couch. And by the time Rubin and Victor reached the square, teenaged beggars had imposed themselves three times.

"Who are these tireless pests?" Victor wondered.

Walking down the steps into the square, Rubin answered, "Why don't you ask them yourself?"

There, in a circle of lamp light, a band of hoodlums stood, smoking cigarettes and spitting on the ground.

Rubin suddenly became earnest. "Listen. All street urchins have nicknames. If you're gonna be accepted, you'll need to have one as well."

"A nickname? Like what?"

"I'll think of something," Rubin promised.

"What's yours?"

"They call me 'Creep.'"

"I should have no problem remembering that."

Victor observed that the vagrants carried similar equipment, except that their baseball bats were customized barbarian implements. Leather had been wound around their clubs, the ends of which bristled with sharpened nails.

Rubin made introductions. "Hey guys. I want you to meet my friend. His name is, uh-h-h, 'Shrink.'"

Shrink!?! Victor was visibly appalled.

"Shrink, I'd like you to meet 'Red.'"

Victor extended his hand, but Red didn't reciprocate. Instead, he tossed his head so that a tassel of dirty hair swept across his face—like a horse tail shooing away a fly. Victor surmised that this kid was probably not on good terms with his parents. Indeed, Red's body language shouted 'I don't need you,' and from the grimy look of his clothing he had rejected help for some time.

Next, Rubin presented a short, pudgy kid in a *Batman* t-shirt and trench coat. "Shrink, this is 'Snake.' Snake, this is Shrink."

"Nice to meet you Shrink," Victor said, self-consciously jabbing his hands into his pockets like the other kids.

"No! *You're* Shrink, and *he's* Snake," said Creep, pointing in turn.

"Oh yeah, heh, heh," Victor laughed uncomfortably. The problem for Victor was that Snake didn't look anything like a snake—unless you consider one of those *National Geographic* photos of an anaconda swallowing a goat.

The last guy was a newcomer in an army jacket who introduced himself as 'Jim.' This, of course, made Victor wonder why he couldn't just have kept his own name in the first place. By appearances, Jim was either brand new to the scene or returned to a loving home when he was not on the grunge-kid clock.

One corner of the square featured a circular arrangement of steps forming a miniature coliseum. Loud speakers were mounted in an overhead trellis in the hope that classical music would drive the teenagers away. Being Portland and all, this simply made it a swank place to hang out and drink Starbucks.

Red cleared his throat and, with a flick of his hand, brushed the mop out of his eyes. Within moments the hair fell again, but with the resolve of a sheepdog he proceeded. "Alright, men. Listen up! Our city is under attack! Protecting it doesn't fall upon the squeamish. Rats spread disease and fuck up the city!" Red shouted, pointing at the group with his cudgel.

"Here here!" Rubin yelled, glancing at Victor.

"Rats carry rabies, plague, leptospirosis, trichinosis, tuburculosis and a shitload of other osis-s-s!" Red preached, pacing. "They terrorize those of us who live on the street."

"Mickey must die!" Snake wheezed with his fist in the air. For a moment it seemed that the kid was going to suffocate until he took a hit from his inhaler.

"Our mission objective for tonight, should you accept it, is to attack Mickey at his base of operation!"

Victor raised his hand. "We're going to Berlin?"

Rubin laughed by himself.

In a momentous tone Red answered, "It's worse than that, gentlemen. Tonight we're going to O'Bryant Square."

"No way!" gasped Snake. He leaned over and whispered to Victor, "That's Berlin!"

Red continued. "As you combat veterans know, O'Bryant Square is within enemy lines. So watch your ankles!"

Victor felt a surge of panic as Red drew an imaginary map with the tip of his bat.

"This is the bus stop on Washington Street where I conducted reconnaissance earlier today. Mickey's dug fortified trenches in the bushes here, here, and here," Red said, his bat tapping the ground.

"We'll take the high ground next to the fountain. But don't let your guard down. There are thousands of fuckin' rat holes in every planter, flowerbox and hedgerow. It's like the surface of the goddamn moon!"

Rubin looked again at Victor's face, savoring the expression. He put his hand on Victor's shoulder. "I remember my first time, too."

"Stay alert..." Red paused for effect then added, "...Mickey's been known to attack." He pulled up his pant leg. A pink lesion above his ankle was clear, even in the dim light.

"Holy shit!" Victor muttered. "Are you guys serious?"

"Serious as a heart attack, so stick with your wingman and there'll be no casualties. Keep your eyes peeled for fresh droppings and smudge marks."

Jim raised his hand. "What the fuck are smudge marks?"

"Someone please fill in the rookie," Red answered with his knuckles on his hips.

Rubin spoke from the corner of his mouth. "Smudge marks are from the oil on their fur. If you see 'em on a curb you know it's a supply route."

Red concluded the meeting the way it began, with drama. "If there are no further questions, this combat mission briefing is over. Gentlemen, man your bats, and may The Force of the Pussy be with you!"

Upon Red's benediction, everyone meowed while striking a claw-like gesture. They gathered their gear and began a solemn procession up Washington Street. As they narrowed the distance Victor sidled up to Jim.

"Excuse me for asking. You don't look like these other guys. How did you end up on the street?"

Jim produced a spliff from behind his ear. "Some of us are runaways, but that's not true for everyone. People want to put us all in the same box."

"So what box are you in?"

Jim sparked the joint. Speaking in measured breaths he answered, "I just rejected my rich-ass dad and his Lake Oswego bullshit. I don't want his money, and I don't want to live in his cold, condescending world."

"What do you mean?" Victor asked, nearly tripping over a fire hydrant.

"You gotta watch where you're going in life. My dad's generation got within a cunt hair's width of actually changing the world, but they sold their souls to the almighty dollar at the last minute. When they seized power they gave it all up for a blow job. Most of us are on the street cuz we're sick of the lies."

"Is it true that people panhandle for drugs?"

"Of course. You'd have to be an idiot to be punked for change in Portland. This city has more programs than New York. We don't use the shelters 'cause they have the same rules we left at home. Plus, that's where the dangerous people are."

"Like who?"

"They tell you, 'as long as you're under our roof you'll go to vocational training,' and other kinds of shit aimed at turning you into a replacement part."

"I know what you mean," Victor replied, dishonestly. In truth he found Jim's politics intellectually lazy.

"In order for capitalism to work they need workers who are willing to follow orders. That's why I dropped out. Why should I become a money grubbing prick like my dad when I can make thirty-five bucks an hour *spanging?*"

Victor secretly felt that people who beg for money are the biggest grubbers of all, but had lived long enough to know that idealism and hypocrisy often share the same bed. He must have looked confused.

"Spare changing," Jim clarified. "People out here are bored, so they do drugs. There's no big important, fuck-all philosophical reason. A ton of these kids are mainlining, shebanging, selling their bodies. There's a lot of heroin addicts, and it costs money."

"You can support a heroin addiction by spanging?"

"I can get a gram of heroin for seventy-five bucks easy. At that rate, it's twenty bucks to get high. Do you want some?"

Victor threw up his hands. "God no! I think it's wrong to take drugs."

"Hey, it's cool. I knew you were a dork the minute I met you." Having said that, Jim pressed his fingers to his lips and sucked the last spark out of the joint.

As public areas go, O'Bryant Park was like a sock that had fallen behind the dryer. Dimly lit, dirty and out of the way, it was hardly missed. Sandwiched between gargantuan buildings on Stark and Washington Streets it was a hangout for those unfortunate souls destined to a life of vagrancy. These were not the tragically hip, World Trade Organization hating martyrs of global commerce like Jim.

Rather, they were the tragically mentally ill common to bigger cities. Because they tended to camp there, well-meaning charity groups often passed out food and blankets. But plenty of crumbs ended up in the bushes, which pleased the rats. So much so, that they held a banquet each night in honor of human kindness.

It was into this maelstrom that Red, the great rat slaying general, inserted his troops. As they entered the park he warned, "That's not gravel you're walking on. A single rat can shit twenty thousand droppings a year."

Once Red and Rubin found a suitable spot, they shed their fishing gear.

Snake leaned toward Victor. "I'm thinking of making a full-length coat out of rat pelts. Wouldn't that be AWESOME?"

"Your mother was frightened by an elephant, wasn't she?" Victor asked.

"I don't think so, why?"

Victor changed the subject. "Why is everyone whispering like it's a golf tournament?"

"You and me are gonna be the *batters*," Snake shared. "Red and Creep are the *anglers*."

Victor looked to find Rubin fiddling with a tiny hook. "What's the bait?"

"Bacon fat. It stays on the hook."

Victor shook his head. "All I can say is thank God you're on our side."

With all players in position, Red picked up his rod and cast the lure. The reel buzzed as the line unwound into the shadows. The bait landed forty feet away, lost beneath a burned out street lamp. Victor began to wonder aloud how they selected targets, but was promptly shushed.

Rubin scanned the war zone with binoculars before slowly winding the reel. Moments later he cast his line on a different trajectory. Again the bacon, drawn by the weight of a lead sinker, sailed through the air. It struck the rear wall of the bus stop before falling into the dirt with a thud.

"This is it. Now all we have to do is sit quietly and wait," Snake instructed soberly.

"Come on you rat bastard," Rubin hissed. "Come to daddy."

Victor stood as quietly as he could, gripping the bat. He trained his eyes on the bushes but saw nothing. Growing tired he muttered to Snake, "Is this normal?"

"What, rat fishing?"

"No! I know THIS isn't normal, I mean the wait. Does it normally take this long?"

"Yeah. Mickey's bluffing. He usually sends out a scout before he feeds openly."

Victor rolled his eyes. Then, to his regret, he saw something scamper. It was a breezy October night, and every leaf that wistfully turned looked like a rat. However, something was hanging palpably in the air—the feeling that they were being watched.

That's when Mickey made his move.

"There he is!" Rubin whispered, his voice shattering the silence.

It was an incredibly large Norway rat—its body a good nine inches long. It appeared on the edge of the platform upon which they were standing, far closer than Victor preferred.

Some people are afraid of public speaking, others shun closed-in spaces, but for Victor it was rats. He hated them worse than funerals. Until now, following Rubin was like chasing a tornado—the lightning was always on the horizon. But suddenly Victor found himself in the very eye of the storm.

For an instant the rat contemplated Victor's boots. It thrust its nose over the concrete edge and gnashed its yellow teeth before deciding against it. Instead, the loathsome creature continued along the step, erratically starting and stopping, sniffing here and there.

Red, in a moment of strategic genius or sheer luck, had placed the group downwind; so the rat was unable to detect them, even at close range. *This was fortuitous,* Victor thought, *since Snake's unwashed hair smells like bacon.*

Then, like a filthy gray tennis ball, the rat darted away and into the courtyard—its plump, shaggy hind quarters bouncing as it went.

"He's heading for the bait," Rubin quietly intoned.

Victor nervously jabbed Snake in the arm. "What does the batter do?"

"Just follow my lead."

"Great." Victor looked downrange, wondering how he got himself into this mess. He never wanted to be so open-minded that his brain could fall out, yet here he was on a rat hunting safari. His knees wobbled, and he could hear blood in his eardrums. For a moment he saw nothing, a fact in which he took great comfort.

But his relief was short lived, for his eyes apprehended not one, but three large rats slinking along the edge of the concrete wall. He squeezed his eyes closed in the hope that it was a dreadful illusion forged of shadow play—but when he opened his eyes there were *four* of them; all scampering toward the bait. They vanished into the dead zone behind the far-flung bushes. The group waited, frozen in complete, all encompassing silence.

"Dudes, this is fucked up," Jim proclaimed, his voice faltering.

With the farcical absurdity of the situation unveiled, the group became unglued. Rubin bit his lip but could not keep from snickering. At once his eyes shone like pools as he chortled through his nose. Humor under stress is contagious, and Victor fell victim as well. Soon Snake was cracking up, and Rubin burst into a full belly laugh.

For Red, the hunt was personal. "Sisters of mercy, will you assholes shut the fuck up!?!"

A brief moment of forced reverence followed as the reprimanded troops struggled to regain composure. This precarious tension lasted until Snake loudly farted. Oblivious to the rats and their keen sense of hearing, the entire group broke into a cacophony of explosive laughter that even Red could not suppress.

Rubin waved his hand before his nose. "Something crawled in you and died, dude." He stepped away from his gear, leaving it on the pavement.

Red threw down his fishing pole. "Mustard gas!"

Snake just stood there looking proud, flapping his trench coat like a bat as he dispersed the vapors.

Nobody was paying attention to the fishing rods, for if they had, they would have noticed that Rubin's line was as tight as piano wire. Whatever took the bait was strong enough to pull the entire rod down the steps. Victor was first to hear the sound. He glanced over as the fishing gear clattered into the courtyard.

"RATS!" he shouted.

The scene collapsed into chaos. Everyone began yelling. Rubin leapt onto his fishing pole and yanked it to set the hook. The fiberglass rod bent into an arc, as if opposing a swordfish.

Jim ran to the safety of a distant street light, while Snake tripped over the tackle box, sanding his face on the concrete.

Red joined Rubin. "I think it's stuck on the bushes!"

"No it's not," Rubin argued. "When I give it slack he takes it up!"

"Keep it upright or the line will snap!" Red hollered. He leapt behind Rubin and repositioned the rod so it was vertical. The fiberglass pole formed a question mark under the strain.

"Keep it like this," Red shouted as he wedged the cork handle into Rubin's belt.

"Dude-yo," Rubin protested, "there is no way a rat is doing this. BATTERS! WHERE ARE YOU? GET YOUR ASSES OVER THERE!"

Victor followed Snake to where the line angled into the bushes. Snake's chin was a bloody mess, and like a battle wounded berserker he waved his truncheon in circles. Victor ducked twice before deciding to get as far away from Snake as possible. He sprinted to the rear of the park where it was safe.

Snake now stood on the front line by himself, panting into the uncharted hedgerow. He stared back at Red, blood now dripping from his chin. "What do you want me to do?"

"Reach in there and un-snag him!"

Snake started to reach into the brush but stopped short. In a rare moment of common sense, he turned on his commander. "You un-snag him, asshole. I'm not getting rabies!"

"FINE!" Red said, snatching the fishing pole from Rubin. He gave the rod one swift tug.

The five men present were never able to agree on what happened next. According to Victor's account, something snapped in the bushes—a twig, probably. As the rod straightened, a humongous brown rat catapulted from the shrubbery. Like a flying squirrel, it sailed over Snake's head. The furry cannon ball also cleared Red at an altitude of ten feet, soared to the back of the park, and struck Victor squarely in the mouth.

Despite the impact, the tortured rodent somehow survived. It scrambled behind Victor, the fishing line crossing his feet. As it scampered around him, the line drew the animal into an ever smaller arc. The rat became frantic, hissing as it raced laps around him. With mere inches of fishing line to spare, a screeching Victor leapt onto a park bench, dislodging the hook. This sudden motion flung the rodent across the pavement where it finally came to rest, motionless.

One could have heard a pin drop. Victor stepped down from the bench, his hands shaking so badly that he could barely hold the bat.

"CRUSH HIM!" Red shouted.

"HIT HIM!" came another voice.

Victor crept toward the rat's body, its whiskers trembling in the dim light. He raised the bat.

Just then the rat opened its eyes and righted itself.

"HOLY SHIT, that's the motherfucker that bit me!" Red gasped, pointing. "What are you waiting for!?!"

But the bat slipped from Victor's grip, hitting the ground with a metallic clang.

"I can't," he breathed, the words falling from his mouth as the beleaguered rodent regained its senses. It shook its head and scampering into the night. "I'm sorry guys. I just can't do this."

THE DANK BASEMENT where Jake lived reeked of cat poop and cigarette smoke. A water stain circled the cinderblock wall—a keepsake from a hurricane that decimated Port Lavaca, Texas forty years before. In the same way that a believer can find the Virgin Mary in the mildew of a gravestone, Jake bragged that the devil leered at him from a cold, damp spot under the stairs.

Long ago, he'd arranged stacks of dad's Playboy magazines to make a nook for his mattress. To call it a rat's nest would be correct. Six years after his parents died in a fiery car crash, the house was a means by which Jake secured control over his friends. The rest of the abode was shared by the members of his rock band, their black t-shirted groupies and an assortment of runaway teens who wandered off the street.

It had been an hour since Violet took the pill. Upstairs in the living room, guitar riffs rattled the floorboards, upsetting the dust. Violet turned her head and sneezed. "That's the craziest shit ever!" she squealed, pulling on her nose. "I want to do it again!"

"Do what?"

"Sneeze!"

"You can't just sneeze on command," Jake growled, stupidly massaging her breast like a radio dial.

Violet's eyes rolled as the MDMA flooded her brain with serotonin. Jake could see the muscles in her jaw.

"You're grinding, Vile." Foolishly, he poked her tongue as her teeth came together.

"Owwwch!"

"I need something in my mouth Jake."

"You feral bitch!" Rolling onto her, he reached for a steel ammunition box. It tipped over loudly as he dug for a pacifier. He popped it into her mouth and buried his face in her neck. Lifting her raven hair, he chewed her earlobe.

"What are you gonna do to me?" she asked demurely, knowing that Jake liked his girls to act young.

"I'm gonna fuck you into the rug," he snarled, looking at her with eyes brooding and intense. He collected her hands and held them over her head.

"Don't cum inside, okay? I can't get more birth control 'till Friday."

"*Trust me,* Vile."

Her resistance fell to his hard body. She parted her legs, controlled by a force that was not her own. As he pushed into her, she raised her hips. Like two snakes under a board, they writhed and tangled as the XTC lifted Violet to pleasures exceeding nature. Jake did his thing, not knowing that making love is more like eating a pomegranate than plunging a toilet. She looked at him, hoping to see his soul, but it wasn't there. So she closed her eyes.

Those who have abandoned their dreams discourage the dreams of others, she heard, from somewhere deep in sleep. She felt her feet growing cold, her jaw aching, and her stomach churning from hunger. With no segue, Violet found herself back in her body. Looking at the red numbers on the alarm clock, she discovered that hours had passed! Rolling to her side, she patted the torn comforter. Jake was not there.

With her tongue ring tapping her teeth she called out, "Jake? Baby, are you here?"

The house was eerily quiet—the music upstairs now softer, more ambient. From the smell of stale beer that seeped through the floorboards, it was clear that the CD release party for *Jalapeno Piss* was over.

Rising to her feet, Violet placed a palm on her forehead. She felt thick and stupid. Hoping to stave off post-XTC depression she kicked her clothing in search of a clove cigarette. Stepping into her panties, she felt a warm trickle.

She finished dressing, then cursed. "Jake you dick. I need this shit like a barium enema."

Finding the stairs in the dark, she located her backpack and cigarettes. The lighter flashed like a comet. Slinging a backpack over her shoulder, she surveyed their love nest with renewed clarity.

"What am I doing here?"

Violet climbed the stairs. The living room looked like someone had detonated a hand grenade. It was a common scene—gangly bodies scattered about on Saturday morning with their boots still on, using crumpled jackets as pillows.

She tiptoed toward Eddie, the drummer for *Jalapeno Piss*. Sighing, she kicked him in the ribs.

No response.

"Eddie! Wake up."

Still no response.

She kicked him again. "Get up, asshole!"

"Huh … What? Violet. What the fuck time is it?"

"It's almost daylight. Have you seen Jake?"

"No sweetie. I'm sorry. He's not with you?"

"If he was I wouldn't ask, dipshit."

Violet was never naïve, but her relationship with Jake was earning her an advanced degree in disappointment. It's never a good thing to misplace your boyfriend.

Eddie looked at her backpack. "You leaving? Do you want me to tell Jake?"

"Yeah, tell him I promised my mom I'd drive her to work."

Eddie was still drunk. He sat up, bracing himself on sinewy arms, squinting like a garden mole. "You okay to drive?"

"Yes. And I love you for asking," Violet said, dropping on one knee to hug him. He kissed her cheek.

Violet dug into her backpack for her keys. She wasn't about to look for Jake if he didn't care enough to spend the night with her.

Screw him.

Besides, Violet knew that if she found him now it would end up in a huge fight. She prided herself on being a world class bitch, and even had a bumper sticker to that effect.

She opened the front door and was about to step onto the porch when she froze. Looking over her shoulder, her gaze drifted up the stairs.

Jakes shirt!

She closed the door. Climbing the stairs stealthily, she dislodged a gold-gilded portrait of Jake's family. She caught it before it fell and dusted it with her sleeve. More than anything she wished for a family like the one portrayed there. She hung the picture and ascended to the landing.

Jakes pants!

Violet peered into the bathroom. People were known to sleep in the tub. She tiptoed past the broken toilet, perpetually tinkling water. She ripped the shower curtain aside.

No Jake there.

Violet walked to Jake's boyhood room. There, she found the other band members—contorted in the dwarfish bunk bed. In the center of the floor, a girl she'd met the night before had fashioned a nest from a beanbag chair.

But where was her young blonde friend?

The master bedroom at the end of the hall had belonged to Jake's parents before they died. He once told her that he couldn't sleep there because it freaked him out. But it had a king sized bed, and if the walls could talk, they'd make a whore blush.

Her hand trembled as she reached for the door. She didn't want to believe what her stomach was telling her. So she took a deep breath, wiped her palms and turned the knob. There, in the center of the bed, she found Jake and the blonde girl.

Violet barged into the room. Shifting to an altered state, her emotions ran amok. She snatched a bottle of black nail polish from the dresser and emptied it onto Jake's head.

Jake sat up, befuddled. He rubbed his head, then looked at his blackened palms. "What the fuck?"

"What the FUCK is right! What were you doing with her, Jake?"

"NOTHING! We were spooning. Why are you all buttsore?"

"Don't pee on my leg and tell me it's raining. You were FORKING, not spooning!"

By now the house had been alerted that Mount Violet had erupted. Knowing the drill, they fled Pompeii with their belongings, the screen door slamming repeatedly.

"I was drunk. I must have thought she was you!" Jake reasoned.

"Let me make it clear for you, since you're obviously a fuck-tard—she's blonde, I'm brunette," she added, pointing at the girl, then herself.

"Honest, Vile. It was dark when I came up here!"

"Oh please! If you were any dumber you'd have to be watered. You left me in the basement, remember?"

"Vile, I was drunk. I mean, look at her!" He motioned toward the girl, whose facial expression changed from fear to bemusement. "Would I tap that?"

Violet snatched the girl's skirt from the floor and threw it into her face. "You've got three seconds before I rip off your head and piss down your throat!"

"You're not *that* goth," the blonde answered, slinking past Violet and lunging for the staircase.

"I fart dead bats, CHILF!" Violet took off her shoe and hurled it down the hallway, shattering the portrait. She turned her fiery gaze to Jake in time to see him stuffing a condom under the pillow.

"Drunk, huh? Pouring alcohol down an asshole doesn't make it stink less!" she said, slapping his face.

Violet didn't count on him hitting her back, yet he struck her so violently that she saw a flash of lightning. Recoiling, she fell across the dresser. Her head hit the mirror, which exploded into a storm of glass. Violet tried to stand, reeling, but collapsed instead.

Jake stood over her. "You're gonna hit me? You're not my mom!"

Trembling, Violet crawled to the foot of the bed.

"I'm sorry. I just want you to be happy with me, that's all."

Jake shook his fist, and she cringed like a salted snail. No longer on the defensive, Jake harnessed the situation.

"A piece of ass is not worth my peace of mind! You're nothing to me!"

"What?" As she cried, she rolled onto her side, drawing her elbows and knees together. Her mascara bled, changing her face to that of a ghost—fitting, for she was dying inside.

"Fuck off, Violet. You drive me crazy with your bullshit," he hissed, lording over her. "Don't you ever talk to me like that again in front of *my* friends!"

Violet found herself beyond reason, suddenly groveling at his feet, with her mop of ebony hair falling over his boots. "I'm sorry Jake. Just tell me what you need from me."

"You need to be cool with me dating other people. I need to have an open relationship."

"N-o-o-o! Please no! I'd rather die."

"I can arrange that." Jake looked away. "I've done it before."

"Are you talking about your parents?"

"I'm telling you that you should get an AIDS test!"

"What does that mean? You're scaring me!" Violet said, her jaw hanging. "Why are you being so mean?"

"Look at you Violet. You can't even take care of yourself. You're all chubby and shit," he said coldly, stepping over her. Then his voice echoed from the staircase, "You acted like a freak as usual!"

Violet bowed her head and sobbed. Lurching, her hand fell into the broken glass on the carpet. Closing her fingers around a razor sharp dagger, she decided in that moment to kill herself or die trying.

She pulled back the sleeve of her blouse and drew the glass across her forearm. The point grazed the tiny hairs, sounding like tearing silk. Its jagged edge violated her skin, so that droplets of red bubbled to the surface. Hypnotized like a snake before a charmer, she turned her arm over to expose her wrist.

This revealed a thicket of scars, like brambles, where she had tried to leave messages in the past—her biography turned biology. The lashes formed symbols like ancient runes. Just the same, there was a story to be read in their mystical convolutions. She touched the trunk of a sky blue artery. Coursing with blood, it was the tree of her life.

This is really going to bleed, she thought with exhilaration. And as her life poured onto the carpet, Jake could only curse himself. She gathered up the corner of the sheet and wadded it between her teeth.

My last breath on the count of three!

Pushing the point of the glass into her wrist, she braced to yank it upward, sharp and fast. The skin dented then flattened with an audible snap as the glass punctured the membrane. She nearly fainted as the blood welled—a stream of crimson trickling to the palm of her hand. Summoning her courage, she breathed, "One, two…"

Then, tipping the shard she caught her own reflection. It was a face so tragic that she felt her heart swell with sympathy. She pulled the glass out of her wrist and sucked the wound. As the salty blood filled her mouth, the spinning room came back into focus.

Jake's a goddamned vampire! He's broken every mirror in the house, he sleeps in a crypt, and he has no soul but for what he takes from people!

She sat upright.

"Vampires can't hurt you unless you invite them in," she murmured. Tossing the shard, she rose to her feet and limped to the bathroom. Flinching, she bandaged her cut before descending the staircase like royalty. Crossing the porch, she retrieved her silver pentacle necklace from the rail where she'd hung it to gather moon rays. She would need strong magic to leave Jake for good.

"I will not be your Renfield, motherfucker." she announced to no one in particular.

As her car raced across the Texas coast, Violet's sadness gave way to indignation. Growing up in Victoria, a smart girl had no choice but to dabble in the occult—drinking beer and smoking pot in the graveyard on Red River. Yet she was living proof that each of us is an acorn waiting to become an oak tree, even if the ground is rocky and infested with fire ants.

Fuck Texas.

A motel sign marked the entrance to the destitute trailer park on I-59 called Shady Hills. She pulled into the park, swerving to avoid the potholes in a road that couldn't decide if it was paved or not. A flea bitten dog with distended teats ran out, barking ferociously.

The mobile home belonging to Violet's mother was the *Taj Mahal* compared to the others. Before his death, an attempt had been made by Violet's dad to disguise it as a house, perhaps to fool a hungry tornado, but the triangular flower box couldn't have been anything but a trailer hitch.

Violet parked beneath a wheezing air conditioner propped up by two-by-fours. Climbing the broken steps, she stopped to pet a kitten.

"Mom, Violet's home!" her brother shouted from the couch.

Violet walked through a hole in the screen door. "Hey Ferret, what's up?"

"Mom's gonna kick your ass. She had to call in sick."

"I'm sure she was happy to have an excuse."

"What's wrong with your face?" her brother pried.

"Nothing." She replied, turning away.

"Mom! Violet got in a fight!"

"Shut up, Dweeb."

Her mother charged into the room, wearing nothing but pink slippers and a bathrobe. She dismissed her daughter with a wave. "Don't even talk to me, young lady. I'm so mad I can't stand the sight of you."

"When could you *ever*?" Violet wondered aloud. "I look like dad."

The woman lurched, coming nose-to-nose with her daughter. "Don't you start that shit with me! Every time something goes good you screw it up. I should never have let you have the car last night!"

"Why not? It's my car!"

"What?"

"I make the payments!" Violet yelled.

"How dare you hold that over me! You want me to lose my job?"

Violet started to cry.

"Violet got in a fight," Robbie added, from the couch.

"Let me see." Her mother's head swung about like that of an ostrich. "What happened to your face?"

"Nothing."

"Don't tell me it's nothing. I'm your mother!" The woman touched the blackened lump on her daughter's face. She nearly burned Violet with her cigarette.

"DON'T TOUCH ME!" Violet said, recoiling.

"Listen to that mouth. I worry and what do I get? No wonder you fight with Jake. Maybe if you acted more like a lady, he'd be a gentleman."

Violet sighed. "It's over. I broke up with him."

Robbie spun on the couch. "No way! Jake's cool."

"Mind your own business, Ferret," Violet snapped.

"Honey, love is *hard work*. You don't just give up."

"He hit me, Mom. You should have seen how mean he was," she whimpered, her tears flowing again. "He said he gave me AIDS!"

"AIDS?"

"You're not even engaged. No wonder he doesn't respect you."

"Nice, Mom. You would know. If you feel that way about your own baby you should have thrown me in the trash and kept the stork."

"Sometimes it takes everything in me not to hit you myself." Her mother added, "Why don't you cool off and call him tonight. It's always the end of the world when you're twenty."

Violet grew numb.

Her mother put her arm around her daughter's waist. "I wish every day that your father was here. If we'd stuck with him he'd still be alive today."

"He was selling my shit to buy heroin." Violet pulled away. "Besides, what's this WE stuff?"

"You shouldn't ditch boyfriends so easily. You're no prize yourself."

Violet glanced around the rummage sale that passed for a living room. "You always stick up for the guy," she said, plaintively. Even when I caught Charlie perving on me in the shower, you stuck up for him!"

"He's not my boyfriend now, is he?" came her retort. Then she took hold of Violet's hands. "Hey, kiddo. We're friends, remember? We used to look out for each other."

Her brother walked to the refrigerator. "Mom's right. Don't give up on Jake. Mr. Hiltz said it took Lincoln seven tries to be president."

"Thanks for that moment of wisdom, Robbie. Lincoln was assassinated."

"Honey, that's not the point…" Violet's mother stopped, suddenly taken by the bloody bandage on her daughter's wrist. "It would kill grandpa if he knew you were still doing this."

Violet closed her eyes. "Well grandpa's not here is he? He left like all men do."

"Honestly, you'll never get married with those marks on your arms."

Violet realized at that instant, *I can either run away now or die in this shit hole, one-horse town.*

VICTOR DIDN'T SLEEP WELL. His dreams were infested by rats. He wanted to call in sick but, with the phone in his hand, remembered it was brain cutting day. It was also Halloween, which would have looked suspicious. So he took a cold shower and left for *The Sentient Bean*. It would take a strong cup of coffee to get him through the day.

"Top of the mornin' to ya!" Rubin said, like a cereal box leprechaun.

"I'm so tired I could die."

"That's not the proper response," Rubin said indignantly. "In Ireland you're supposed to say, 'and the rest of the day to you, good sir.'"

"Just give me the usual, but make it a quad."

"Not until you say it."

Victor acquiesced. "And the rest of the day to you, good sir. Could you *be* any more annoying?"

"You should know better than to challenge me. Who pissed on your cornflakes, anyway?" Rubin asked, tapping coffee into the filter.

"Nobody. I'm just exhausted." Victor closed his eyes and put his hands on his head. "I think I'm dreaming right now."

"Doubtful. Given the choice, would you dream of me?" Rubin busied himself. "I've always had a superhuman ability to function without sleep."

"Your humility is your most redeeming quality."

"It ain't braggin' if you can do it. By the way, tomorrow is *Demonic Submission*," he added excitedly, "so make sure you get plenty of rest."

"How could I forget? After last night I expect Satan himself to be there."

"As a matter of fact, he will be."

Victor laughed uncomfortably.

"He has a goatee trimmed like a French topiary."

"You're serious?!?"

"Of course. Do you own anything leather?"

"Whatever for?"

Rubin sighed for effect. "Good morning, Herr Doctor. For tomorrow night."

Victor thought hard. "A belt, maybe."

"Good. Wear that."

"Just a belt?" Victor asked, smiling now.

"Oh, and shoes."

"Lovely."

"Hey, I want you to know that we're all deeply moved by the compassion you showed last night. Well, all of us except for Red. He thinks you're a treasonous bastard."

"Captain Ahab will have to take his revenge another day. Just because you *can* do something doesn't mean you must."

Victor picked up his coffee and pumpkin-shaped cookie before wishing Rubin a Happy Halloween. When he finally arrived at the hospital, he discovered that his eight o'clock patient, Jesus Cortez, was not there. Victor chuckled at the note.

Dr. Albrecht, Jesus will not be coming in today. He
had to be in court.

Wishing Jesus luck, Victor went to the restroom to splash cold
water onto his face. Rising from the sink he heard a voice.

"Hey, hey, watcha' doin' buddy?" It was Dr. Clifton.

"Oh I don't know. What are *you* doing?" *Stupid question.* Dr.
Clifton was standing at the urinal.

"I'm physically expressing my opinion of Dr. Lindsey who, inci-
dentally, is looking for you."

"She is?" Victor asked, tearing a towel from the dispenser.

"Yeah. She was slithering around asking where you were."

"That woman is like a human time clock," Victor complained.

"I *wish* she were a time clock. Then I could punch her twice a
day. You remember that assessment I did for the court case? I got it
back this morning. There was so much red ink it looked like she'd
slaughtered a goat. You'd think that by this point we wouldn't be
micromanaged." He flushed the urinal with his foot.

"Well, Sam, until we get licensed we're doctors in title only. This
too shall pass."

"Like a gallstone." Standing in front of the mirror, Dr. Clifton
wet his hands and preened his hair. "If you ask me, I think she needs
the touch of a man."

Victor gave him a weary look. Projection is a neurotic defense in
which a person attributes their own secret desires to others. Freud
would have much to say about men who talk to other men while using
the urinal. "Go easy on the contempt, Sam. It's high in cholesterol."

Later, Victor knocked on Dr. Lindsey's door.

"Come," she said, as if adding the word 'in' was wasteful. There
was no place to sit, as usual. All the chairs were piled with charts.

"I've been rearranging my files," she explained, dryly.

That's what obsessive compulsives do when they're anxious about something, Victor mused.

"I have to finish this so I can visit my sister in Detroit. They think she has cancer."

Bingo! "I'm sorry to hear that. Is she going to be okay?"

"They found a mass on her spinal column. She's to undergo surgery this weekend. It couldn't have happened to a nicer person. It really should have been me."

Christ, what a strange comment! In whose opinion? he wondered. Victor noticed an opened pack of cigarettes.

"Is there anything I can do?"

"No. Dr. Hammon will supervise your work until I get back. That means she's gonna need your help at the nursing home starting Monday. I don't want to lose this contract. We're getting Medicare referrals already so there should be plenty of people for you to see.

"Sounds great," Victor said, listlessly. The last old person he had to spend time with was his third grade piano teacher. Mrs. Sutter was a mean spirited old shoe with halitosis that could peel paint. Five minutes with her and Mozart would have taken up the guitar. Victor didn't like old people.

"You'll be doing neuropsychological testing as well as seeing folks in therapy," Dr. Lindsey said, wiping her brow. She resumed her supervisory timbre. "Now, the REAL reason I called you here is to tell you about your new patient. She's on the locked unit."

"Psychiatry referral?"

"Well, it used to be that we got lots of referrals that way. But that was before Dr. Moran, who thinks he's God's gift to psychiatry."

"So who referred her, then?"

"The head nurse, Asha, has been there for some twenty years. When she thinks a patient can benefit she sends 'em our way."

Dr. Lindsey dug through a stack. "Ah, here she is," she announced, opening the file and scanning the cover sheet. "She refuses to talk to Dr. Moran, and becomes violent whenever he's around." Then she smiled. "I like this girl already..."

Victor suddenly felt uncomfortable. "What's so funny?"

"I hope your vaccinations are up to date. It says here that *she bit him!*"

"Nice," Victor said, pinching the bridge of his nose. He was getting a headache.

"Twenty year-old Caucasian female, a hundred-and-forty pounds. From the ER intake, she's apparently bulimic."

"She makes herself puke?"

"Yeah, can you imagine doing that?" Dr. Lindsey quipped, sticking her finger down her throat in crude parody. "They're still trying to pin down a diagnosis. Rule-outs include Borderline Personality, Schizoaffective Disorder and Bipolar Disorder. Whatever she is, she's a firebrand. Looks like a perfect opportunity for you to grow as a clinician."

"Interesting." That was all Victor could say. From his experience, Borderline Personality Disorder was the most untreatable disorder of all. Those patients were emotionally volatile, prone to infantile rage and self-destructive behaviors. Worst of all, they have an uncanny ability to draw unsuspecting people into their drama.

"Is she psychotic?" he asked.

Dr. Lindsey thumbed through the intake report. "Dr. Moran says she has delusions of being Cleopatra."

Victor raised an eyebrow.

"You know, the Queen of Denial?" she joked, grinning. "She engages in magical thinking. Apparently she thinks she's a witch, and can do magic as well." Dr. Lindsey wiggled her fingers in the air. Then she closed the file and handed it to Victor.

"She's crackers, alright. Is she on meds?"

"Yeah. She's to be started on 5mg of the Zyprexa this week. Wow, it looks like she had a haloperidol lactate injection last night."

"Haldol? They still use that stuff?" Victor asked. "I thought it was a neurotoxin!"

"It works on agitation, and there's plenty of it to get rid of. She's on Level Three Supervision—suicide watch. Apparently she slashed her wrists."

Victor's lips grew taught. "Razor?"

Dr. Lindsey tossed the file at Victor. "The wire in her bra."

"Yikes. Anything else before throwing me to the alligators?"

"Don't turn your back on her, and don't let her get between you and the door."

"I'll be careful," Victor muttered. "Should I see her right now?

Dr. Lindsey smiled. "It doesn't matter. For once you have a captive audience."

Victor excused himself and walked across the parking lot of the decrepit old wing. A 1930s portrait in beige, it should have been demolished years ago. However, in the same way that people say they have 'palmetto bugs' instead of cockroaches, the antiquated structure avoided demolition under the pretense of being a historic site. To Victor, the lobby looked like a New York subway station.

"Excuse me," he asked the receptionist. "Could you tell me how one gets to the psychiatric unit?"

"Follow this wall behind me to the bank of elevators. Go to the second floor and turn left. There's a hallway that leads to the 'B' wing," the bookish woman said, refusing to look up from her needlepoint.

"Thanks," Victor mumbled, remaining at the counter. He drummed his fingers nervously and cleared his throat again. "Also, could you tell me how one arrives at the morgue?"

Nearby, a man with a cane looked at him fearfully. The woman put her needlepoint down and removed her glasses. They dangled from a chain as she trained fierce blue eyes upon him.

"Time," she replied. "All it takes is time."

"You're a funny lady."

"The *pathology lab* is on the third floor. Go left for a bit and you'll see the sign for 'C' wing on your right." Satisfied with herself, she doled out a wee smile.

Following her directions, Victor arrived at last on the locked unit. Procuring the cipher code from a housekeeper, he entered the digits into a keypad. The powerful magnetic lock released and Victor pulled on the heavy door. He was greeted by the pungent odor of urine and a committee of partially clad patients shuffling in tissue slippers. Victor walked along the polished floor until he found the nurse's station. It was a fortress behind which those who claimed good mental health held dominion over those deemed infirm.

Victor stood at the counter, balancing his briefcase on his knee. "I'm Dr. Albrecht. I work for Dr. Lindsey. I'm here to see, um…"

The portly nurse looked at him with freckled cheeks that were rosy despite her African complexion. "You must be the new psych resident!"

Victor nodded. "Yeah, I got here two months ago." He wasn't about to let anyone overlook the hours of excruciating labor he'd already put in.

Asha faced the other nurses. "They just get younger every year." Then she glanced back. "You don't mind me givin' you a hard time, do you honey? At my age I figure the good Lord won't mind."

Victor smiled, also suspecting that the good Lord had better things to do.

"I know who you're here to see. Her name's Violet Cain. Poor thing, that child's upset about something."

"Any info that might be helpful?"

"She came to the ER at ten o'clock last night. Saddest thing you ever saw. Urinalysis found marijuana and alcohol."

"Was a drug panel ordered? Any hallucinogens?"

"Should have been, considerin' how she was carrying on last night." Pursing her lips, she added, "She's not exactly into needles right now."

Victor thumbed through the report. "It says here she cut herself with the wire from her bra."

"She used a razor at first. The paramedics bandaged her up at the party, but when they got here she was bloody again. It's hard to believe, but she nearly pulled the veins out of her arms on the way over."

Victor turned white.

"Fifteen stitches, bless her. She's calmed down a lot now that the pain's hit her. We have her on ten minute checks. She seems pretty stable now."

"That's good."

Asha performed for the other nurses, who had obviously heard the story before. "This morning I moved her to a normal room. I told her, 'You listen to me, child. I'm puttin' my job on the line, so you'd best behave. Don't be killin' yourself and makin' me look bad.'"

"And that worked?"

"Listen, Dr. ... I'm sorry. What's your name again?"

"Victor."

"Victor, that's nice, when you've had as many kids come through as I have had you learn to keep it real."

"Where is she?"

"Room 217," Asha answered, pointing across the counter.

"Thanks. I'll go see her now..."

"Oh, and Victor..." she interrupted.

He was growing impatient. "Yes?"

60

"You might want to take off your tie," she said, pulling on her collar and flopping her tongue about. The other nurses laughed.

"Thanks," Victor answered, fiddling with the knot.

This place is harsh, Victor reminded himself, *designed for people in the most deteriorated condition.* If Violet was less of a threat, she might have been considered for the open unit. There she would attend mandatory psychotherapy groups, earning her way back to freedom by collecting poker chips for good behavior. But her current intentions were too clouded for her to go unmonitored.

Victor dismissed the Red Cross volunteer sitting by the girl's door. Cautiously, he knocked and entered the unnaturally bright room. It was empty except for a poster of Timberline Lodge, a mattress on the floor, blankets and a crescent-shaped bowl containing toiletries. The bathroom door was locked. She couldn't be trusted not to drown in the toilet.

The patient was sitting on the mattress with her back against the wall. Victor saw a Baroque young woman with shoulder-length black hair and pretty features. Her eyes were dark, and Victor surmised she had Mediterranean blood. Both arms were bandaged and her mascara had run from the sobbing. Wearing nothing but a hospital gown, she repositioned her blanket as Victor entered.

"Hi, I'm Dr. Albrecht."

She stared at the floor, trying her best to resemble an angel she once saw in a New Orleans cemetery.

"Can you tell me why you're here?" he queried.

Saying nothing, she turned her face away.

"I understand you tried to kill yourself last night."

Still no response. Victor waited several minutes before sitting down on the floor. He wanted to be at her level. It's important when working with adolescents not to talk down to them—literally or figuratively.

"One of the problems with suicide is that it's a permanent solution to a temporary problem," he said.

Barely breathing, Violet stared at a tiny crack in the floor. Another ten minutes passed, well into that realm where silence becomes deafening. Not knowing what else to do, Victor began telling a story.

"When I was a kid we had a dog named Fritz. He was a dachshund. You know, kind of a sausage with legs. He wasn't jumpy or annoying, but just small and, well, optimistic ... shall we say ... regarding his abilities. He really thought his bark was something."

Victor tapped on the heel of his shoe and watched her for a response. There was none, so he kept talking. "Well, one day a man came from the gas company to check the meters. You know, those burly guys with tool belts who step on the azaleas...?"

Violet stirred. She pulled a tissue from a roll of toilet paper and blew her nose. It took considerable effort as only the tips of her fingers protruded from the bandages. To Victor this meant she had blinked. She'd given up pretending to be catatonic.

"...anyway, something happened to Fritz. We never knew exactly *what*, because I don't speak dog, but his personality changed. For some reason he got timid and depressed." Victor shifted on the cold tile floor. His legs were falling asleep.

"He flinched whenever we pet him. Something happened. Maybe he barked and got kicked by the guy. We didn't know what to do, but it was obvious that he was really sad."

Violet began playing with the tissue. She tore off little strips of paper, dolefully lining them up on the corner of her mattress.

"So, I tried something different. Every day, for an hour, we just sat together. I wanted to show him that he was worth my time, and that I wouldn't hurt him."

Victor stopped there, having made his point. Another twenty minutes passed without a sound. Eventually, Victor got up and dusted off his pants. He felt okay about the session. She didn't attack him, and that was a good start. As he turned to go, Violet's voice rang like a bell.

"So what happened to Fritz?"

Victor stopped with his back toward her. He turned his head and smiled, trying not to gloat.

"What happened to Fritz is not as important as what happened to you." Victor had to play this hand very cautiously. For adolescents, the single greatest point of leverage is found in the question 'who are you to me?'

He quickly added, "I know that you don't know me from Adam, but, believe it or not, I care deeply about you the only way I can at this point—as one human being cares for another. That's about as honest as I can be with you."

Violet played with her toes, refusing to make eye contact. Then she startled Victor, breaking the silence for a second time.

"Why the *fuck* should I tell my secrets to someone who clearly has none of his own?" Violet asked.

Victor stayed on target, thinking fast. In a neutral tone he replied, "Because you've already tried everything else and it hasn't worked."

"How do you know what hasn't worked for me? You haven't lived my life!"

"You're right, Violet. I haven't lived your life. I'm sure you have good strategies, but for most people, killing themselves is not on the list."

The most beloved word in any person's lexicon is their own name. It's a way to build instant rapport and trust. For a split second, Victor panicked at the thought that her name might be Veronica, and that he had blown the session.

"Why run from death?" she asked, with surprising force of presence. "We're all on death row, Doc."

"There's a difference between running from, and running toward death. We all get to take the big dirt nap, you know? What's the rush?"

Victor was afraid that this was beginning to sound too much like an argument. He knew that the more pro-life he became, the more pro-death she would have to counter. Obviously, she was casting him into the role of an argumentative parent. It was incumbent upon Victor not to play the part of her dad.

"We can't keep you here forever," he sighed. "If you persist in wanting to do yourself in, you're as good as dead. We both know that. I just hope that you're here long enough to consider other options." Victor felt good about that comment. The best way to end an argument is not to argue.

Victor was halfway out the door when Violet asked again, "So are you gonna tell me what happened to Fritz or not?"

Victor felt cocky. "If you let me come tomorrow, I'll tell you."

"I have a better idea. Why don't you tell me right now, and *I'll decide* if you ever talk to me again," she said very matter-of-factly.

Checkmate. "You want the truth? Never mind, of course you want the truth. The dog died. He got run over."

"Fucking figures," she said, reclining on her pillow. "Anything you say about God you'd better be able to say over a dead puppy."

"The point is, Violet, that he didn't slit his paws like you did. In fact, he had many more years of life before the end. I just wish the same for you."

Violet broke eye contact.

"Now let's figure out how we can get you off this ward. I'm guessing you wouldn't mind having your own bathroom."

Violet's bravado melted into reticence. "I'll decide when I'm ready to go. I don't trust myself yet, and I sure as Hell don't trust you."

Like his rat, she was on the hook, so Victor backed away. "Good. Take your time. Don't let anyone rush you."

"Don't worry. I won't. And tell hoochie mamma that I need more Tylenol. My fuckin' 'paws' are killing me."

She used my metaphor. That's good! Victor thought. "I'll get right on that, Violet. But before I do, I want to thank you for talking with me. I'll do my best not to be a poser."

"Hello! It's not difficult!" she shouted as the door clicked behind him.

Standing at the nurse's station, Victor briefed Asha.

"I think she just wants the pain to stop. Her argumentative nature is a healthy sign. She's actively looking for a reason to live. I'm willing to let her beat up on me if it gives her a sense of purpose."

"Well Doctor, it sounds like you had a good meeting," Asha complimented.

"I'm not saying it wasn't tricky."

"Don't I know it," Asha said, her laughter sounding like music. "Did you hear any of that crazy talk?"

"I didn't really get a chance to ask about it, but she didn't volunteer anything that would lead me to believe she's psychotic."

"Me neither, but I'll keep my eye on her. Will you come tomorrow then?"

Victor spoke over his shoulder. "You betcha. There must be a reason someone with that much life in her would want to die, and I'm gonna find out what it is."

Chapter 7

VICTOR WAS HAPPY WITH HIMSELF. For a few hours the torment of school, indeed of life, seemed worth it. He wanted Violet to succeed with all his heart, and as he reflected on their session, he gained a spring in his step that carried him to his next appointment.

Long ago Victor noticed that there are days when every patient seems to be working on the same issue. It being Halloween, the theme *du jour* was death. So for the rest of the morning Victor preached that mortality was a gift—a clarion call to live a richer life. It was a fruitful approach, and all of his patients left smiling, albeit nervously.

Shortly before one o'clock, Victor bid his last patient a hasty farewell. He didn't want to face the morgue on an empty stomach, so he rushed to the cafeteria. Unfortunately, the salad bar had been dismantled.

Damn!

"I guess we're fated to have lunch together after all," came a voice from behind.

There stood Angelita in skintight bellbottoms and a washed out 1970s t-shirt. Complete with a faux fur vest, Victor marveled at her hipster sense of style.

"I'm afraid not," he said, nervously. "The salad bar just closed. You look GREAT, though!"

"Um … Okay," she answered, bashfully. "You look great too, Victor."

"No, I mean it. I love this vest," he said, petting her shoulder.

"If you want to touch me, Victor, all you have to do is ask."

"What is this, teddy bear skin? Did you make this?"

"No. I found it in the thrift bins," she bragged, turning her body as if at a fashion show.

"I wish I was as cool as you," Victor said.

"Um, thanks, I guess."

"What are you doing here?"

"What are YOU doing here?" Angelita echoed.

"I work here, remember?"

"Oh. That's right. I forgot you said Pioneer. That's so-o-o cool Victor. For a moment I thought you were stalking me."

"How about you?"

"I'm here to see one of our long-time residents from the nursing home. She had a heart attack. I brought Cerberus!"

She lifted a canvas bag with an art museum logo. The Chihuahua thrust its velvety head from the sack and looked at Victor with beady eyes.

"How adorable! She just sits there like that?" Victor asked, secretly hating little dogs.

"Yeah. I take her to the nursing home. The residents are crazy about her."

Victor reached in, letting the cur lick his hand.

"Do you wanna come with us?"

Victor hesitated. "Um, sure! I should have time."

It was a boldfaced lie. There were assessments to score before brain dissection. Since she was Rubin's fiancé, he assured himself that no harm could come from hanging out for a bit.

As they walked, Angelita sashayed with one foot in front of the other, so that her hips swayed like Freud's pocket watch. She clearly understood that the key to being sexy is the ability to arouse yourself.

"So, what do you do?" Victor wondered, feeling dizzy.

"I work for the activities director. You know, art therapy, holiday decorations and stuff like that."

"Sounds fun."

"Old people are very lonely." She bunched up her nose. "I have a bumper sticker that says, 'Be nice to your kids. They'll be choosing your nursing home someday!'"

"I never wanted kids. It terrifies me that they'll hate each other," Victor replied.

"Really? You should reconsider. I think you'd make a *great* father."

"How can you be so certain?"

"Oh, I can tell. You like to help people. Plus you're great with four-year-olds," Angelita answered.

"Why do you say that?"

"You get along with Rubin, don't you?"

"Oh, come on now. Rubin's at least six."

Both laughed, uneasily. It seemed to Victor that she never spoke kindly of her boyfriend, and he considered exacerbating this problem. He waited for the proper moment—an uninterrupted stretch of hallway.

"So tell me more about Angelita. I mean, life is too short to be mysterious."

"There's not much to know, really."

"Oh, come on. What ignites your passion?"

"Passion? Well, I'm working with my professor on an art exhibit. It's gonna be unveiled at Christmas. Professor Epson is *amazingly* gifted with his hands," she said, hugging her body as if to quell a chill.

Victor had only known Angelita for two days, and yet he was feeling jealous. There are women who have this effect on men, and she was a member of that tribe.

"Tell me about him…" Victor said, faltering then correcting himself, "…I mean *the exhibit*."

Angelita grinned, shrewdly. "We're against the war in Afghanistan. The project was my idea, really, but Professor Epson has all the connections. He's a very important man."

Victor nodded politely, but his inner-brat wanted Epson's head on a pike.

"Basically," she continued, "he's taking credit for it. But my name will still be on it, and that's good enough. I'm just thrilled to be working with an artist of his caliber."

I knew there had to be something wrong with that bastard, Victor thought.

"That sounds a little unethical," he said. "In psychology we have strong codes against exploiting students. He shouldn't be allowed to get away with it."

"Oh, he's not a bad guy. He's just under a lot of pressure…"

Victor interrupted her. "Tell me about the work."

"It's a flag of Afghanistan made of colored sand. Think of a Tibetan mandala, except between two sheets of Plexiglas," she said, holding her hands together in illustration.

"Like an ant farm?"

She kissed her finger and pressed Victor's brow. "You get a gold star! We're gonna release ants into the exhibit so that they slowly take apart the flag…"

Victor finished her thought, "...in the same way that Russia and the United States have meddled in their affairs. I get it. It's abstract, but brilliant!"

Victor didn't appreciate her politics. He wondered how she would like being stoned to death for leaving an abusive husband.

"What? You're looking at me funny," she said.

"Nothing. Go on."

"I can't take *all* the credit. There's a whole genre of art in which the medium is the work itself. Last year we went to Tillamook and wrote words on the sides of cows with paint. The idea was to let them walk around forming sentences."

"Where, pray tell, did you find cows to use?" Victor asked, smirking at the image of cows playing Scrabble.

"We had to get permission from the farmers. They were afraid that we would mess up their milk production—which it didn't, by the way."

"So what did the cows say?"

Angelita chuckled. "Mostly nonsense. Although four of them spelled out the phrase, 'cows wait and hope.'"

"That's intense," Victor said, privately wishing that the hospital was a never ending labyrinth. But it was not, and soon they stood on the geriatric recovery unit.

Angelita became morose. "Just so you know, Ms. Paluch is a demented Holocaust survivor. She has no short-term memory. Things that happened sixty years ago are as real as if they happened yesterday."

"I think you might be right about that," Victor said, fallaciously. He knew damn well the implications of dementia.

"In her twenties, she was captured by the Nazis. She and her friends were driven to the countryside, and forced to wade into a bog. The Nazis opened fire with machine guns, and she had to play dead, only to be later sent to a concentration camp. Now she's very suspicious of doctors, and being locked-up in a nursing home plays on the very worst of her memories."

Victor was touched by the woman's story, but felt a tinge of defensive guilt that all Germans feel.

"Just follow my lead," Angelita said, reaching into the tote-bag to pet Cerberus. The hound had been so quiet that Victor forgot it was there.

Together they entered Ms. Paluch's room. Being a double accommodation, the only other furniture was a wheelchair and a nightstand. Some well-meaning family member had hung Halloween decorations. But of all the things they could have chosen—from cats to happy pumpkins—they chose a crepe ghost. It hung above her headboard, giving the appearance that her spirit was leaving her body.

"Hello Ms. Paluch. Do you remember me?" Angelita shouted, as if to a classroom of kindergarteners.

"Who are you?" the delirious woman asked in a panic. She gestured that Angelita should speak into her right ear, which was apparently the only one still functioning.

"Do you remember me? I'm from Whispering Pines Nursing Home," Angelita shouted, leaning over the crone's fossilized ear.

Whispering Pines! Who thinks up the names for these places? Victor wondered. He understood nursing homes, and if there was any 'whispering' or 'pining' going on, it was usually by mortified family members. There's nothing fun about watching a parent slip into obscurity as their brain rots.

"You're who?" she asked again, blinking blood-rimmed eyes at Angelita.

"An-gel-i-ta. I'm from the nursing home where you live. Look here, I brought my baby!"

Angelita lifted the mousey canine and held it over her lap so that the woman could get a better look. Usually the puppy's goofy antics made even the most entrenched curmudgeon smile, but the woman only squinted unfeelingly.

"Honey, she don't look nothing like you," she muttered, exposing a scattering of tombstones for teeth.

Angelita suppressed a giggle, which made her seem all the more adorable to Victor.

"Perhaps 'baby' wasn't the best choice of words," he whispered. "You might want to tell her that she ain't nothin' but a hound dog."

Angelita looked at him, then back at the old woman. "That's because she takes after her father!"

The woman strained to raise her head, scanning Victor from head to toe. Finally, after considerable effort she responded, "Yes she does…" Then she pressed her wispy head back into the pillow, content to have put the question to rest.

Victor checked his watch. He was not a big believer in therapy with the elderly. Besides memory problems, their generation was not prone to therapeutic navel gazing. Then he remembered what Dr. Lindsey had told him.

"Is Whispering Pines near Tanasbourne?" he asked.

"…185th and Fascination Street," she answered.

Victor's face brightened. "You won't believe this, but I'm gonna be working there!"

"No way."

"I'm serious as a heart attack…" Victor looked at Ms. Paluch. "um … sorry."

"What a coincidence."

"We have something else in common. I LOVE working with the elderly, so I asked my boss to find me a gerontology rotation."

"I'm not sure, Victor, but something tells me there's an angel looking over us," Angelita said.

"I agree."

Angelita returned her attention to the woman in bed. "So, Ms. Paluch. I was wondering if you could teach me something today. Do you have any words of wisdom?"

"Nice and dumb?" the woman shouted back, her silver cataracts reflecting the sterile light.

"No, Ms. Paluch. Wiz-dom!" Angelita straightened in her chair to better project her voice. "Do you have any wiz-dom?"

Victor secretly wondered if Angelita was upsetting the poor woman. *Hasn't she been through enough already?*

"O-o-o-o-h, w-i-s-d-o-m!" she shouted. "Well..." Then she tarried in the same way that farmers do when they're watching the corn grow. Both Victor and Angelita bent their ears so as not to miss the pearl of advice that such a thoughtful delay would surely secrete.

"I always say. When life gives you lemonade you have to make lemons!"

That was it. That was the sum and substance of her life experience. Victor chose his words carefully, hiding behind an impenetrable poker face. "On that profound note, I need to go."

Angelita stowed Cerberus into the canvas tote. Making sure to hold Ms. Paluch's hand as a sign of thanks, she looked up at him and asked, "Why so soon?"

"I get to poke at a human brain in ten minutes!" Victor noticed Ms. Paluch's shock and covered his mouth. "Sorry … I don't know why I'm so irresponsible around you."

"Don't apologize, silly," Angelita answered, standing from the wheelchair. She stretched her arms and yawned, holding the pause longer than necessary. Victor surmised that she did this to make her breasts look larger.

"I think the things you say are cute, Victor," she added with a glance that bordered on a caress.

"So I'll see you next week at Whispering Pines?" Victor asked, trying not to sound too hopeful.

"You'll see me before then. Tomorrow is *Demonic Submission*. I assume you're coming to the house to get ready."

Victor slapped his forehead. "That's right! Of course. Have you changed your mind about going?"

"Nah. Once you've been to a few of those things they lose their appeal. Why do you ask?"

"Because I've never been and I thought it might be fun to go as a group." This was chess, and Victor just saved his bishop.

"Well, this is where we part." Angelita walked to the end of the hall. She stopped, turned, and crossed her arms. Her bangles bunched up at her wrist. Then her face acquired that same sideways smile that he saw on the porch. Like before, it made him want to kiss her. "As for tomorrow, I might just change my mind..."

Victor's heart jumped.

"...although I doubt it. I have a lot of stuff to do for Professor Epson."

Damn the both of them!

Like an emotional Bermuda Triangle, Angelita rendered Victor confused and directionless. It wasn't until he was out of her range that he regained his bearings. Cursing, he vowed on his life that they would never be lovers.

Chapter

8

V ICTOR ENTERED THE MORGUE to find medical interns donning aprons. Dr. Schramek stood in the midst of his acolytes,
preoccupied with a textbook. Closing the cover, he spied Victor in
the doorway.

"Ah, there you are. We're still waiting for people, so go ahead
and get robed up. Masks, eye protection and latex gloves are in these
bins," he said frenetically, pointing to the shelf.

The self-satisfied demeanor of the medical students tainted the
room like a dead mouse in the drywall. Smiling politely, Victor studied their aprons so as not to make a fool of himself. As he fumbled
with the knot, he noted a stench worse than their arrogance, that of
pickled death.

Eventually the group followed Dr. Schramek into the laboratory.
The pathologist centered himself behind a ceramic table with a shallow lip. On the floor sat a bucket of formaldehyde.

"Why do a brain autopsy?" he asked in a long, drawn out rhetorical
prose. "Due to the complexities of neurologic illness, our diagnostic
uncertainty can only be resolved post mortem."

His love for the subject was evident in the way he rocked on the balls of his feet, occasionally gaining altitude to emphasize points of importance. Grasping the dowel rod over the bucket, he lifted an inverted human brain from the mire. For him, it was like Aphrodite had risen from the sea. The brain swung for a moment, dripping from a bundle of ventral arteries.

"What we have, ladies and gentlemen, is a three pound super-computer comprised of one-hundred billion neurons with ten trillion neuronal connections."

Dr. Schramek handed the brain to one of the students. When Victor got his turn, he cupped it in his hands like a religious artifact. It was lighter and smaller than he imagined a brain to be—barely two hand-fuls. Swooning, Victor realized that an entire life rested in his palms.

Dr. Schramek continued. "If I might sin by oversimplification, there are two kinds of people who come to this hospital: those with hardware problems, and those with software problems. If a patient's symptoms are not surgically or pharmacologically amenable, we refer them to the likes of Dr. Albrecht."

He shared a wink with Victor, to the annoyance of the interns. Victor was surprised by Schramek's magnanimity. Until now, his only consolation was that the stethoscoped egomaniacs at Pioneer were equally dismissive of one another.

"Today we're going to take a look at the hardware, so gather around," he said, setting the brain upon a paper towel. Using a knife he began cutting it into slices, explaining that it had belonged to a patient with Parkinson's disease. "I'm looking for abnormal anatomy, especially swelling, tumors or lesions."

Then he cut away the brainstem and the wrinkled, cauliflower-like *cerebellum*, laying it to the side. Turning the brain upright, he made vertical cuts, shaving sections from the *frontal lobes* so that they fell like slices of bread.

"Coronal cuts, again, looking for abnormalities in the tissue," he calmly explained. "We want to check the *cortex* for any sign of infarct," he declared, pointing at a pockmarked area of gray matter.

"This is probably necrosis right here. It may have been a stroke," he said, fingering the holes.

While Victor had acclimated to the pungent smell of the lab, the walls closed in on him. He stepped back to fight off a wave of vertigo. In all his years of dealing with anxiety, this was an unexpected reaction.

Dr. Schramek then isolated a lump in the center of the brain which he called the *basal ganglia*. Commenting on its atrophy, he pointed.

"A patient's symptoms are a map. Please look closely at the treasure," he said, summoning the group with gloved hands.

"These pigmented areas are the *substantia nigra*." He removed his gloves and pulled a dog-eared volume from the shelf, quickly leafing to a page of photographs marked with a paperclip.

"You can see that our patient does not have these dark areas. We conclude that the dopamine producing neurons are gone—hence, the presenting symptoms of tremor and postural instability."

While he took microscope samples, the interns poked at the brain as if it was a dead animal on a railroad track.

"I hope you found this exercise useful. If you have no further questions you may excuse yourselves to the washroom. *Be certain to scrub down!* Brain pathogens are the most infectious threats, some even passing through latex!" he added with a Transylvanian accent. The interns laughed.

Victor lingered until they filed out. As strange as it was, he wanted a few minutes alone with the brain. Circling like a vulture, he stared at it—wondering who the person had been. He was so quiet that Dr. Schramek breezed past him, slipping through a swinging door. Taking this as an invitation to ask further questions, Victor followed him into the ice cold morgue.

The snapshot taken by Victor's eyes would haunt him for the remainder of days. It was a naked, waxen body of an old man, sprawled out on a metal table with a drain. A ghastly china doll with thinning hair, the cadaver's impoverished fingers curled downward. Its mouth was agape; its eyes terminally opened in a fishy stare. The rubbery body was resistant to the exertions of the doctor's assistant as she bullied it into position on the table.

Without warning, the blood left Victor's head. Overcome with apprehension, he felt suddenly detached—alien to himself, as if life were a dream. As his vision narrowed, his knees folded. He held onto the door frame, stumbling backward.

"Breathe slowly, bend at the knees and put your head down as low as you can," came a compassionate voice. "It happened to ME the first time," Dr. Schramek admitted.

"I'm okay," Victor lied, struggling to get enough air into his lungs. "I'm sorry. I just wasn't ready to see that."

"Few people are. That's why our culture hides the dead. My father was a country minister. In *his* day it was common to keep the body at home, sometimes for days. Can you imagine such a thing?"

"No," Victor breathed, his legs slowly finding roots again.

"That's where we got the idea of flowers at funerals," Dr. Schramek added. He dawdled for a moment, carefully considering his words. "I was just about to do a *post mortem*. You're welcome to join me if you'd like to face this fear."

"I must admit, I have a strange hang-up with death," Victor said. "I'd love to watch, if it's not an imposition. I need to get over this."

"That's what psychologists are, right? Voyeurs?" he jested. "You sure you're okay? You still look a little tepid."

"Yeah, I'm fine," Victor answered, finally standing without support. "I want to understand the big picture, you know?"

"Cradle to grave?"

"Womb to tomb," Victor rejoined, smiling.

The room was tiled in ceramic stone that gently sloped to a silver drain. Against a far wall, two gurneys had been shoved; one of them sporting another body in a zippered bag.

Before long, Dr. Schramek was teaching again, this time with a naked carcass as a lectern. Holding the scalpel gingerly he made a t-shaped cut, half an inch deep, from shoulder to shoulder; then from the neck to the pubic bone. What little blood rose to the surface was wiped away. Then, digging his fingers under the flap, he began to tear it from the pink ribs beneath. The old man's hide resisted, so Dr. Schramek helped it with carefree, crisscross incisions; lifting the sheet of skin and hair as he spoke.

"What we have here is an 85 year-old Jewish male with a history of lymphoblastic leukemia, osteoarthrosis, hyperplasia of the prostate, hypertension, and peripheral vascular disorder."

Soon the man's breast was flayed open. He laid there with his xylophone exposed to the air like a Sperm whale aside the Pequod. The internal organs were safe for the moment, still locked within the sinewy chest—but not for long.

Gripping a bone saw with two hands, Dr. Schramek applied the screaming blade to the chest, spitting bone dust and speckling the man's neck with blood. When the acrid smoke cleared, and with an audible cracking sound, the cemetery gate finally swung open. Cutting through a thin membrane, a collection of shimmering pink and gray organs were exposed, piled together like pillows on a loveseat.

"This guy's an interesting case. He overdosed."

"You can tell by his stomach?"

"No, I read his chart. He committed suicide."

"That's sad."

"Some of these seniors have closets full of expired prescriptions. Medication compliance is a serious problem for the elderly."

Using scissors, Dr. Schramek began cutting organs free with well-rehearsed efficiency. While waiting for his aide to suction the stomach cavity, he placed his thumbs beneath an elastic gray mass. Stretching it thin like a balloon, he invited Victor to take a closer look.

"This is a lung. See those black specks? They're carbon deposits."

Victor nodded. "It looks like pepper. Was he a smoker?"

"Maybe. Or, he lived in the city. We want to take a good look at the lungs to see if there's any fluid in them." He cut them out and handed them to his assistant. "Most of us will die of pneumonia."

The woman took the organs and placed them onto a grocer's scale. Recording their weight, she dropped them into a basin. It was outfitted with a stream of running water where organs could be cut into pieces, sprayed off and prepared for later examination. Cleaning the organs of feces and unwanted debris, she placed samples into Tupperware containers filled with formalin.

"This guy was in pain. We can prescribe opiates, but ten percent of suffering can't be anesthetized. The leading indicator of suicide is being a white male over fifty with a health problem."

As Dr. Schramek removed the intestines, he knotted each end to retain their content. Victor felt vindicated to learn that people actually *were* full of shit. When the smell became overwhelming the doctor's assistant sprayed a citrus-scented deodorant above the carcass.

Victor's face pruned. "It smells like someone crapped on an orange."

Dr. Schramek looked over his glasses. "The coroner wants to know what killed him, so we'll be writing a toxicology report. We'll send samples from the heart and blood vessels, the gallbladder and vitreous gel from his eyes. Of course we want to examine the stomach and especially the liver."

Victor stepped back to make room for the assistant as she carried a section of the large colon to her work bench.

"Wanna know where your prostate is?" Dr. Schramek invited.

80

"Sure," Victor answered uncomfortably. If nothing else he figured it might be a novel experience that he could throw at Rubin. Looking inside the body, he saw that it was completely ransacked. Only the spinal column remained, deeply nestled in muscle tissue. The old man's body looked like the looted hull of a Spanish galleon.

Dr. Schramek guided Victor's hand into the dark cavern within the pelvis, locating an egg-sized bump. "This guy must have had one heck of a time peeing. This is nearly twice as large as it should be."

Victor grimaced and removed his hand from the body, feeling that he had gone beyond a simple violation of privacy.

"Dr. Schramek. You said your dad was a minister. Do you believe in God?"

"Well, I used to be Protestant. Then, one day I was praying and it occurred on me that I was talking to myself. I've been a humanist ever since."

"So you don't believe in an afterlife?"

"You're a biological machine, Victor. The way that you deal with this fact is a measure of your maturity."

Victor felt the need to explain himself. "On my drive here from Tucson I heard a radio program called *Tales from the Afterlife*. Some guy collected hundreds of stories from people who died and came back. Apparently it's hard to get into Hell because most of them said dying was a wonderful experience."

"Of course they did. It feels good to have your brain unplugged. Every crummy thing you ever did is erased as the brain loses oxygen. That's why people do drugs—to stifle the inner tyrant. When you die you get to see that cursed slave-master driven into the abyss before you."

Victor considered the idea then countered, "Not me. I plan to live forever. So far, so good."

Dr. Schramek kept working in silence, and to Victor it seemed that he'd become contemplative. Victor went with the feeling, and for the first time since the autopsy began there was an aura of piety—even reverence.

Victor felt compelled to humanize the experience. This had been a person, after all. He stepped closer and allowed his fingers to mingle with the boney, ice-cold digits of the old man's hand. The texture was similar to chicken parts, and he suffered an odd realization that the difference between flesh and meat was at best semantic. He closed his eyes, and projected compassion instead.

The dead hand closed into a fist!

Victor yanked himself free, leaping from the table as if a cobra had struck. The unflappable Dr. Schramek barely noticed. His eyes casually rose to find the young psychologist ashen-faced, standing several feet from the table.

"You look like you've seen a ghost, my boy."

Victor debated sharing his thoughts. Struggling to gather his senses, he observed that the corpse looked more peaceful than ever. Its face was tranquil—no, smirking—and its hand was definitely closed into a knot of fingers!

"Um, Dr. Schramek?"

"Yes?"

"Do bodies get *rigor mortis?* You know, sit up, jump around, that kind of thing?"

Dr. Schramek was too busy with his thoughts to hear what Victor really wanted to know. That is, do the dead ever shake your hand during an autopsy?

"*Rigor mortis* is a chemical change in the muscle tissue."

"I see," Victor said, vexed by the gratified look on the dead man's face.

"We usually find it in facial musculature during the first twenty-four hours. After that the tissue breaks down."

"How long has this guy been dead?" Victor asked, wary of the answer.

"He killed himself three days ago," Dr. Schramek answered. Suddenly a line of cherry red blood trickled from his right nostril.

Victor pointed. "You're bleeding!"

Dr. Schramek looked down, which caused the blood to splatter on his white sleeve.

"Blast it," he cursed, wiping his nose with the back of his wrist. "We need to get the ventilation system fixed." Running off, he spoke to the ceiling. "Formaldehyde is caustic! Hold on a minute while I get a tissue."

Victor was now less frightened than feverishly curious, and was beginning to suspect that his mind had played a trick. So he leaned over the old man and peered into the milky, dry eyes. Placing his fingers onto the fragile eyelids, he pressed them shut.

As he always did in times of profundity, he drew upon his college experience with Shakespeare—particularly Hamlet, a character in whose torment he had always found kinship.

"O that … the Everlasting had not fixed His cannon 'gainst self-slaughter…" Then glancing to make sure nobody was watching he finished, saying, "…Lay him in the earth, and from his fair and unpolluted flesh may violets spring."

Returning with cotton in each nostril, Dr. Schramek startled him. "Shall we close him up, then?"

"Sure. It all makes sense to me now," Victor muttered.

"What do you mean?"

"Nothing. Nevermind. I was just talking to myself."

Secretly he thought he'd shared a profound moment with the old man. He felt somehow tied to this stranger; bound by the fragile cord of human destiny—to be born, to love, to have dreams and ambitions, to make mistakes and then to die.

Dr. Schramek retrieved a plastic bag containing organs that were not useful. He stuffed it into the chest cavity and returned the ribcage to its proper position. Like a rotten jack-o'-lantern, the lid fell inside the body with a hollow thud. Then he threaded a curved needle with what looked like packing twine. With wide arcing movements he knitted the horrific gash. The elastic flesh, pink on the edges, stretched and bunched together as he pulled it tight, knotting it firmly at the neck.

"That's all she wrote," he said impiously. "Off to the funeral home!"

Victor left, finishing his work day in an altered state of mind. He ruminated on his brother's funeral and how the tiny casket had been closed. Some say that all emotions stem from the same source, anxiety, indistinct until we name them. Victor didn't know if he wanted to laugh or cry. There were so many secrets.

Driving home, he rolled down his window, breathing deeply of the autumn air. As the trees rushed by he enjoyed the sights and sounds of life; his thoughts calmly wandering from place to place, like a dragonfly on a pond.

On Hawthorne Boulevard, the street light changed. Victor slowed to a halt, curious that the leaves had changed in the same progression—green to yellow to red. What did it all mean? It was a season for contemplation. He opened and closed his fist on the steering wheel, seeing it for the first time as a component of a biological device.

Just then, a whimsical parade of trick-or-treaters entered the crosswalk. The costumed children waddled like dwarves on their way home from the mine, proudly swinging their sacks of saccharine gold. Toward the rear of the group, a tall ghost in a bed sheet held the hand of a boy who was dressed as a doctor. As the phantom led him to the other side, Victor began to cry.

He struggled to control the flood, but when the light changed to green he openly wept for the loss of his innocence. It was decades overdue.

Chapter
9

*T*HERE'S NOTHING FUNNY about a funny farm. In truth, mental illness is two-dimensional and uninspired. Violet waited in the activity room, reassembling the same puzzle to keep from going insane. It was a *Pre-Raphaelite* painting of an angel visiting St. Agnes in prison. Sadly, she couldn't finish it because the piece with the seraphim's face had been stolen by the obsessive-compulsive kid. Violet wasn't about to rough him up.

She pried her elbows from the sticky table and dropped her bandaged arms into her lap. The television had one channel and the knob was broken off. Disinterested in watching game shows through scratched Plexiglass, she turned to the dazed woman next to her and narrowed her eyes. Violet had learned one thing on the ward—in the land of the blind, the one-eyed girl is queen.

"Hey!" she called, not expecting a response.

The woman had arrived that morning in a manic, psychotic state and was now chemically lobotomized. The lady continued to stare at the television, her inner world flowing like molasses. Violet hooked her fingers into the corners of her mouth and unspooled her tongue.

"Miss Cain!" Asha reprimanded. "I came to bring you a cigarette on account of good behavior, but I must have the wrong girl!"

"Not so Nurse Ratched. I did everything you asked—even talking to Dr. Moron!" Violet crossed her arms in a huff, regressing to a thirteen year old.

"I'm Nurse Henson, and it's pronounced Dr. Mor-anne, young lady. Look, I know you don't want to be here…"

"That's not true! It's positively glamorous to live in a gated community."

"Very funny. Now get your butt in gear, or we're taking a smoke break without you."

Violet stomped into the hall where the other cattle were waiting. This was to be a chain-gang affair. Asha pecked a code into the cipher and the door popped open. Soon Violet found herself pressed against Asha's pillow-like bosom as everyone jammed into the elevator.

"Honey, push the lobby, will you?"

"I DID already!" Violet whined.

"Child, you're killin' me."

Violet turned her head, "Nurse Henson? Is that shrink gonna see me today? He *promised*."

"Who, that handsome man? I don't know, honey. They usually come before lunch."

"That figures. Well, *fuck him* then. I don't need fixing."

"I'm fixin' to get me a bar of soap," Asha warned, tussling Violet's hair.

Before long the group walked across a courtyard at the center of the hospital complex. They gathered beneath a gazebo while Violet pinched a cigarette between her nicotine stained fingers.

"I can't smoke these trailer-trash menthols. Don't you have cloves?"

Asha's patience was wearing thin. "Hey Betty Boop, do you want a light or not?"

"Alright, then." The tobacco crackled as Violet inhaled half the cigarette with one drag. She closed her eyes and breathed out.

"It's nice to see you getting sun," Victor said.

Startled, Violet opened her eyes. She went into a fit of coughing. "I hate the sun. It fucks up my moon tan."

"I wanted to come earlier, but I had stuff to do this morning," Victor explained. "How are you?"

"Peachy!" Violet pulled on her hospital gown. "Can't you tell? I'm wearing pastels!"

Victor wasn't sure what to say next. Therapy is more difficult when patients are captive. His first task, beyond establishing rapport, would be to convince her that there was something in it for her.

"Care if I join you?"

"Whatever you want," she spouted, examining her finger nails.

Victor scoured his memory, trying to recall what technique had worked so well the day before. Coming up empty he sat next to her on the table, taking care to stare into the distance just like she did. "How can I be of service today?"

"I could use your opinion."

"Absolutely."

Violet rose from the table. Jutting her hips provocatively, she struck a pose. "Tell me the truth. Does this cigarette make me look fat?"

"Are you trying to lose weight?"

"Trying? I've already lost twenty-one grams, which is the weight of a human soul."

"Nice."

Small talk in the beginning of therapy is okay if it serves a larger purpose, and Victor felt it was important to mirror her disinterest. Young people are repulsed by fake familiarity, so he decided to share something from his life. "I did something cool that I'm sure you've never done."

"Like what?"

"I got to cut up a dead guy on Halloween."

"Don't be so sure I haven't."

"Did you know that your lungs are really small?"

A plume of smoke escaped Violet's mouth in place of a witty comeback.

"I've held one. They're about the size of your palm…" Victor said, holding out his fingers.

Violet was watching him obliquely. "Doc, are you a necrophiliac?"

"No, it wasn't a sexual thing. And when you inhale smoke, your lungs get these little black specks that never go away. Smoking is a kind of slow suicide."

Violet held up her bandaged arms, "What do you think I'm trying to do, here? I'm stalked by the Grim Reaper."

Victor retreated into contemplation.

"You remind me of my grandfather…" Violet said out of the blue.

Victor felt a rush of emotion. He wanted her to see him as a boy, and the thought frightened him.

"…he used to say crazy shit like that. He was always thinking about important stuff."

Victor tried the key in the lock. "Tell me more about him."

"I'd rather not."

The key broke off. *Her grandfather must have been special to her. Go wider, not deeper,* he thought. "So, I heard you're interested in history."

"Who told you that?"

"It's written in your chart. It says you have an affinity for Egyptology."

Violet found this curious. "It does, huh? I wanna see what it says."

Victor returned her discomforting stare. They both knew that he had the power, and she didn't seem to like it one bit. He was gauging her reaction. If she WAS psychotic he would soon know. "Dr. Moran wrote that you think you're Cleopatra."

Violet grunted. "I like *Nightmare Before Christmas,* but that doesn't make me Tim Burton. The next time I see that dick I'm gonna show him what a harpy I can be."

"I don't think that would be in your best interest, Violet."

"Stupid Dr. Moron! I thought it might be romantic to die like Cleopatra. Not that zombie, Liz Taylor, mind you. I was thinking more of Vivien Leigh," she said, fluffing her hair.

"Go on."

"I was scoping out the Egyptian cobra at the Portland Zoo, and they called the cops. That's all. What a dick. He totally blew it out of proportion."

"You actually did that?"

"Yep. I got the lid off the cage. They revoked my zoo membership."

It didn't matter if it was true. To Victor, the girl demonstrated intelligence, creativity and passion—all predictors of a good outcome in therapy. However, she was at high risk for completing suicide for the same reasons. As the group began to make their way back indoors, Victor put a finer point on the discussion.

"You know, Violet, what fascinates me is that you're not dead yet. I mean, you're obviously bright and resourceful, yet you're still alive. That tells me that you have coping skills. If I'm right, the only reason you're here is that you had a lapse in judgment."

"Just one, huh?" Violet replied, incisively.

"Have you done this before—attempted suicide?" Victor pressed.

"It runs in the family. So, what's your name again?"

"Victor," he answered, desperately wanting her to remember.

"Well, Victor, my whole life has been one giant lapse in judgment. I kicked my twin to death *in utero,* and since then everything I touch turns to shit. Who knows, I'm probably making a huge mistake talking to you." Violet became teary eyed.

She just admitted that she's agreeing to talk to me! Victor was euphoric. "Don't be so hard on yourself. Most of life is out of our control. The only thing we can count on is change."

"Unless you're me and you're at a vending machine," she said, trying to be funny again.

But it didn't work. Victor had seen her tears. He continued. "It's just the truth. We can't control the weather, but we *can* set the course, and decide whether or not to raise the sail."

"Aye, Captain Blackbeard, aren't you supposed to be cheering me up?"

Asha announced that it was time to go. Everyone crushed their cigarettes.

"My job isn't to cheer you up. We all kill ourselves for one damn fool reason or another; some for their country, others for their children. It's your sense of timing that has everyone upset. It's like the casino just opened, and here you are—young, smart, full of potential—and you're cashing in your chips. It defies logic, it really does."

"They're my chips! I have problems, okay?"

"It's not the problems that are messing you up. It's your solutions. It's true that the chips are yours, and I will never challenge you on that, but I can't help but wonder who would be hurt by news of your death."

The group had reassembled by the elevator. Victor knew that people commit suicide for different reasons—to punish themselves, to end pain, or even to hurt someone else. Soon they were back on the unit, and Violet invited him to her room. She sat on her mattress and crossed her legs. The sparsely outfitted room had not changed from the previous visit, save for a toothbrush and a pot of delicate flowers with a brightly colored Get Well Soon card on a stick.

"They're letting you brush your own teeth now. That's good."

"I'm anal about my oral hygiene."

"Are those flowers from your mother?"

Violet grew agitated. "Gee, I don't know. Let's find out." She picked up the pot and read aloud, *"Dear Rosemary, your father and I miss you very much.* Nope, not from my family!"

"Who gave them to you, then?"

"They arrived this morning after some bitch was Medivac'd. They were at the nurse's station, but Asha said they were meant for me because they're violets. You know the poem, roses are red, violets are blue…"

She hung her head in despair.

"Not *all* violets are blue. They come in different colors," Victor said as earnestly as he could. "My finely honed senses tell me that you and your mom don't get along."

"I don't want to hurt her. I just wonder if she would finally appreciate me if I was in the ground."

"It's a good question. The problem is you wouldn't get to gloat."

"My mom is disgusted by me, Victor. She thinks I'm a failure. And the sad truth is she's right."

"And your dad?"

"Never knew him. He blew his head off with a thirty-aught-six on my birthday."

"My God."

"Don't sweat it. I've been through all the stages of grief—drugs, alcohol, promiscuous sex. I'm fine now."

"If Dr. Moran thinks you're Cleopatra, then it's possible that your mom is equally confused about you."

"No, Victor. She's right. I'm a world class fuck up."

"It's okay to fail, Violet. It doesn't make you a failed human being. Maybe I'm going out on a limb, but your mom carried you for nine months. You came out of her body, and yet you claim she finds you disgusting?"

"Shit comes out of your body, Victor." Then Violet became businesslike. "Tell me the truth. Before I say anything else, are you gonna write about me like Dr. Moron did?"

Victor became disoriented in a sea of conflicting roles. What part was he going to play; psychologist, friend, teacher, father-figure or Judas? Who was he working for? He gave her question thoughtful consideration.

"I'm obligated to chart what we talk about. But, I keep it very general; unless of course you tell me you're going to hurt yourself. That's the truth, Violet. I hope it's good enough for you."

She looked at him blankly.

Victor sighed. "At some point you're gonna have to take a leap of faith, or I can't help you."

"I never asked for help."

"Not with your lips."

Then came silence. Victor was going to say more, but opted instead to let it ride.

"Fair enough, Victor. But before I say another word I want you to answer a question."

"You can certainly ask me whatever you want."

"Now you're starting to sound like me," she quipped.

Victor didn't laugh. He cleared his throat and waited with trepidation as she ran a bandaged hand through her onyx hair.

"Have you ever smoked pot?" she finally asked.

"I'm wondering what you're looking for. What meaning would you give my answer?"

"No way, man. You're dealing with a pro. I've had counselors since elementary school, motherfucker. Fair is fair, it's a simple question. Yes or no. Did you ever toke the ganja?"

Victor was aggravated. Although he tried to keep it to himself, her impudence clouded his judgment. He'd let the horse out of the barn, and the filly was too wild to harness.

"No. To be perfectly honest, no. I don't think it would make me a better person if I did. I have a strong personal ethic against drug use, and although marijuana may seem perfectly safe, research suggests otherwise. Shall I go on?"

"Please do."

"Even casual users suffer anterograde amnesia, and brain scans show deactivation of the frontal and parietal hemispheres. That means that as long as you smoke pot you'll never make anything of yourself, because your get-up-and-go will have got-up-and-went. Any more questions?"

"That was saucy." Violet looked subdued by his candor. "I'll let you know if I think of anything else."

"Good," Victor said, weighing the merits of his diatribe. There's a fine line between enforcing proper boundaries, and making the mistake of opposing a teenager.

"Oh, I remember what I wanted to ask you…"

"Isn't it my turn to ask YOU a question?" Victor rejoined, looking tired.

"In a minute. You asked if I had any more questions and I do," she insisted.

Victor deeply inhaled, then slowly breathed out his irritation. Closing his eyes, he invited her to continue. "Fire away."

"Do you have a girlfriend?"

How could the session have gone so wrong? Victor wondered. He decided it was time to take control. "I'm not going to answer that. It's inappropriate."

"Come on, Victor. What's the big deal? How can we get to be friends if you don't share basic things with me?"

"We're not going to be *friends,* Violet."

A look of sadness flashed across her face.

Victor no longer cared if he lost her today. The way she was behaving was at the heart of her illness. He was finished building rapport for the day.

"We're never going to be 'buddies,' Violet. This is serious business. You're not well, and although you refuse to take yourself seriously, I do. I'm a psychologist. I have training and experience that you might find helpful in your search for answers. If you don't want me to help you, then tell me, and I'll walk out of this room right now."

Violet shifted.

"But if you're interested in a tomorrow, or even another hour that isn't as bloody awful as today, I suggest you sit back and let me do my job—even if it's not on your terms. I won't abandon you, but I'm not here to play games either."

"So you're single, then?"

Victor stared at her, and if looks could kill...

Violet averted his eyes, and for a minute Victor wondered if she was crying. Then she whispered, "For some people tomorrow never comes."

"I understand, but if we're going to do this I need some assurance that you're dedicated to getting healthy. You don't have to become America's sweetheart, but you do need to try. I think you owe it to yourself to give therapy a chance."

She seemed to be absorbing it all.

"I typed up an informal contract that I want you to sign. It basically says that you won't kill yourself for the next six weeks. That should give you plenty of time to decide if this is bullshit or not."

Violet finally answered, sniffling, "I don't plan to be here that long." When Victor did not respond, she gave in. Her mordant sense of humor returning, she mouthed, "I love a Faustian bargain."

Victor produced the contract. Removing the fountain pen from his pocket, he handed it to her. "I have no intention of abandoning you, Violet Cain. The question remains, will you abandon yourself?"

She scribbled her name, speaking as she drew a unicorn on the border of the page. "Don't you think I'm tired of being fucked up? Every time I look in the mirror the same fat-cheeked bitch ogling at me, keeping a diary of my stupidity. I *wish* I was a vampire. Then I'd have no reflection."

"If you were a vampire you wouldn't have a soul either. Then again, keep doing drugs..." he added, his mouth twisting.

"Look, man, it's been almost two days since I freaked out. I don't even *use* drugs, Victor. I just don't like pain. I'm not one of those stupid bitches who fantasize about giving vaginal birth in a bathtub full of rose petals. I'll take the epidural, thank you."

"I can agree with you there. Home deliveries are for pizzas."

"Don't you realize that if I wanted to kill myself I could have done it a dozen times already today?" Violet added.

"Please don't take this as a challenge, but it's not like you have the means. They took the laces out of your shoes for crying out loud. You don't even have a bra on."

"You noticed?" she asked, coquettishly.

"Like I said, they took the laces out of your SHOES," he repeated. He was all through playing hopscotch in Violet's minefield.

"You forgot the piercings," Violet asserted. "I had a tongue ring, earrings, eyebrow post, navel ring, and ... well the other one," she said, looking downward.

Victor rolled his eyes.

Apparently Violet realized that he was not going to take her bait. She closed the session in a way that allowed her to regain control. "You're a good psychologist, Victor. But if you're gonna make it in the shrink business you need to pay closer attention."

She pulled the pot of flowers into her lap. Reaching into the violets, she withdrew the six-inch long plastic spike that held the greeting card in place. To make her point, she dragged the sharp end of the spear across her bandaged wrists with the Get Well card still attached.

"Poetic somehow," Victor breathed, shaking his head. "Now hand it over," he added, showing his palm.

"Can I keep the flowers?"

"As long as you promise not to eat them."

"I prefer oleander. The poison is quicker," she said smugly.

"One last thing. If we're going to work together I want you to keep a diary. I just want you to spend five minutes a day writing about what a miracle it is that you can breathe, okay?"

"They won't give me a pen."

"You can do it at the nurse's station. See you on Monday; and *for the love of Christ*, behave yourself!"

Violet flopped on her bed, shouting at the ceiling, "Why does EVERYONE say that to me?"

Victor strode from the room feeling content. Asha handed him Violet's chart in exchange for the plant spike. There was now a special tab in her records called *Psychology*, so he busied himself with a vague outline of what had transpired. Using a two-hole punch he inserted the no-suicide contract and slapped the binder shut.

Victor then tapped his pen on the counter. "Asha, I have a question."

"I have an answer if you ask real nice," she replied, eating leftovers from a plastic container.

"Are violets deadly?"

Asha orbited in her swivel chair. "They can be if you make 'em mad."

"Seriously now."

"Nope."

Victor slipped the pen into his pocket. As he retraced his steps to the outpatient clinic, he obsessed over the session. Something about it bothered him, and it wasn't until he reached his office that he figured it out.

Patients often pretend to be someone they're not—a fountain of jokes, wit, or profound insight to avoid dealing with uncomfortable feelings. Carl Jung famously called this 'the persona.' In Violet's case, she played a streetwise punk; someone far different from the scared, desperate girl who'd gouged her wrists with a rusty wire. Victor had not yet gotten to know *that* person.

But the week was behind him. Thus freed from business, he looked forward to a night on the town with Rubin. He could never have guessed what *Demonic Submission* would turn out to mean.

Chapter 10

IKE SO MANY OF THE CITY'S YOUNG INHABITANTS, the sky above Portland never commits to anything. Instead, and without thunder, the drizzle gathers on power lines and branches like crystal beads. Splashing down the curb, Victor rolled to a stop. The music blaring from Rubin's house might have been made by a wolverine in a trash can. *Gothic/Industrial Music,* they called it. He let himself in to find a flock of ravens gathered in the kitchen, clutching beers and clove cigarettes. Yet despite the preponderance of black fabric, their pirate shirts betrayed their nerdy, thespian souls.

He spied Persephone at the sink. When their eyes met, she pointed to the ceiling. "Rubin's upstairs!"

Victor ascended the staircase, again treading dirty laundry. He was relieved not to have seen Angelita yet. Feeling like himself, he barged into the bedroom to find Rubin illuminated by a dozen candles in glasses and jars.

"Courtly love!" shouted the king of *non sequitur,* leaning against the vanity with a stick of eyeliner in his hand.

"I'm sorry." Victor began, seating himself on the bed. "You look nothing like Courtney Love."

"Not Courtney Love, you imbecile. *Courtly love,* as in the days of old. You know—true love without ownership or attachment. Like the Knights of the Round Table had!"

Rubin put one foot on the chair. His hand dropped onto Victor's shoulder. "Tonight, I am King Arthur; and you, my erudite friend, shall be my Lancelot…"

"I shall?"

Rubin continued, "…and fitting, too. I don't know how you do it. My boss, Jenn, is obsessed with you. It's been very good for me at work."

"Really?"

"Yes. If you want, I'll hook you guys up."

Victor found the topic dangerous. There was a hint of jealousy in all of this posturing. Rubin was now standing in front of the mirror, teasing his black hair with gel. He was wearing a dog collar, a miniskirt, torn fishnet stockings and a long-sleeve t-shirt with the midriff cut out. Sitting on the bed next to Victor, he bent to fasten the dozen-odd buckles on his boots.

"So, this is kind of a gender-bending, gothic King Arthur thing that you're doing?"

"Yeah. I was gonna wear a sword, but I doubt they'd let me in with a three foot knife after 9/11!"

As Rubin said this, he motioned toward the wall. An array of medieval weapons hung there and, being a boy, Victor couldn't resist pulling down a sword. He swung the blade to check its balance.

"I still don't get the King Arthur angle," Victor said.

"It's Angelita's idea. She decided to go at the last minute, and has it in her mind to be Guinevere."

Was the significance of my being Lancelot completely lost on them? Victor coughed. His heart was in his throat. "Weren't there other knights I could be, like Perceval? I want to be the guy who finds the Grail."

"Don't we all know," Rubin said with sarcasm.

Just then Angelita pranced into the room, painted in a licorice polyvinyl outfit. Shining like a black candied apple, her knee-length dress was slit to the thigh. With matching arm-length gloves and stiletto fuck-me boots, she was a prurient delight.

"Lancelot, my champion!" Angelita gushed, laying her hand upon Victor's. It took him a moment to realize that he was supposed to kiss it, which he eagerly did.

Caressing her fingers, Victor whispered, "You look like a mermaid after Exxon Valdez..."

"I said the same thing! Did I not?" Rubin gushed.

"No, Rubin, if my memory serves me correctly, you called me a ninja sea cow."

"Same thing!"

"Talk to the hand," she said, holding her palm in Rubin's face. "I could use some lotion, darling. And you owe me big time."

"Why bother? It doesn't work," Rubin quipped. "Does one of my palms look smoother than the other?"

Angelita recoiled. "Since you're such a pig, I wonder if *Sir Lancelot* would be so kind as to assist me with my corset."

"I'm not sure I can. What do you want me to do?" Victor asked, nervously. Imprisoned within the strapless gown, her breasts already seemed to be under a dangerous amount of pressure.

"Just pull it," Angelita said, resting her elbows on her knees so that her *derriere* presented.

Rubin grinned lasciviously. "Put that in your spank bank, Victor!"

Victor sneered. He pulled the cords forcefully—bringing their bodies into contact.

"O-o-o-h, Victor's happy to see me," she muttered, grinding her butt against his groin as Victor finished lacing.

Rubin snarled, "Victor can't tie a knot. He made bunny ears and tied them together!"

"Bunny ears are cute," Angelita countered.

"Me thinks Victor is too sober," Rubin answered in frustration. "We've all gotten a head start. Let the nectar of the vine soothe thine furrowed brow, for tonight you are my *Fortunato!*"

"I thought I was Lancelot, and you my lord and king," Victor replied, trying his best to be a good sport.

"But I am. As Angelita is my queen," he announced, lifting a crown of black silk roses from the dresser. He placed it upon her brow.

A tumbler was thrust into Victor's hand as more people filed into the room. A ruby liquid poured from a wicker decanter. Victor threw his head back, downing the wine with a splash.

"My own private stock. I call it *Amontillado*," Rubin said, promptly recharging the glass. "It's fermented grape juice and bread yeast."

Rubin then addressed the gathering, holding his glass high. "I call upon you, faithful knaves, to devise a costume for Victor! Look at him! My God, I've seen wounds that were better dressed!"

"I'm okay," Victor insisted. "Really."

"Nonsense! You can't wear blue jeans to a goth club! They'll revoke our Hot Topic membership!" Saying this, Rubin leapt upon the bed. With wine dripping down the wall, he lowered an accusing finger.

"As King of Camelot, I find you guilty of the crime of modesty. Your sentence…" Rubin stopped short to take another drink, then shouted to a jackbooted anarchist in the doorway, "Drum roll please!"

The black-maned graver executed a drum roll, his silver rings rapping on the dresser.

"Off with his pants!" Rubin shouted to raucous cheers.

"No, really. I'm fine," Victor begged, backing away from the encroaching mob. With Rubin in the lead, and taken by a kind of *folie à deux*, they pounced—tearing at Victor's clothes until the bed frame cracked. This pandemonium continued until tears of laughter poured from his eyes.

Before he knew it he was sitting on the floor in his underwear while strangers tossed garments at his feet. Angelita perched herself on a chair with a cigarette in her hand. She took it from her mouth and offered it to Victor. He dithered for a moment before accepting it.

Speaking in puffs, he admitted, "I've never had friends, Angelita. I think, in this moment, I'm happier than I've ever been."

"I know," she replied, falling silent. Her eyes mingled with Victor's for a dangerous minute, and he thought he saw the pulse rise on her slender neck.

Thankfully, Rubin returned from the hall with a floor length Jesuit's coat. He refilled Victor's glass and took another swig. Handing the jug to Angelita, he dropped the coat into Victor's lap.

"Hurry up now. We wanna get a good spot in line."

With Angelita's help, Victor dressed himself like a post-apocalyptic homicidal cyborg, complete with mirrored shades.

"I'll have to fend off the girls with pepper spray," Angelita said as she painted shadows under Victor's cheekbones with burnt cork. She crowned his outfit with a leather dog collar, similar to the one worn by Rubin, and placed herself between the two men.

Hooking arms she said, "Getty-up ponies, it's time to take your queen to the ball."

Drunk on wine and ardor, the bridled men followed her into the rainy street. As they climbed into the moldy backseat of Persephone's car, Angelita wiggled between them. After some fussing about seat belts and the selection of music, they traversed the river Styx on their way to *Hades,* the Northeast Portland nightclub hosting the *Demonic Submission* event.

The absinthe and water they now drank from a Gatorade bottle washed away any hint of boundaries, and the conversation collapsed into ribald innuendo. At one point Rubin tipped over, flopping into Angelita's lap. Running her fingers through Rubin's hair, she commanded Victor to retrieve a cigarette from her purse. It rested on the floorboard between her knees.

"I want a dragon kiss," she proclaimed.

"What's that?" Victor asked, lifting his face from her lap. He tried to get the lighter to spark.

"Just inhale smoke and kiss me."

He didn't need to be coerced, although the cigarette lighter slipped through his fingers twice before he finally got a flame. He took smoke into his lungs and planted his mouth upon hers. With their tongues entwined she sucked the vapors out of him. It might as well have been his soul. Holding it for a moment with her eyes closed, she kissed him again, breathing it back. Victor nearly lost consciousness, his world spinning from lust and hypoxia.

Rubin shouted from Angelita's lap. "Hey, where's mine, princess? I want a dragon kiss too!"

Leering into her lap, she spoke enticingly, "I'm sure Victor would LOVE to kiss you, darling."

"Um, that's okay," Victor said, stiffly sitting upright. He reached into her lap and placed the cigarette directly into Rubin's mouth.

Rubin coughed and sat up, flicking ash from his eye. "I have another idea. As king of Camelot I hereby declare that we each must have a favorite word tonight!"

"What do you mean?" Angelita asked, giggling.

"My favorite word has always been 'lugubrious.'" He waved his fingers like a butterfly. "Loo-goo-bree-us."

"Nice and mournful," Victor acknowledged. "How about you, Angelita?" He watched her think, finding irresistible the way she chewed her lip.

She turned her head and pinned Victor to the seat with a sultry glare. "I've always been partial to the word…"

Victor's mouth hung in anticipation.

"…'moist,'" she said as suggestively as possible, her lips glistening in the passing streetlights. "It's a perfectly salacious word, don't you think?"

"I have to agree," Victor said, swallowing hard. "Although I'm fond of the word 'assiduous.' It means diligent, which I have to be…"

An uncomfortable silence settled upon the car.

"…Plus it has the word 'ass' in it, which I'm desperately trying not to be," Victor added. "Hey Rubin, are Shrink and Creep going to be at the club tonight?"

"They'd better be, cause *you're* Shrink and I'm Creep! You mean Red and Snake, you ignoramus."

"Exactly. That's what I meant."

"NO! Those assholes never have money," Rubin said with his nose in the air. "Tonight we mingle with Portland's dark aristocracy!"

Persephone craned her neck from the driver's seat. "Rubin, could you spread it any deeper? Most of these people work at the mall."

Rubin put his fingers in his ears. "Like Portland's weather I pay no attention to criticism."

Persephone resumed, "I heard Lord Faustus is gonna be there tonight."

"Where did you hear that?" Angelita wondered.

"I'm dating the owner again. It's a seasonal thing."

Rubin popped up from behind the seat. "That's kick ass! Tonight's your lucky night, Victor. Faustus knows *everything about the occult!*"

"Huh, I thought that distinction was yours. Is he that Satan guy you told me about?"

Angelita seemed annoyed. "He's not a Satanist. He's a *Promethean!*"

"It's the difference between flesh and meat," Rubin said.

Weaving through a subdivision, the car emerged at an obscure industrial park. They piled out and walked down a dingy, weed conquered sidewalk. Rubin ran his hand along the chain link fence, summoned by a deep pulsating rhythm in the distance. Rounding a cluster of dumpsters, a queue of goth clubbers came into view.

Nearly everyone in line had expended great effort on their costumes. Several wore leashes. One woman had a torn wedding dress with red paint splashed on it. Another, clearly pregnant, wore a nun's habit. Her partner came, of course, dressed as a priest. Others expressed their fetishes for rubber, leather and plastic in multitudinous ways. The primary colors were red and black, although white dresses were tolerated if torn or sullied somehow. To Victor, the whole assembly was a seminar on the long-term effects of spanking your children.

So it was, that on rare occasions the bondage/discipline and gothic/industrial scenes, theoretically divested, came together along the sordid frontiers of suffering, guilt and hedonism. The idea that pain and pleasure were indiscernible was a philosophical point of agreement for both subcultures.

A massive African-American man in football armor and leather pants cased the line. Obviously part of the event staff, he menacingly lumbered as if inspecting new recruits. Wearing an executioner's hood and slapping his hand with a ping pong paddle, he smiled at Victor.

In your wildest dreams, buddy! Victor was unsure of how much of this was showbiz.

Rubin stole behind Victor to rub his shoulders. "The problem with too much morality, my friend, is that you cheat yourself out of living."

"But you live longer."

"Victor, it's clear that you're interested in breaking out, but I think you're still holding back."

Victor felt annoyed, as he always did when someone with half his education endeavored to teach him something. He felt that the much vaulted 'school of life' was an idea promoted by those without ambition. He had not yet learned that knowledge speaks while *true* wisdom listens.

"How can you say that, Rubin? I went on your rat hunt. I'm standing in line at your spankfest, drunk on your cough syrup. Just because I don't want to be paddled by a gay prison guard means I'm closed minded?"

"Cough syrup? You see, Angelita, what happens when you throw pearls to swine? Never again, Victor. Never."

Angelita interjected, "He's right, Rubin. Stop picking on him. You've been at it all night."

"I'm just saying that in order to find yourself you have to become lost. Follow me. I'll get you all turned around."

Rubin then looked at Angelita in a way that made Victor sick. As if they shared a dark secret, the two began communicating in nods and winks. Victor suddenly felt in danger.

Angelita opened her purse to produce a yellow highlighter. She snapped off the pen's cap to reveal a marijuana cigarette. Looking at Victor, she said, "When forced to choose between evils, I always pick the one I haven't tried yet."

Victor's face was a mask of fear. He did NOT like doing illegal things.

"Relax. *Magic* dragon kisses," she explained.

"Oh, magic. I get it," Victor croaked, nervously. Astonished by their brazen disregard for the law, it became clear that his friends had nothing to lose.

"You smoke, don't you Victor?"

The question came too quickly. He didn't have time to prepare one of his pseudo-intellectual rebuttals. "Yeah, of course," he lied, growing paranoid. "You sure you wanna be doing that out here, though? I mean what if…"

Before he could finish speaking the joint was lit—its acrid smoke wafting through the crowded line. Angelita sucked at the spark then leaned over to kiss Rubin.

Victor was upset. When offered a chance to kiss those lips again, he decided that he would seize the prize. Soon it was his turn, and Angelita took an extra deep breath, sucking the joint until she nearly burned her fingers. She motioned for Victor to close the gap.

This time Victor took control, forcefully taking her face into his hands. Tilting her head, he kissed her mouth with possessive hunger. For a moment she tried to pry loose; but then relaxed, her body melting in his embrace. They breathed into one another for several minutes, oblivious of the world.

When they finally broke apart Angelita looked sleepy. "Damn, Victor. A girl could get used to that!"

Rubin was several yards ahead, holding their place at the head of the line. "Hurry up, my little morning doves!"

The cashier at the gate blurted, "Three of you?"

Victor threw a glance at Angelita. He wished there were two.

"That'll be twenty bucks each," said the ogre, flames leaping at his face. The cash register was literally on fire. The drawer was extended, filled with candle wax and bits of paper. He took their money and stuffed it into his shirt. Then he checked their driver's licenses and stamped their wrists with the number '666.'

"The mark of the devil will get you into the beer garden," he snarled.

The trio pushed their way through a maze of torn linen, opening to a scene of unbridled decadence. A dark, jagged opening in the cinderblock wall of the warehouse marked the entrance of the nightclub. Outside, the fenced parking lot had been transformed into a beer garden.

Picnic tables were crowded with the usual patrons—felicitous fairies, fallen angels, punk rockers, post-pubescent pallbearers, mistresses, and makeshift *Marquis de Sades*. The tables were decorated with multi-tiered, candelabras. Either the owners had proven to the Fire Marshal that there was no danger in burning down the condemned garage, or they were in gross violation of the law.

Most interesting was the scaffolding in the center of the alley—an eye-level platform with medieval stocks. The neck and wrist holes were uncomfortably low to the ground, placing a voluptuous young redhead in a very compromising position. Her fiery mane covered her face, but did not muffle her whimpering.

Behind her, two topless mistresses with riding crops towered over her naked ass, delivering a barrage of blows in perfect tempo to the music. Victor was already high; his muscles buzzed, and his thoughts weren't clear. For the second time in as many days he grew weak in the knees—first from death, now from lust. Recognizing the look, Angelita snapped a leash onto his collar.

"Down boy," she said, whispering to Victor's subconscious. "You see, men are no different from puppies."

"How's that?" Victor asked, struggling to maintain his dignity.

Angelita's lips were swollen. "When you feel mommy's teeth on your neck, you'll know."

With Rubin in the lead and Victor happily tethered, the threesome sauntered into the cavern on the side of the building. It was hardly a nightclub at all—more like Satan's ballroom. Aside from the strobe lights, smoke machines and laser effects, cauldrons of fire flickered from dangling braziers. They shed an eerie light upon the brawl and completed the effect of one's complete decent into Hell.

The music sounded like an amplified lawnmower. Dripping with the distilled angst of post-modernism, it violently engaged the dancers. Victor looked across the sea of bobbing heads, obscured by fog and cigarette smoke. He was a boat awash in a hurricane, and the needle on his moral compass was spinning.

Thus, through the combined effect of alcohol, pot and flashing colors he achieved what Rubin had promised—a deep inner chaos. Neither self-conscious of his desire, nor empathic of Rubin's jealously, he was finally open to whatever would happen. He was a salmon, tired from too much swimming. It was the inevitable fate of a moralist. Giving in, he drifted with the current to a dark and swampy reservoir.

As they clamored to navigate the swell of people, they passed a candy store of sexual oddities and delights including a bicycle with a dildo for a seat, and a shadowbox—a screen behind which a young couple did the dance of creation. Victor stood like a deer in headlights until Angelita yanked him away.

"I want you to meet a friend of mine," she shouted, standing at the base of a wooden platform.

Victor looked up to see a man chained to a crucifix, his arms splayed-out like a human animal hide. His back was covered in rivulets from the abuse rained upon him by the Amazon warrior that stood there. She was a big-boned woman of Scandinavian stock. Her blonde hair flowed over her shoulders like a waterfall, and upon her feet she wore stilettos with heels like deck nails. Upon seeing Angelita she stopped whipping.

"Oh my GAWD, you guys! Hi Angelita!" she cried, stepping down from the platform to hug them. "How are you? I haven't seen you in ages!"

To Victor, it seemed uncanny how easily her personality flipped from the Whore of Babylon to valley girl.

"Victor, this is Sophia," Angelita shouted. "Most of the girls working here are from her troupe. She's the top dominatrix in Portland!"

"I'd say she's doing a good job," Victor answered genuinely. He shook her hand, noticing that she had a grip like a man.

"So what did this guy do wrong?" Victor asked, pointing to the side of beef hanging from the cross.

"Oh, he just needed a good beating. Most guys do," she added, elbowing Angelita. "Care for a ride?"

"No thanks, I'm not into abuse," Victor quickly answered, shocked by the welts on the man's back. "How do you know when to stop?"

"We use 'safe words.' We're going pretty easy on him 'cause it's a public event, but if you were a private client we'd agree upon a word that you could say when it got too intense."

"Why not just say 'stop'?"

"Because sometimes 'stop' means 'go.'"

"It does?"

"Hand me the power, Victor. I'll look into your eyes and show you that everything you believe about yourself is a lie."

Victor tried to speak, but found no voice. He cleared his throat. "So how do you guys know each other?"

Angelita broke in, "We had a yoga class. Sophia turned me on to this whole scene. This is how I met Rubin."

"Yes, my darling. It was here that the gods deemed our paths to intersect," Rubin inserted, squeezing himself between Angelita and Victor. "I'm gonna look for Lord Faustus, if you two don't mind."

"I don't mind," Angelita said, coldly.

Sophia looked Victor over as if he was on the dessert cart. "So, is this the hot professor I keep hearing about?"

Victor smiled.

"Who, Victor? No. He's my pony boy," she joked. "Actually, he's a friend of Rubin's."

Victor knit his brow. "I thought I was a friend of *yours!*"

Angelita was about to apologize when the Valkyrie offered her the cat-o'-nine-tails. "Care to give him a couple strokes?"

"But of course, my lady," Angelita answered with fervor, and for a minute Victor feared that *he* was to be flogged next.

Before he could protest, Angelita snatched the implement—nine knotted cords, fastened to a handle—and hopped onto the platform. Stretching the polyvinyl dress to capacity, she assumed a batter's stance. Victor winced as she brought it, cruelly, across the man's rear end. The pain was so intense her victim nearly climbed to the ceiling.

CRACK "That's…"

CRACK "What you get…"

CRACK "For every girl…"

CRACK "You ever lied to…"

CRACK "You piece of shit…" Angelita shouted with surprising venom.

"That's my girl!" Sophia cheered, handing her a goose feather to replace the whip. "Now tickle him until he repents!"

Angelita took the feather and pounced on the man's back like a panther. She took the man's hair into her fist and yanked his head back. "Tell me you're sorry, you fucking child molester!"

The man was unable to escape her capricious torment. He pulled against his bindings as she applied her artful inhumanity, dancing the feather across his ribs. Eventually the soul was broken and the man complied. Then he collapsed, hanging like a wet rag.

Sophia praised her. "Hey, you're pretty good at that. Want a job?"

"No thanks. Getting paid would take away from the intrinsic pleasure," Angelita kidded as she jumped down from the platform. She handed the feather to Victor. "Use this on the next girl who turns you on."

"Will she be ticklish?"

"Yes she is," Angelita teased. She pointed to the laminated card that hung from Sophia's neck. "Are you gonna use your VIP badge?"

"I doubt it. We're all tied up here."

"I wanna show Victor the VIP room."

"Oops, silly me! I just lost my VIP card," Sophia clowned. She turned her head and dropped the necklace into Angelita's hand. "You kids have fun!"

The exercise of whipping a man had stoked Angelita's fire, for she coarsely took Victor's leash and led him away. She plowed through the teeming throng as if on a mission, at last climbing a set of rickety, wooden stairs leading to a loft. Angelita flashed her badge to the guard at the door, and pushed her way through a beaded curtain.

Furtively, she turned to Victor. "Just act natural, and try not to stare."

"Yes, ma'am," Victor replied.

Chapter 11

T HE DEN WAS GILDED with Victorian *chattel*, complete with rope tassels and burgundy velvet tapestries. Darkly upholstered couches lined the walls of the chamber, and a dim chandelier hung from the ceiling. Outfitted with flickering bulbs, the gold-leafed sconces offered little light—so it took a moment for Victor's eyes to adjust.

He found the room starkly quiet in contrast to the pumping night-club. A Persian rug framed a mattress on the floor, around which a dozen couples fed their libidos. Some knelt while others sat with their drinks, all quietly enraptured by a pair of women who were making love. Were it not for the moaning it might well have been a church.

Victor and Angelita tiptoed around the assembly, the floor creaking in their wake. They found an opening in the circle, and Angelita knelt. Victor crouched behind her. Watching the writhing knot of arms and legs before them, Angelita lay back, sinking into his arms.

The two women on the mattress lay side-by-side, each with her face obscured by the legs of the other. Their tongues darted, and the excitement they raised in each other was contagious. Afloat on the tide of ecstasy, the assembly took to slaking their own private hungers.

A man across from Victor cupped his girlfriend's breast, kneading it tenderly. On the mattress, one of the women began rocking her hips. Then, seeking better leverage, she rolled on top of the other. Victor heard a gasp escape from Angelita's throat, and from the ensuing gyrations, it was clear that the dominant girl was pursuing an orgasm.

Victor was now fully aroused, his thinking clouded and confused. With no consideration for Rubin, he began kissing Angelita's neck. Licking the salt from her skin, his mouth delicately brushed her shoulders.

"Sir Lancelot. I thought you were my protector," Angelita protested meekly. Her neck was bristling.

"My Lady, you need to revisit your Celtic history," he answered, wrapping his arms around her waist. Angelita rolled her head to the side as he nibbled.

The woman on her knees was cooing now—short little cries as she moved on her lover's face. This proved more than the crowd could bear, and several couples moved to shadowed corners to pursue private agendas. As the spell blossomed, so did the musky fragrance of sex.

Angelita pushed away from the mattress, urgently turning to face Victor. They devoured one another with brutal, open-mouthed kisses. She took Victor's hand and placed it under her dress. Following her lead, his fingers dove up her thigh, fluttering like a butterfly. She raised her knee as far as the dress would allow. Flushed with desire, Angelita breathed shallowly. Teasing her for several minutes, Victor's hand finally came to rest on her sweltering wetness.

"You're very naughty, my queen," he murmured, chewing her earlobe. "No panties?"

"In this dress?" She was barely able to thread words.

"You're the hottest woman I've ever known."

She flicked his nose with her finger. "I believe you'd drink my bathwater."

"Only to get to you."

They kissed again, his finger slipping into her silky valley. Angelita's breath hitched.

"Fuck me," she blurted, her eyes pleading.

"HERE?" Victor asked, sobering up. "We can't do that!"

Angelita pulled Victor toward the couch.

"Sit down!" she commanded, pushing him into the cushions.

The springs were broken, and Victor sank as if on a cloud. Oblivious to the couple fucking next to them, she deftly unbuckled his belt before pulling his pants down with one impatient tug. Then she hiked her dress and straddled him. Awash in bliss, Victor pushed into her as far as the couch would allow.

"Goddamn!" she cried.

Victor looked up at her. "Did I hurt you?"

"Don't be a fucking ninja."

"What?"

"I want to hear you talk dirty!"

"Do what?"

"CALL ME A BITCH!"

As she pleaded, the women on the mattress began to squeal as well. The couple next to them began jarring the couch with their rutting, and the strange woman laid her head on Victor's shoulder. Not to be out done, Victor seized Angelita's ass with his hands. He pulled on her violently, fucking her with abandon.

"You're a bitch," he said, looking at her to confirm that he'd said it correctly. But her eyes were closed. Victor saw in that moment that he wasn't doing her—she was doing him. So he said it again, with conviction.

"You're a fucking bitch!" he snarled, burying his face in the bouncing cleft of her bosom. He felt anger.

"Don't you fucking move!" she answered, moving with purpose, driven by hunger. He felt her body shake with tremors as her nails tore at his back. "Yes! Yes!"

Then she sat heavily in his lap and pressed her forehead against his. With their eyes nearly touching, she panted, "Cum, Victor. I'm on *Depo*."

Gripping her hips, Victor used her body to please himself. With an exultant groan, he came. Holding her so tightly that she could barely breathe, a wave of clarity overcame him. *I just fucked Rubin's fiancé!* He opened his mouth, but she pressed her finger to his lips.

"S-h-s-h-s-h-s-h! You can't have virtues if you don't have vices," she said, rising from the couch. "We all have secrets, Victor. It's okay. I need to go to the little girls' room. You staying?"

That's it? "I'll follow you," Victor insisted, drying himself with the ends of his shirt. "Rubin's waiting for us, remember?"

She laughed. "Oh, yeah. Rubin. I forgot all about him."

If Rubin was the king of non sequitur, Angelita was the queen of understatement. Just as they reached the bottom of the stairs, Rubin appeared.

"Ah, Guinevere and Lancelot! You guys won't believe what I learned at the Sex Positive Booth. Did you know that a pig's orgasm lasts thirty minutes?"

"No it doesn't," Victor answered.

"So, I take it you've seen the VIP room!" Rubin said, elbowing Victor. Playing the fool to a degree beyond comprehension, he added, "Anything going on up there?"

"Just the usual," Angelita interrupted. "Nasty people fucking."

Victor cringed.

"It couldn't have been *that* boring! Your cheeks are rosy, my love," Rubin said. He reached for Angelita's face but she backed away. Undaunted, he bragged to Victor, "Pretty amazing stuff, huh?"

"I can see why you like it," Victor replied.

"Look boys, I really gotta go to the girls' room!"

"Ah, but of course, my darling," Rubin offered with a bow. Then he faced Victor. "I've found Lord Faustus."

"That's great."

"I talked you up. I told him you were a well known psychiatrist."

"Yeah, I'm a real pillar of the community."

When Angelita was out of sight, Rubin frowned. "Thought you could hide it from me, did yah?"

Victor became ashen.

"You spilled a gin and tonic on my shirt!" he said, pointing at Victor's stomach. "The shirt I loaned you ... Hello, tonic glows under black light. That's alcohol abuse, you know?"

Victor was burnt out on lies. "I need some fresh air."

"Good. Faustus is outside."

Walking into the night air, Victor trailed a few feet behind. His head was spinning. "I kinda wish you didn't tell people I'm a shrink."

"Don't be ashamed. There are worse jobs."

"No, it makes people defensive."

"Relax!"

They passed through a checkpoint in the chain link fence and entered the beer garden. Victor immediately spied a bald man with a cropped goatee sitting on a picnic table. He was dressed in a fascist ensemble with black shirt, pants and tie—his pale head, seeming to float in the shadows. With a commanding presence, the man stood to greet Rubin.

Victor was not in the mood to have stars placed in his eyes. He was used to thinking circles around people, and had particular contempt for pretentiousness. Offering a hand, he fired the opening volley, "You stood up when we arrived. Are you well-bred?"

The surfeit smile faded. Faustus said nothing. Holding Victor's hand captive, he turned it from side to side.

Victor smirked. He was enjoying the game. "Perhaps you're a palm reader, too?"

A sinister grin spread across the occultist's face. "Despite the impression you wish to portray, my good doctor, you are an anxious man. You pick at your fingers."

"Impressive," Victor admitted with a toothy smile. He retrieved his hand. "What else do you see?"

"Blue-collar origins. Your teeth are crooked. You struggle with inferiority, despite the titles you hang upon yourself. I think you're uncertain of your purpose."

"And you can tell this how, exactly?"

"Your posture. Your body looks like a question mark, perhaps from bumping your head too long on a ceiling that was set too low by your father. So now that we're on equal terms I'm hoping that we can speak more—how shall I say—honestly?"

"That's very impressive…"

Rubin nudged Victor. "I told you so."

"…My name's Victor."

"Victor! That's a pretentious name. It must be exhausting." The dark figure resumed sitting. Placing a hand on his chest, he announced, "I am Lord Faustus."

Victor's shoulders popped audibly as he straightened. "MY NAME is pretentious? I imagine your parents didn't name you *Lord Faustus!*"

"Anyone deriding hypocrisy in others is a hypocrite by default." Faustus closed his eyes and added, "Faustus is the name of my soul. You would do well to discover the name of your own."

"The name of my soul is *Victor*. I can say that with certainty," he said, hooking his thumbs in his pockets.

"So, what can I possibly offer *a psychiatrist who has known only victory?*"

"I'm a psychologist. I've known victory because I have the wisdom to ask questions, and I've decided that you can help me."

"Appealing to my sense of vanity?" The frown reversed. "Well played. Sit down."

The goth kids who surrounded Faustus made room for Victor to sit. They seemed to recognize that their mentor had met an equal.

"So you study the occult?" Victor asked.

"To put it mildly," he answered smugly, "I have the world's largest collection of Satanic artifacts in my underground studio."

"Sounds interesting. I'd like to see it."

"Fellowship is not the aim of my spirituality. You had a question for me?" Faustus reminded.

"Yes. I have a friend who I'd like to help, but I'm not sure I can until I better understand what she's talking about. First of all, she says she's part of the 'gothic subculture,' which I'm not sure I understand."

"Good luck with that. Ask five goths and you'll get five answers. Being goth is about being real. We prefer the harsh reality of existence."

Victor balked. "Which reality? In my experience, the limits of one's mind are the limits of one's world."

Faustus uncrossed his arms that he might emphasize his words like an orchestra conductor. "Everything that you've ever known, loved or achieved will be taken from you. The meaning of life is loss! We are a group of outcasts who celebrate that fact."

"I thought the word 'gothic' was a reference to literature."

Faustus pursed his lips. "And architecture. But as with any subculture, it's also about music, ideas, and a way of being. In the

'70s, journalists had no way to classify this new kind of music they were hearing. The band members wore black, and the melodies were morose—similar to the gothic writers. So the name stuck. In time, a subculture gelled along these themes, which includes an interest in the supernatural."

Victor squinted. "Aren't a lot of these kids just out to annoy their parents?"

"When you dance with death you foment a certain urgency to be truthful. But the less fake people *try* to be, the more artificial they become. It's now fashionable to look like us. A lot of sheep wake up in the morning and say, 'I think I'll be alternative today.'"

Victor nodded. "It's paradoxical."

Faustus cheered, hammering his fist in the air, "Of course! *True* authenticity is rare, even between you and me. We're constantly on the edge of being full of shit so who are we to judge? We may have *moments* of clarity in our lives where we enjoy interludes of self-determination, but then we fall back to sleep. We must be ever vigilant, especially with ourselves!"

"If it's such a battle, why bother?"

Faustus closed his eyes. "No one can answer that question for you."

"Why not wear bright colors?"

"We're dark people. Mysticism is rooted in sadness. Why else would we *cry* in the presence of the inexplicable?"

Victor fiddled with his chin. "What about body piercings and tattoos?"

"Ask your friend what her piercings mean *to her*. We alter our bodies to mark our lives—break ups, new beginnings or a spiritual awakening."

As he said this, he hooked his arm around the shaven head of a young woman. "Lilith here has an interesting tattoo."

The girl was hesitant, showing surprising bashfulness for her rough-and-tumble look. Eventually she put her head down so Victor could see her scalp. The back of her shaven dome displayed a retail barcode.

"It actually scans," she chirped over her lip ring. Batting electric blue eyelashes she added, "It's my birth date."

"But what does it mean to you?" Victor asked.

"When I turned sixteen I got a job to support my mom. I became part of the system that day."

"I see. It's the mark of the Devil!" Victor muttered. Then he threw his hands in the air. "Of course, you're Satanists."

Faustus chuckled, ominously. "No. We're Prometheans. The angel Lucifer was a light bringer. The God of the Bible is the enemy."

Victor wondered if the windbag hadn't created his own religious niche so that he could be the head of something.

Faustus continued, "I don't sacrifice animals unless I'm eating a cheeseburger."

The group laughed, probably out of procedure.

Victor wanted to know how to help Violet. "This friend I told you about claims to be a witch. Is that the same thing?"

"Witches are gothic hippies," came Faustus' reply. Again, the crowd laughed. He smiled at them and added, "they're Catholic Pagans."

"I see."

Faustus' face darkened. "This person you're asking about is a patient, isn't she? Perhaps I know her."

Victor lips tightened. "Why do you ask?"

"No need for concern. I have an enormous amount of respect for psychology, in truth. You're what priests were in the Dark Ages— except you're doing a better job. I assure you, your reservation in Hell is confirmed."

"Good to hear. I'm no priest, but I deal with spiritual crises all the time," Victor expounded. "In a way, I like it when people are upset with their beliefs. It's an opportunity for change."

This excited Faustus. He lunged. "Yes! Now contrast that with Christianity, where a spiritual crisis is a problem! You should be suspicious of *any* group that calls people sheep."

Victor saw many parallels between Faustus' philosophy and his own. "You know, in psychology, it's common for people to look at doctors as if they were angelic. It's called 'transference.' Of course it's unethical to encourage such fantasies."

"Why not? Jesus did. And he used that power to heal."

Victor shrunk from the blasphemy. "You're not suggesting that Christ benefited from transference, are you?"

"Why not? He was a victim of the hopes of his time, like Kennedy or Martin Luther King."

"You have to admit that Jesus' ministry of forgiveness was revolutionary."

"Please, doctor. It was completely self-serving," Faustus said. "Why do you suppose he *taught* forgiveness in the first place?"

"Because it was his mission?"

"Come on Victor, you're losing stock."

Victor scratched his earlobe. "I honestly don't know."

"He was born in a Middle Eastern country, to a twelve year-old girl, out of an illicit affair with a celestial being. Everyone in the dusty markets of Nazareth was talking about it. I'm sure he had a few stones cast in his direction."

"And?"

"He was an angry little pistol. It frightened him, so he taught the very thing he most needed to learn—FORGIVE, FORGIVE, FORGIVE!"

Victor's face brightened. "In psychology we call that *reaction formation* … although I think most Christians would have a problem with your theory."

"When I meet a Christian who gives away all of their money I'll care. Their dominion over the public discourse will soon end. Nietzsche was correct to note that there has only been one Christian in history, and he died on the cross. Everyone since has been a fraud."

"That's funny."

"And sad."

"So you're saying Jesus *was* God after all?"

"Of course he was. So are you."

Victor grumbled. "I find that hard to believe. Trust me. I'm no God."

"That's why you slouch."

Victor saw Angelita at the entrance of the beer garden. He extended his hand. "Maybe we can talk again sometime."

"It's inevitable," Faustus said, looking away dismissively. "You didn't get what you came for, and you're a diligent man."

"Assiduous," Victor corrected. "I'm assiduous."

Victor and his friends spent the rest of the night dancing. Watching Rubin broke Victor's heart. He seemed to hang on Angelita more than usual, as if sensing that something had happened. It was nearly sunrise when they finally piled into Persephone's car. As they rambled homeward, Angelita laid her head upon Victor's shoulder. He enjoyed her warmth, but upon closing his eyes could only think of Violet.

Chapter

12

THE BROOM CLOSET where the interns worked was hardly big enough for two people, let alone Dr. Clifton's ten-speed bike. Victor fell over the clutter, slamming his *Sentient Bean* travel mug on the desk. Before he could bite his breakfast scone, Dr. Clifton shattered the peace.

"So how goes your little vacation over at Viagra Falls?"

Victor turned his head. "Now that you've coughed up your morning fur ball, I assume you're referring to my important work at the nursing home?"

"Don't take offense. I just hate to see someone squander vital waters on barren soil."

"I appreciate your concern, Sam. Actually, it's the best rotation ever."

Dr. Clifton finished typing a sentence as if he was squashing a bug. The wheels on his chair squeaked as he pushed away from the desk. "That's not what you said last month."

Victor nodded like a bobble-head. "Yeah, so? I had a change of heart! Suppose I actually *like* the elderly."

"Suit yourself. I'm just warning you not to tell Dr. Lindsey. If she finds out you *enjoy* doing something she'll feel obligated to transfer you elsewhere."

"Well, that will be hard for her to do from Detroit."

"*Oh contraire, monsieur.* She's back. As a matter of fact, she graced me with her foul countenance this morning. And let me warn you, someone's lit the fuse on her tampon."

"I suppose I'd better go and say hello, then."

"Good idea. It's always better to meet with her on *your* terms," he answered, resuming typing.

"Hey Sam, can I ask you an unrelated question?"

"Sure," he answered, his face blue from the computer screen.

"Why are you such a miserable son of a bitch?"

"*Cogito Ergo Doleo.* I think, therefore I'm depressed."

Indeed Dr. Clifton spoke true. As with most compulsive personalities, Dr. Lindsey found it impossible to stay away from work. Her distrust for mankind was like a rock in her shoe. By the second week of her visit home, she'd come to believe that the hospital could not exist without her.

"My sister's very sick," she told Victor. "She's undergoing chemo, and doesn't need me pestering her. So what's new with you?"

"We're all glad to see you back," Victor said. He thought about the hospital morgue which was filled with people no doubt holding similar delusions of importance.

In truth, work had been pleasant with her gone. He wasn't doing *real* therapy in the nursing home, so there was nothing to report. His testing clients were open and shut cases, well supervised by Dr. Hammon. This left his work with Violet, which he was reticent to discuss.

"Okay. First off, I'm pulling you out of that nursing home. Now that I'm back, there's no reason for you to be out there."

125

"But I *want* to be there!"

Dr. Lindsey gave Victor a suspicious look. "We can arrange it if that's how you honestly feel, although it'll be in addition to other things I've planned. I have you scheduled to do a lot more testing before Christmas."

"Okay. I don't mind extra work."

Dr. Lindsey scowled. "So, what's going on at Whispering Pines?"

"Well, I started seeing folks three weeks ago, twelve patients in total."

"Uh huh."

"They're pretty demented, but I'm learning a lot."

"So what kind of therapy are you doing?"

"I'm doing *nice-young-man* therapy," Victor said as a matter of fact.

"What's that?"

"I invented it. People are dying of loneliness there, and because they have Alzheimer's, every visit's the first and only one."

"Go on. I can't wait to hear the rest."

"After I meet with them, I listen in the hallway. The roommate usually asks, 'Who was that?' If the patient answers, 'I don't know, but he sure was a *nice young man*,' I call the session a success."

In truth Victor had serious doubts about whether he was doing any good at all. His real reason for being at the nursing home was, of course, to be near Angelita. In the three weeks since their tryst at the nightclub, she had chilled considerably. This made Victor want her even more.

"By the way, what's the diagnosis of that girl on the locked unit?" Dr. Lindsey queried, fumbling with a spiral pad.

"I gave her an *Axis I* diagnosis of 296.22 *Depressive Disorder, Single Episode, Moderate.*"

"That's all? It seems a little weak. She's dysthymic at least. Are you sure you weren't influenced by her? Dr. Moran said she's a nut roll."

Victor bristled.

Dr. Lindsey became droll. "Just because she acts cute when *you're* around doesn't mean she isn't mentally ill. She gets by on youth and beauty, but believe me, by the time she's forty she'll be fat and on Lithium."

The bitch was obviously in a wretched mood. Victor wanted to stand up to her, but didn't want to deal with her flying monkeys. "I think her ideas come from a spiritual place," he said, timidly. "She's Wiccan. It's part of her religion to have magical thinking."

"I think she has a personality disorder."

"What do you mean?" Victor asked, livid at the idea of her diagnosing a patient she had never met.

"Adults dabble in magic when they're impotent in real life. It's like in Haiti where everyone is poor, so people practice Voodoo. In this country people who study the occult are usually ineffective human beings. They do this to feel special."

"What's so wrong with wanting to feel special?"

"Diagnosis isn't about feeling sorry for people, Victor. It's about calling a spade a spade. Psychics are mostly schizotypal people. They practice Reiki on their dogs for crying out loud."

"How is the practice of magic different from a Christian believing in prayer? And would you say the same things?"

Dr. Lindsey ignored his question. "She's obviously taken you in, Victor. She's got *Borderline Personality Disorder.* She's manipulative, emotionally volatile, has delusions of being a witch, cuts on her arms, and is splitting you and the psychiatrist—and me for that matter. I'm a little surprised that you haven't put it together. You're usually on the ball."

"You've never met her. What if Dr. Moron actually *is* an asshole? You've said it yourself. Even paranoid people get followed."

"It's pronounced 'Mor-anne,' and he may be an asshole, but you work for the hospital. Never, under any circumstance, should you ally with a patient against a staff member!"

"I didn't. I'm just asking the question."

"Victor, what's happened to you? This job is about pattern analysis. After you've seen a thousand patients like I have, you'll find it disappointing how uncreative people are when it comes to being nuts."

Victor looked dejected.

"Look, it's a simple matter of statistics. The average person has twenty-seven dollars in their wallet. Like it or not, it's a fact. Knowing facts allows you to predict things. I'm willing to bet my lunch that Violet says mean things behind your back."

"I'd rather not find out," Victor answered, bitterly. It occurred to him that Dr. Lindsey was the one doing the splitting. "I do best when I take people at their word."

"Good luck with that. So what are you guys working on anyway? You need to have goals to do therapy."

Victor realized he had to be careful. Three weeks had passed since Halloween, and he'd already met with Violet on ten separate occasions. She always did well during the session—listening and putting concepts into her own words so Victor knew they were truly hers. He felt that he could say anything to her at this point, no matter how probing. In short, they were primed to do truly good work together.

Yet when they were apart, Violet forgot her lessons and regressed to broken patterns of problem solving. Her childhood nest of dysfunction was still where she came to rest at the end of the day.

"We're still getting to the goal-setting phase," he breathed. "I've established good rapport, and she's ready to do the work..."

"But?"

"She tends to relapse when I'm not there. But she is getting better. Asha said they're moving her to the open unit."

"That doesn't mean a thing. They're short of beds. If she isn't acting out, they have to lower her level of care. There's a waitlist of people in *real* crisis."

Victor felt angry. "I'm glad to hear that the patient's needs are driving this hospital's decisions."

"What do you expect, Victor? I'm sure your little shrew doesn't have insurance. Oregon Health Plan's probably been footing her bill—and that's assuming that coverage has been authorized. If not, the hospital's been eating the cost. She's been here for three weeks and frankly that's a little long for a suicide crisis. It sounds to me like she's scamming us to keep seeing you."

"I'm not sensing that, Dr. Lindsey. I'm not sure she would survive on her own if we discharged her. She's just not there yet." Victor was torn between defending Violet and damaging a relationship with his supervisor. He hated to admit it, but Dr. Lindsey was starting to make sense. "If you see this more clearly than I, then give me some ideas."

"It's not your problem, Victor. Once she's discharged you'll never see her again. It's not like she's going to open *her* purse to pay for therapy with you."

"She might."

"The pattern says otherwise. In all my years I've never seen a patient do that."

Maybe it's because you suck, Victor thought. Stewing, he abdicated. "Well, then I need to give her something that she can take with her if she leaves."

Dr. Lindsey put down her pen. "I seem to recall something from my grad school days," she said. "It's called the *black feather technique.* Have you heard of it?"

"No."

"Basically, you link your discussions in session to a transition object that the patient can focus on when you aren't around. It keeps them from bugging you with phone calls."

"You mean like a teddy bear?"

"Why not? It worked when you were a kid."

"Doesn't that place the healing power outside the patient?"

"Oh please, Victor. I don't see you holding a teddy bear anymore."

"Good point," Victor admitted, feeling a little better. He relaxed a bit, which was always a dangerous thing to do around Dr. Lindsey.

"I still think she's manipulating you. Do you have a crush on her?"

Victor was in shock.

"I don't want you seeing her more than once a week, starting today," she ordered.

Now Victor was fuming.

"Psychology is about patterns, just like the insurance business. Remember Victor, *twenty-seven dollars!*"

Eventually the torture ended, and Victor slogged to his next appointment. Halfway to the waiting room he dug for his wallet. Inside he found a driver's license, a credit card, a coffee club membership, Angelita's broken feather, and *eleven dollars and twenty-six cents*. The bitch was wrong.

Odds were, Violet was no average patient. Victor couldn't have guessed how true this was.

Chapter

13

VICTOR COULD BARELY CONTAIN his contempt for Dr. Lindsey. She had a lot of nerve telling him how to conduct therapy. Even worse, her insinuation that he only cared about Violet because she was attractive was an outrage.

"Word up, Victor? You seem different today," Violet asked, pouring herself a cup of water.

"I hear you're getting off the locked unit soon," he answered, keeping the bigger news to himself. "Congratulations."

"You heard right," Violet said, closing her hands around her journal.

They're letting her use a pen! Victor also noticed that her bandages had been removed. Reflecting on the pink ridges where the stitches had been, he said, "The best predictor of future behavior is past behavior. You need to start using the skills we're working on."

"Believe me. I'm more sick of this nuthouse than you are."

"It's not enough to be free from the cage. You have to know how to fly. It takes practice, you know."

"What if you're a chicken?" she joked, looking out the window.

"The best way to fail is to never try," he replied. "Can you think of *anything* of value that doesn't take a lot of work?"

"Yes. It takes many nails to build a crib, but only one screw to fill it."

"There you go again, making jokes."

"Lighten up Victor! Who says I'm joking?"

Victor raised an eyebrow. "Is there something you've not told me?"

"Perhaps I'm waiting for the right time."

"What if I told you that we're running *out* of time?"

"Okay, Mr. Rabbit. If you must know, I got *hoovered* right after I got to Portland. Are you happy now?"

Victor scratched his head. "Please translate, 'hoovered'?"

"An abortion," she groaned, pulling her hair.

Victor's face fell. "Oh no! What was that like?"

"It sucked, excuse the pun. Or as we say in Texas, stirrups are for rodeos."

Admiring her inky eyebrows, Victor wondered if the carpet matched the drapes. He rubbed the image out of his eyes. "Are you okay with it now?"

"I guess, aside from all the guilty girly stuff. I smoked pot and drank like a fish before I found out. I'd never do what my mom did to me. She smoked like a factory, which is why I was born underweight and dyslexic. I hate her for that."

"You're dyslexic?"

"Yeah. Some devil worshipper I am. I've rejected Dog and make sacrifices to Santa!"

Victor looked at her, perplexed, then tiredly remarked, "I just got the joke."

"Honestly, I have to use a ruler to read," Violet said, adjusting her pillow. "Anyway, I broke up with my boyfriend right before I moved here. He got me pregnant to keep me around; or maybe just out of disrespect, I'm not sure. But I won't spend the rest of my life hating my son cause he looks like an asshole."

"So *that's* the reason you tried to commit suicide?"

Violet looked up, her mouth open. "Dude, have you ever *been* to Texas?"

"You know what I mean. You mentioned the abortion, but I'm still not clear on why suicide was the only way."

Violet paused, hanging her head. "There was some other shit that went down in October. It seemed like I was dead inside already, so I figured 'why bother going on with the charade?'"

"And now?" Victor probed, hoping that she wouldn't disregard ten sessions with a flip remark.

"I still cry a lot, but I'm not in crisis anymore." She held up her journal and tapped on the cover with newly painted fingernails. "Writing in this journal helped me because I don't have to work through the same shit over and over."

Victor squinted. "Where did you get black nail polish?"

"I used a *Sharpie* at the nurses' station."

"Sorry for interrupting. You were telling me about the journal," Victor said, marveling at her resourcefulness.

"I love to do it, but I'm scared a friend will read it. There's a lot of private stuff in here," she revealed, hugging the book.

Victor didn't want to sabotage the one thing that had worked. "The kind of person who would read your private stuff is not a friend at all."

"Victor, when you asked me to write about the things I have to live for, I finally realized that my fucked up family has nothing to do with me."

"Bravo! At some point we just have to go out and find our own paths."

"I already know which path I'm on."

"Which is...?"

"The psychopath."

Against his better judgment, Victor smirked. "You're an adult now. You can create the family you wish you'd had. I have a small group of friends who care for me and that's good enough."

"My best friend Ashley and me are like that. She's so cool. She knows everything about angels! We're renting a room from some guy we met in Hillsboro. We call him daddy, even though he isn't much older than we are."

Victor couldn't resist. "Do you think you missed out by not having a dad? This seems to be a theme."

"I was *lucky* not to have a dad. Half my girlfriends were molested. All that shit turns a girl into a feminist. You know, 'the crazy idea that women are people.'"

Victor crossed his arms. "I'm a humanist. You know, 'the crazy idea that people are people.' I can assure you that evil women exist."

"A-w-w-w. Victow got his heart bwoke," she teased, impishly. "Is that why you're still single?"

"You should try testing a thought in your mind before you say it out loud. I was referring to a molestation case where the perpetrator was the grandmother."

"That's some sick shit, man. My mom may not be a saint, but she never diddled my fiddle."

Victor pressed his temples. "On one hand you say you benefited by not having a dad, yet it clearly warped the way you see men."

"I can see dads being important for boys, but why girls?"

"Because dads provide a once-in-a-lifetime chance to learn the skill of being a girl *in relation to* a boy. If that's missing, girls go through life getting hurt. Then, of course, they take it personally."

"Gee, you think so?" Violet bunched up her pillow.

"It's the only love affair you'll ever have that doesn't involve sex. That's why it's so important."

"I had a grandfather who was like a dad. He promised to move to Victoria when I was a teenager, but never did. It was a big disappointment for me." Tears dropped from Violet's eyes. "I guess that's what guys do. They lie."

"You're entitled to your opinion. But if I said the same things about women you would call me sexist."

"What if it's true?"

"What, that *guys lie?* That's kind of a simple philosophy, don't you think?"

"Got a better one?"

"How about 'people lie sometimes'? I'm wondering if blaming half the human race doesn't get you off the hook for your own misbehavior. This whole time you've been telling me that you have a lot of secrets. I'm curious how many of them involve lies that *Violet's* told."

Violet contemplated Victor's statement. "I fucked Eddie once. He was the drummer for Jake's band."

She grinned, then finished, "But it's different 'cause I really didn't want to have sex with him."

"He raped you?"

"Well. No. Not exactly," she mumbled, pensively. "I kinda raped him."

"Uh huh."

"Okay. My bad."

Victor self-consciously uncrossed his arms. He didn't want to project disapproval. Instead he moved to the edge of the chair. "Love and fear are oil and water, Violet. They can't coexist. You have to choose."

"My grandpa used to say something like that. 'A ship is safe in the harbor, but that's not what ships are for.'"

"He was right, so why don't you set sail?"

Violet scowled. "I kinda feel like you're blaming me for my life. I didn't ask my dad to paint the wall with his brains."

"You're all we have to work with. We have to let go of disappointment, plain and simple. It's an anchor."

"Look, I've got shitty luck."

Victor walked to her bed and looked out the window. High in the sky, silver tufted clouds were breaking, and a column of sunlight shined upon the hospital grounds.

"All you have to do," he said, "is open yourself to new things. Show a little faith."

"Faith leads to disappointment," she argued, fanning her fingers.

"No. Faith without action leads to disappointment. I wonder if you've ever really known a man. I wonder if you're brave enough."

"I've had *lots* of boyfriends," she said, glazing over as her mind replayed the squalid details.

"But did you relate to any of them?"

"It's called 'falling in love,' Victor."

"Don't fall! You'll only skin your knees!"

"What the fuck are you talking about? All my life I've loved *too much*. I see colors more brightly than normal people."

"It's not *real* love if you throw yourself into the pyre. That's called an offering."

Violet's face darkened. "Have you ever had an STD? Now I know why Jake's band was called *Jalapeno Piss*."

Victor shook his head.

"Looking back I always put myself in danger with Jake. Can you imagine not using a condom in this day and age?"

"No, I can't," Victor answered. He felt ashamed.

"I need a way to judge guys before I get involved. Is there a litmus test?"

"Why not pretend that you have a daughter. Then imagine that she brought home the guy you're considering. Ask yourself if you would approve of him."

Violet closed her eyes. "Hmmm. I would definitely discourage my baby girl from dating Jake. Come to think of it, I wouldn't let my turtle date Jake."

"It's uncanny, isn't it? We're unable to show ourselves the same compassion that we have for others."

Violet began to cry.

"I'm leaking again," she whimpered.

Victor looked for tissues, but there were none. He entered the bathroom, wound toilet paper around his hand and gave it to her. Her eyes were dark and bottomless.

Sniff. "I should know better than to sleep with a guy who would sleep with me."

"That's not the point I was making, but you can freestyle it."

Violet was lost in thought. "I just can't get over how much time I wasted. We were together four years, man." Again the tears flowed.

"If the purpose of life is for us to discover who we are, then bad relationships are more helpful than good ones. Have faith."

"You talk a lot about faith. You don't have an imaginary friend in Christ, do you?"

"I've never been concerned with what a person believes. It's how they *behave* that matters."

"Do you believe in angels?" Violet asked.

Victor was careful. "I suppose such things could exist."

Violet's eyes grew large. "Supernatural gifts run in my family," she bragged, rising from the bed to pace the room.

"My grandpa was obsessed with Kabbalism! He studied angels at the university in Israel, and had a theory about how they built the pyramids. He wrote a couple books that got him in trouble."

"Tell me more about your beliefs."

"I'm a witch, although I joke that I'm *Jewitch*. I fell in love with Wicca after reading a book on it. It's a beautiful, Earth-based religion."

"So you think you can do spells and stuff?" Victor asked, trying to be respectful. Secretly he feared that she might have psychotic tendencies after all.

"Yeah. Mostly we worship Mother Nature as a duality of a god and goddess. Halloween, for example, is a holiday from ancient times when my Celtic ancestors would slaughter the animals for the year. It was a magical time when the door between this world and the next was thin and could be easily crossed by ghosts."

"I thought you were Jewish."

"I'm not thoroughbred. My dad was Black Irish. I told you he had addiction problems, remember?"

Victor realized that Violet's heritage was an important source of strength, so he left it alone. "It sounds cool, but does Wicca work for you?"

"Do you ask your Christian nut jobs if *their* religion is working?"

"No. I don't. Sorry. It just sounds weird when you say that you're a witch. You must admit you're fighting a long history of bad press. It certainly freaked out the psychiatrist."

"It's not my job to conform to society, and if Dr. Moron doesn't believe me he can suck my tit."

"Umm. Okay. But I don't think it's fair for you to be *surprised* when people don't respond in the way you hope they will. It's hard to take a person seriously when they say they can perform spells."

"But I *can* do spells," she insisted.

"You can do spells," he repeated flatly. The bottom dropped out of Victor's heart. Perhaps she *was* delusional. Some patients are extremely well versed in hiding psychosis, but it always shows up eventually.

"That's what I said," Violet grumbled.

"Would you be willing to demonstrate?" Victor asked, abandoning the supportive role he was supposed to be playing.

"Now, who's lacking faith? Real magic doesn't work like that, Victor."

Victor hoped that he could force her into reality. That way, she would either have to admit that she was lying, or would have a psychotic breakdown.

"I've always thought it would be cool to be invisible. If it's not a bother, I'd like you to cast a spell that makes me invisible—just for fun."

"If you insist," Violet said. The playfulness vanished from her face. She climbed onto the bed and turned her back to him. Facing the window, she crossed her legs to make herself comfortable. Neither said anything for several minutes until Victor realized what she was doing.

She is ignoring me. Making me invisible!

He stared at her obsidian ponytail for several minutes longer before breaking the silence. "Okay, I get it. You win. How do you reverse the spell?"

"You have to say the magic words," Violet responded, dryly, her voice bouncing off the window pane.

"And those words would be...?"

"The two most powerful two words in the English language, Victor. *I'm sorry.*"

Victor apologized. He knew in that moment that she had enchanted him. She turned around and dropped her bare feet to the floor with a slap.

"So how did you like it?" she asked.

"Like what?"

"Being invisible."

"It sucked."

"Welcome to my world."

"I'm wondering if there's a way to use magic to help you get better. Honestly, Violet, sometimes you seem more together than I am, and yet you keep relapsing into depression whenever I'm not around."

"What can I say, Victor? I miss you."

"You also keep focusing on me, which makes me very uncomfortable."

"What's so wrong with me wanting to be like you? You've got your shit together, you're not an asshole—Hell, you're even a guy. Isn't that what therapy is supposed to be?"

"Yeah, but I'm concerned that you're on an emotional rollercoaster. I think you need a daily reminder of what we're doing here. Something you can hold in your hand."

"Like what?"

"It's called a *black feather* technique. Basically we give you a transition object to anchor you when the emotional storm comes."

Violet chewed her lip. "What should we use?"

"Anything—a coin, a necklace, or a drawing maybe."

Violet covered her mouth. "For a moment I thought you were gonna give me a black feather."

"Actually that's not a bad idea," Victor said, opening his wallet. He pulled out the broken feather from *Demonic Submission*. Straightening it, he ran his fingers across the pinnate fibers to make it smooth.

"Except it's a *white* feather technique," he joked.

"In Wicca we call that a *talisman*—a magical charm. I'll think of you whenever I see it."

"I want you to think of *Violet* whenever you see it."

"Okay. I will. I'll keep it with me forever," Violet promised, holding it to her heart.

Disempowering a patient can be perilous. Victor felt like he was juggling flaming hatchets. "No. Keep it until you no longer need it."

"Okay. It's a lot like me—broken, out of shape, and kept in a man's pocket for too long."

Victor smiled. "Good. I need to go now. So until next Thursday keep writing in that journal, okay?"

"Next Thursday? That's Thanksgiving! Aren't you coming tomorrow?"

"That's something we need to discuss. My boss told me I can only see you once a week."

"There's something else. Don't beat around the bush, Victor. We're tight."

"She thought you might be manipulating the situation so that you can stay. The point is, after all, for you to get better and leave here."

"How is not seeing you supposed to help me? Does that make any fucking sense to you?"

"You can always see me in the outpatient clinic after your discharge."

"I'm fucking broke, Victor. I don't have a job. I happen to think I'm learning a lot from you. If I'm taking a little longer it's 'cause I like what we're doing."

"Violet, listen…"

"Why is it that I always have to listen?"

"Violet, I believe in you."

"Cut the shit, Victor. It's about the money." She covered her face with a pillow and screamed.

"You know I can do a job and be sincere at the same time! Artists do it. I'm on salary. My pay doesn't change no matter how many times I come see you. Besides, I'm coming on Thanksgiving. Most people call that a holiday."

"This sucks ass, Victor," she added, derisively. She blew her nose, and it sounded like a fog horn.

"You're right, it does. But I still want you to get off your meds and grow up to be a happy, healthy fairy princess. I care about you,

Violet, so just hold onto that feather and you'll make it through. We need to be more efficient, that's all."

"Whatever. I'll make it alone. I always do."

"That's the spirit. Think of this as a trial run for being on your own, but with a safety net."

"Can I write poetry in my journal?"

"Of course!"

"Alright, Victor, you're forgiven." Violet then assumed a Texas accent. "Now git, and don't let the door hit yah where the Good Lord split yah."

Dr. Lindsey is wrong about her, Victor thought. *Her problem is that she has a high I.Q.*

As he left the psychiatric unit, Victor encountered a schizophrenic man loitering at the door. He was standing as rigid as a gargoyle, his bulging, dilated eyes brimming with inflammation. All at once the man leapt from a catatonic state and asked, "Do you believe in ghosts!?!"

Unnerved, Victor doubled his pace.

"You really should, boss! You really should!"

Chapter
14

THANKSGIVING IS NOT A BIG HOLIDAY for vegetarians. Victor hoped Angelita would be at the nursing home. While his heart ached whenever he saw her, he projected indifference. This was his role in their game of cat and mouse. To the contrary, Angelita had become flirtatious of late. Her favorite ploy was to prance off, stopping and glancing over her shoulder to ensure that he was still looking. It was tiresome and stupid, and Victor began to wonder if he wasn't simply in love with desire itself.

What the fuck am I doing here? This woman doesn't just have Alzheimer's, she has Rectal Myopia.

"Here it is, Thanksgiving, and nobody visits me!"

"I'm visiting you."

"You don't count, Doctor."

"Oh, you mean your children?"

"That's right. Do you have any of your own?"

Victor was going to have fun no matter what. He scrunched up his mouth. "Not that I know of."

"Well spare yourself the trouble," she complained. "Kids aren't worth it."

Victor saw a cross on the wall. He thought himself clever. "It's clear that you're upset, Ms. Roosevelt, but you might find it surprising to learn that the Bible talks about depression."

"David said unto the Lord in PSALM thirty-two, 'for when I kept silent my bones WASTED away through my groaning!' Amen."

Victor interrupted her, incisively. "I was thinking more about Lot's wife. God warned that if she kept looking back at the past she would become bitter like a pillar of salt."

"Oh no young man," she protested. "God hates the fags!"

Victor swallowed.

"Say, you want my banana?" she asked, pointing to a brown fruit on her nightstand. "It's gonna be lunch soon."

Normally it would have been inappropriate to eat a resident's food, but Victor no longer cared. He shooed away the fruit flies and ate her banana. He sincerely doubted that he would *ever* find value in rehashing the good old days with people who brought us black-and-white drinking fountains and the Holocaust. The more time he spent with these dinosaurs, the more he feared becoming demented by association. *The Greatest Generation, indeed.*

He spent the next moments pushing wheelchairs into the cafeteria. Then he returned to the nurse's station to record the events of the day. It was a good spot for bumping into Angelita.

"Hey stranger," she purred, stealing from behind.

On the counter in front of them was a large bouquet of flowers. It was a gaudy collection of grasses and long, pointy tropical blossoms.

"Oh, Victor. You shouldn't have," she joked, turning the vase.

"I think it looks like a space alien's genitals."

"You speak as if from experience," Angelita said.

"That's from Mr. Claus' funeral. I only got to see him twice before he died."

"Oh no! Santa died?"

"Of course … and the Easter Bunny too," Victor answered, drolly. His pen scribbled a signature. "You know, the guy with the air tank on the golfing dolly?"

"Oh, William. Yeah, that's sad."

"He passed in his sleep."

"I guess. I'd like to die while making love," Angelita added, burying her nose in the flowers.

"That would kinda suck for your partner, don't you think?" Victor's pen danced in the chart. "Most people die at the wrong time. Some too soon, most too late."

Angelita simpered.

Victor continued, "Can you tell me where the records room is? I have to close Mr. Claus' account with Pioneer."

"Why don't we go to lunch first?" she offered.

"I suppose I have time." Victor was secretly thrilled.

Angelita insisted on driving, opening her passenger door before Victor could protest. He plopped heavily into the bucket seat. The old convertible reeked of smoke.

"My dad bought this car when I graduated high school."

"Really? Must be nice to have a dad with money."

"Oh, Victor. You're not gonna hold that against me are you? I'd give it all up just to have a normal family."

"'Normal' is a clothes dryer setting." Victor was feeling snarky, so he waited until she'd merged with traffic. "I'm buying lunch if that's okay."

"No you're not," she snapped, looking over her shoulder to change lanes.

"But I'd like to."

Grinning, she let go of the stick shift and cupped his knee. "It's okay, Victor. I have a job."

Victor suffered her rejection in silence. He saw a restaurant that looked promising and pointed. It was an Italian joint on the railroad tracks known for oversized portions and a roaming accordion player. Making themselves comfortable in the darkness, they received menus. The meatless fare was limited, so they decided to split the *pasta primavera* with mushrooms.

Victor excused himself to the restroom. Returning, he joked, "You know you work in geriatrics when you have to wash your hands *before* you pee."

"No kidding. CNAs get the worst of it, changing diapers and all."

Victor caught his breath. His heart beat twice as fast in Angelita's company. In the four weeks they'd worked together, neither had spoken about their tryst at the nightclub.

"Say, you're welcome to join me in arts-and-crafts today," Angelita offered, holding her chin higher than usual. "I'm running the whole thing myself."

"Where's the activities director?"

"You're not gonna believe this. She fell off a ladder." Angelita giggled, covering her mouth with her hand.

"This is funny?"

They were interrupted by the waitress, who brought their drinks. Angelita took a sip. "You know that sign that says 'injury free work place, seventy-four consecutive days?' Well, she was changing the number to seventy-five when she fell. Now it's back to zero."

"Well, congratulations on moving up the rungs," Victor responded. "Maybe now you can do something about that awful music."

"It's music that was popular when they were young."

Victor huffed. "Where is it written that you have to be stuck in one time zone, forever? By that logic, in 2060 we'll still be listening to Madonna."

"Then it's a good thing Oregon has an assisted suicide law," Angelita joked, blanketing her lap with a napkin.

Eventually the food arrived. Angelita picked at her lunch like a bird.

"This is a lot of food. Too many carbs." She fretted, lifting the bread and placing it on Victor's plate. "I don't know how you stay so thin."

"Oh, you know, the usual—exercise, eating right, attachment anxiety with self-induced vomiting."

"You too, huh? So anyway, last night I boiled clear glass marbles. Now they're covered with little cracks, like snow balls. We're going to glue them together to make snowmen."

Victor loved how she quickened at the mention of art. He wanted to lean over the table and kiss her.

He must have looked desperate, for Angelita tilted her head. "What's wrong? It's like you're not here."

"I'm kinda bummed. I honestly think you're doing more important work than I am."

"How's that? You're a doctor."

"The whole premise of our involvement at Whispering Pines is bogus. I'm given patients who are demented and told to help them using cognitive therapy. I get the worst of the worst—the ones who don't even respond to medication."

"You sound frustrated."

"I am. The caregivers don't get it. Take Mr. Keller. The CNAs are pissed because he makes sexual comments during his bath; but if you think about it, it's perfectly understandable. He's confused. Suddenly he wakes up from his nap to find himself in an Elysian pool being lathered up by water nymphs. I sure as Hell would make sexual comments!"

"Oh, I agree. Just 'cause you're old doesn't mean you don't have sexual needs. I should know," Angelita said, pushing on her crows feet. Then she shifted her gaze from side-to-side to ensure that nobody was listening. "You know how the ladies get bananas at snack time? I hate to tell you this, but they're not for eating, if you know what I'm saying."

Victor coughed up his bile.

"Scouts honor. Here, drink some water."

"Thanks. I think I just lost my appetite." Victor pushed his plate away. "There's just something about the whole system that feels like a massive scam."

"How so?"

"When I was a kid my mom used to tell me German children's stories—you know, to teach about life and stuff."

"You mean *cuentos!* In Latin America they say that folk tales can heal."

"Yeah, but this *Cuervo* isn't so healing because it doesn't turn out the way it's supposed to. It's the story of the grasshopper and the ant."

"Yeah. The ant works all summer, while the grasshopper is lazy and starves."

"Exactly! But that's not what happens in reality. Here, a person who worked his whole life gets a homeless bum for a roommate. The guy who spent his money on booze is put on Medicaid, while the conscientious man has to cough up three thousand dollars a month. It's disgusting."

"It's disgusting that we help people?"

"No, dammit. It's disgusting that the ant doesn't get to gloat!"

"Maybe you aren't cut out for geriatrics."

"That's not true. I love the elderly," he said, thinking about how good it felt to be inside her.

"It's your attitude," she pressed, pointing with her fork. "You just don't have the sensitivity for it."

"Give me one example," he insisted.

"Remember '60s week when we made tie-dyed shirts?"

"Yeah."

"There was a patient you wanted to see, so you told everyone to hurry up and finish dying."

Victor blushed. "I guess I'd better not come to your snowman workshop; lest I tell everyone not to lose their marbles."

Angelita reached for the salt. "Don't take it wrong, Victor. I'm sure you're a great therapist. I know it makes *me* feel better to see you."

He'd had enough. Speaking with a mouth full of bread Victor replied, "There you go again, saying things you don't mean."

"Of course I mean it. You're special to me."

He swallowed, wiped his hands and reached across the table. Placing his hand upon hers, he pleaded, "Then let's go out Saturday! Just you and me. We'll hit some clubs … maybe Voodoo Donuts."

"I can't, Victor. I'm going to the Rose Garden with friends. We've had tickets for a while."

"Who's playing?"

"I forget," she said, waffling. "Oh yeah. Jeff Buckley. Eva Cassidy's opening."

"I'd *love* to see Jeff Buckley! He's my favorite!"

"I'm sorry, Victor. It's kind of a private thing. Maybe some other time." She registered his disappointment, and quickly added, "Don't get me wrong, I really like you."

"Then tell me you care about me! I can see it in your eyes," he blurted, crossing the point of no return.

Angelita set down her fork and wiped her mouth. She sat quietly, intently listening.

"Dammit Angelita, when I look at you it's like there's a light shining on you from Heaven. Sometimes I think the passion I have for you was there at the dawn of creation. It feels that strong."

"You fell hard, dincha?"

"Yes I did. There, I said it. Fuck it. I LOVE ANGELITA TORRES!"

The busboy looked up.

Victor went for broke. "What else can I say? You're gorgeous, you're funny, you're interesting, you're awesome in bed—well, on the couch at least."

Angelita remained silent. Victor wondered what she was thinking, if anything. She began rolling linguini on her fork. Finally looking up from her plate, she asked. "What else?"

"What else? What else is there? I'm screwed because you're engaged to my best friend!"

Her fork dropped loudly. "What are you talking about? I'm not engaged!"

"Rubin! I thought you were his fiancé."

Angelita fumed. "In his dreams, maybe! Where did you get a crazy idea like that? I wouldn't go out with a guy named after a sandwich!"

Victor looked inside himself. "I'm not sure where I got the idea, but I thought you were together."

"Well, we're not. Although I'm getting pretty sick of Rubin's shit. He's had a major crush on me since he moved into that house—bringing me gifts and shit. I thought we took care of it."

"But you kissed him and stuff."

"This is Pornland, Oregon! Kissing doesn't mean shit."

"So you're single?"

"Of course," she said, clearly fatigued by the topic.

The gears turned in Victor's head. Months of guilt lifted.

"Wow! Damn. I mean, on some level I knew you weren't together or I never would have gone with you to the VIP room."

"Uh, huh," she said patronizingly. "It's okay, Victor. You're a guy. That's what guys do."

The guilt returned like a wet bag of sand. "Now wait a minute! I've loved you from the minute I laid eyes on you."

"I know you dig me."

"And!?!" Victor prodded.

"And what?"

"How do you feel about me?"

Angelita's laugh lines deepened. She strained for a minute, shrugged and answered apologetically, "I can't tell."

"What do you mean you *can't tell?* It isn't complicated. All you have to do is say how you feel."

"Why are my feelings so important?"

"Because how you *feel* is the train that takes you to what you want!" Victor exclaimed, too short-sighted to see that emotional distance was her defense against anything real.

"Look Victor, I think you're a really great guy. But I've got so much going on with the art show coming up at Christmas. The last thing I need is a serious boyfriend."

Victor became incredulous. "So *Demonic Submission* meant nothing to you?"

"I'm sorry. I'm not saying that. You just can't push a river. I don't know what I was looking for, maybe affirmation."

"Affirmation?" Victor warbled with emotion. "Got any more clichés? How about 'you'll call me in the morning'?"

"Victor, don't be like that."

There was no hiding his desire. The more he tried to suppress it, the worse it got until tears rimmed his eyes.

Angelita took his hand and let out one long breath. "Oh Victor, that's so sweet. That's what I like about you. You're passionate."

"Let's go. I'm embarrassed."

"Don't Victor. Those were the nicest things a man ever said to me."

"I'm glad you enjoyed it, because it cost me plenty."

"Then let me pick up the tab," she offered, opening her purse.

He agreed because he was unable to string words together. He was not used to losing, and resolved himself to someday winning her love. When they got back to the nursing home, Victor apologized. They hugged in the parking lot, which only made things worse. With her arms around his body everything felt so perfect—like the night they made love.

"I love you with everything I have, Victor. The problem is I don't have much to give," she said, lighting a cigarette in the drizzle. With a stream of smoke, she added, "Timing is everything, you know?"

Once inside, Victor busied himself with closing Mr. Claus' file. The records room was a tomb-like chamber, lined with shelves. Rows of manila folders, some as thick as phone books, had names written on their spines. The left wall featured the living, and the right wall, those who had perished.

It was a mausoleum—the word 'DECEASED' darkly scrawled across countless names in red ink. A chill ran up Victor's spine as he walked the length of the row, fanning their lives with a finger.

Brenner.

Bryant.

Cafferty.

Cain.

Claus.

Victor galvanized as he registered the name, his fingers crawling backward.

Cain, as in Violet Cain?

Closing his hand around the bundle, he pulled the chart from its resting place, folders collapsing into the gap. Victor slapped the chart onto the table and noisily dragged a chair. He was sweating now beneath his raincoat, but too enthralled to care.

On the top of the records he noticed a red sheet of paper with two-inch high letters, 'DNR.' Do Not Resuscitate. Beneath that he found a medical report:

Psychiatric Consultation   10/25/02

Patient: Efron Cain, Ph.D.   DOB: 09/03/1917

Chief Complaint: Patient is an 85 year-old Jewish-American male referred by Dr. Williams for psychotic behavior and delusional thinking. Specifically, patient has delusions of speaking with angels, and is considered an elopement risk. Patient is increasingly isolative. Behavior has become worse over the past week.

Past Medical/Psychiatric History: Dr. Cain arrived at Whispering Pines on 07/14/02 after being diagnosed with advanced Lymphoblastic Leukemia at Pioneer Community Hospital. At that time he was also diagnosed with Schizoaffective Psychosis, NOS—and it was determined that he could no longer manage his own medications. He has shown decreased interest in self-care and social activities since his arrival, and complains of severe pain…

Beneath the report lay a brief handwritten account of the incidents surrounding his death:

On the morning of October 27, 2002, resident Efron Cain was found not breathing by the housecleaning staff. Nursing Supervisor Janet Ormond, LPN, found the patient unresponsive with weak femoral and carotid pulse...

Victor leafed through the pile, his eyes resting on a typewritten note. It looked like the page of a diary—undoubtedly procured as evidence of Dr. Cain's insanity. Victor consumed its contents, his eyes unblinking. He tore out the page and stuffed it into his pocket. Once back at Pioneer Hospital, Victor hurried to make his afternoon appointment with Violet. Pausing in the hall outside her room, he read it to himself once more.

26 October 2002

One feather short! My life is finished, although it will not end the way I'd hoped. Last night I dreamt of Enochian Angels. Standing in their neon courtroom the one called Metatron passed his verdict. I am not to be admitted to their flock. No silver gilded wings for me. No chance for appeal.

It's hard to believe that my life's work shall amount to nothing. By what stroke of foolishness was I so involved that I overlooked the damning testimony of my own conscience? It's too late for me to be a father to Violet now; she's all grown up. Even if she wasn't, the pain in this Judas-of-a-body has rendered me useless to her.

I've been hoarding pills. All that remains is to pray for God's mercy. The Hosts of Heaven are clear on the punishment for self-murder: Neither death nor rebirth for the natural course of my days. Then, like a flame, I shall be extinguished. Unless...

Purgatory may buy me the time I need to set things right. In haunting my celestial prison I may yet conceive a way to fulfill my promise to Violet. In ways that a living man cannot, I shall yet make amends!

—Efron Cain

Although its meaning was cryptic, Victor concluded that the note was something Violet had a right to see. It was up to her to determine its significance.

"Is Violet around?" he asked Asha, excitedly. "I went to her room, but it's being cleaned."

"What in the world are you doin' here on a holiday? Don't you have family?"

"Not worth mentioning."

"We downgraded Violet to the open unit last week. She wasn't there for twenty-four hours before she escaped."

Victor was in shock. "Do you think she'll come back?"

"Oh yeah. And someday we'll have a black president!" Asha said, sardonically.

He dropped his fist upon the counter. "Damn. I had something vitally important to give her. Did she leave a forwarding address?"

Victor thought of mailing the page, but quickly abandoned the idea. What if she was not of the proper mindset to receive it? Plus, he had no proof that Efron Cain was, in fact, her grandfather. He could be sending unauthorized medical information about one patient to another. It was a stupid idea. The mystery would simply have to go unsolved.

"You might get a copy of her driver's license from the records department. Other than that, Victor, I don't know what to tell you," Asha concluded with sincere regret. "Have you eaten yet?"

"Yeah. Italian."

Victor's heart had been broken three times in a single day. The first time came with his realization that Angelita harbored contempt for his best friend. The second was when she rejected his love. Now this, which made him wonder if Dr. Lindsey was correct after all. Perhaps his relationship with Violet *had* bordered on self-serving. Now that she left without saying goodbye, he felt foolish for caring. And, he missed her.

"Not good," he mumbled, "not good at all. Fate makes a game of our lives, Asha."

The woman lovingly set a paper plate in front of Victor. "Looks like you need some of my pumpkin pie."

Chapter

15

SHIVERING TUBA PLAYERS gargled the closing notes of *Good King Wenceslas* before dumping out their horns. Dwarfed by the eighty-foot tall Christmas tree in the center of Pioneer Square, the band looked like toy soldiers. Endowed with the same immutable spirit of those who drove their oxen across the Blue Mountains, the Portland audience exuded contentment as though it was a balmy day. They stood shoulder-to-shoulder, sharing umbrellas and lyric sheets like a scene from a Norman Rockwell portrait.

Rubin turned up the collar on his waistcoat as he glanced at the clock on Jackson Tower. "Ten after eight. The art show just started."

It had been three weeks since Angelita and Victor shared their unpleasant lunch date. As it happened, she confronted Rubin as soon as she got home. The housemates fought while Victor played mediator, which meant that he apologized a lot. In the end, Angelita stormed off to her room, implementing what the men would later call "The Big Chill."

Victor and Rubin, on the other hand, bonded over their shared rejection; leaning on one another like addicts in recovery. They prowled the gothic scene like wolves, taking turns with girls from the small pool of heroin-chic spider kittens that Rubin knew. It was a contest in misogyny, except when the thought of Angelita made Victor fall off the wagon.

"In truth, she's one of the most compassionate people I've ever met," he said in a dream-like state, his ten-speed bike ticking at his side. "She cares a lot about the elderly."

"Oh please," Rubin said, rebuking him. "So she has a job, finger painting in the morgue. This makes her Mother-fucking Teresa?" Rubin's speech was slurred, his blood pickled from drinking since morning. "It's all part of a conscious effort to simulate a personality."

"You think Angelita's fake?"

"I'm saying she's an activist 'cause it makes her feel morally superior. She's posing, not juxtaposing. Most women are like that."

"You think so?"

"Indeed," Rubin answered down his nose. "I've had it with their stupidity. Angelita once told me that she was against women's suffrage because women have suffered enough. I can't take conversations like that anymore. I'm revolting against women altogether!"

Victor laughed. "No. You're revolting *to* women altogether. You meant to say 'rebelling'!"

"Okay, I'm rebelling 'cause straight women find me revolting." Rubin hiccupped. "Dip me in chocolate and throw me to the lesbians—that's what I'm basically saying!"

"How can you say that after last Friday? Those Japanese twins were all over us."

"I know what you're trying to do, Victor. But the girl who kissed me was just taking one for the team."

"That's not true..."

Rubin straddled Spike and began pedaling. "Sailor Moon wanted to fuck you, Victor, plain and simple. Her friend snogged me 'cause chicks hunt in pairs. It's okay, I'm not into Orientalism."

"Self-pity doesn't become you," Victor said, jumping onto his own bike. "You're a nice guy!"

"Women ask nice guys to fix their computers. They save their libidos for undiscriminating assholes like you."

"I don't sleep with every woman who offers," Victor answered, defensively. He pedaled harder to catch up with Rubin.

"Oh yeah? Then look me in the eye and tell me that you never fucked Angelita."

Victor looked into Rubin's soul. He found a desperate sadness there.

"Go on. Say it!" Rubin implored, slamming on the brakes.

Victor came to a stop next to him. "I've never slept with Angelita. I swear!"

"Swear to God?"

"...I don't swear to God."

"Jesus Christ, you fucked her, you pig!"

"I did not."

"*Then swear by your life!*"

"Okay! May Spike run me over if I'm lying!"

"Spike? My trusty steed? Death by mountain bike is kinda improbable, don't you think?"

"Alright, dicknose. May a mountain of bikes fall from the sky and crush me if I'm lying! How's that?"

"Well, good, 'cause it would have broken my heart if you'd said yes."

For a fleeting moment, Victor felt bad. Then he remembered that their roles could easily have been reversed. "Excuse me for playing psychologist here, but it's pretty clear that you hold a candle for her as well."

"Of course! I'm in love with her. That's why I HATE her. Look at us all dressed up to go to her stupid art show. Admit it, we're still her lap dogs."

"We're her *friends*. She would do the same for us," Victor tightened the knot on his tie. Both men had spiffed up for the event—Victor in his suit, and Rubin in an 1810 gentlemen's costume, complete with riding boots, cane and a silk cravat.

Rubin protested, looking at the cracks in the road. "Ever read the poet Rilke? *How shall I hold onto my soul?* Victor, our souls have been stolen. She's a sorceress."

In his drunken state, Rubin's foot slipped from the pedal and into the gutter. Shaking the water from his boot, he added, "Did you know that Rilke died after pricking his finger on a rose?"

"He must have lost a lot of blood."

"Speaking of blood, do you like vampires?"

"Never met one."

"A while back I was telling you about my amazing vampire LARP."

Braking at a crosswalk, Victor smiled. "You have a vampire fish?"

"Not carp, you idiot. LARP. Live action role play. Each person creates a character. We meet once a month and pretend we're vampires."

"Adults do this?"

"It's like those mystery dinner games. Everyone comes dressed as a character to solve the riddle."

"Kinda weird. I suppose it could be fun."

"I'm glad you think so. It's totally realistic 'cause nobody breaks character all night."

Victor looked at him quizzically. "Do you drink each other's blood?"

"Cranberry juice."

"Would I need a cape?" Victor asked with a sidelong glance.

"Vampires don't wear capes! They're like rock stars now. They wear trench coats, ride motorcycles and play guitar."

"Play guitar? If you were immortal is that what you would do?"

"No. I'd fight werewolves."

Victor became incredulous. "You guys fight each other?"

"Not physically. If vampires have a disagreement it's solved by rock, paper, scissors."

"I see." Victor waited, then asked what he really wanted to know. "I don't want to go to a pole party of the living dead. Will there be girls there?"

"Shit yeah. Vampire chicks suck, if you know what I mean," Rubin said, his eyebrows dancing.

Victor stopped pedaling. "I feel like you're trying to sell me on this!"

Rubin stopped and folded his hands piously. "I just need you to play *one teeny part*."

"I KNEW IT! How teeny?" Victor asked, pulling along side.

"It's the role of the Vampire King."

"You scheming bastard!"

"Hear me out! You have a theater background. You're intelligent and well spoken. Plus, you're downright creepy when you get into people's heads. You're perfect, Victor."

"Thanks. I think."

"Just don't say no before you consider it."

"What's my character's motivation?"

Rubin was in his element. "The Vampire King is the supreme father of all Vampires. The original patriarch, he's a powerful and seductive creature. It's not like it would be a leap for you."

"I can't do it. I know nothing about vampire lore."

"I'm hosting it at my house in March, so we have plenty of time to catch you up. Imagine their surprise when they put the clues together and discover the crypt of the Vampire King in *my own* basement!"

Victor searched for a reason not to do it. "I don't have the orthodontics."

"We use fake nails—the pinky finger ones, and denture glue. They look just like real fangs."

"We'll talk about this later."

"Splendid."

Victor grinned.

"What?"

"The crazy shit you do," Victor said, shaking his head.

"You love me and you know it."

The funny thing was that Rubin was correct. Soon they reached the South Park Blocks. They hiked through the park, shrouded in fog, until Rubin rested his bike against Lincoln's statue. Above the pitter-pat of icy rain, the murmuring of a large crowd was heard.

Across the street, the art museum was bustling with well-dressed, high-society types. A white tarp made of spandex had been erected to ward off the rain. Stretched over poles and anchored in the bushes, the canopy adroitly assumed eye-catching conical shapes. Glowing red, blue and green from within, the museum courtyard looked like a futuristic circus.

Hanging from the eve of the building, a spot-lit banner gently flapped.

Winter Solstice: Darkness and Hope
~ A Portrait of Local Talent ~
Saturday, December 21st

Victor looked at the sign. "Do you suppose they'll sell tickets to us hoi polloi?"

"Speak for yourself. I shined my boots for this thing," Rubin said, tapping them with his cane.

They walked through the crowd and purchased tickets. Victor was eager to find Angelita's exhibit, but Rubin insisted on finding the bar instead.

"I need to get good and pissed to stomach what passes for art here," he said.

Weaving through the drove, they ended up in the *Albert Arnold Sculpture Mall.* A cellist was playing inside the stuffy café, and the rain had let up. Museum goers congregated outside, chatting and drinking champagne in the cool air. Rubin returned from the bar with two glasses of cola.

"I thought you were getting champagne!" Victor protested.

"At four dollars a glass? They must be out of their minds. Don't worry, I've got us covered."

He removed the handle of his cane and pulled out a vial of rum. Unscrewing the cap, he poisoned Victor's soda, then his own. Victor grimaced and threw back the cocktail. It splashed in his stomach, lighting fireworks in his head.

Victor spotted Angelita through the bottom of his glass. Spitting ice into the tumbler, he pointed. She wore a dazzling floor-length beaded gown; dark blue with shimmering sequins. The man she stood with was also coiffed to perfection. Dark and saturnine, he was dressed in a tuxedo, clean shaven with the kind of face you see in a brandy commercial. He was drawing a lot of attention, especially from Angelita.

"Who's that asshole?"

"That's the great Professor Epson."

"No kidding. We should introduce ourselves," Victor said, rolling the empty glass between his palms. He stood up.

"Hold on, I need another drink." Rubin tipped his cane and a second bottle appeared.

"Jesus Christ, Rubin. How much have you had today?"

"Yo ho, a pirate's life for me," he sang, dumping the liquid fire into his gullet.

"Just let me do the talking, okay?"

"Yes sir," Rubin snapped, saluting like a British sailor.

"And tuck your shirt in!"

They approached the self-important gaggle with Rubin staggering behind, one hand down his pants.

Angelita was first to notice them. She seemed genuinely pleased. "Victor! I'm so happy you guys made it!"

"Us too," Victor replied. "I can't wait to see your artwork."

Rubin said nothing, leaning on his cane like J.D. Rockefeller. Swaying slightly, he swallowed a belch.

Angelita eyed him scornfully. Looking at Victor she smiled. "I'd like you to meet Professor Epson. He's the head of the art department at my school."

The men shook hands. "It's a pleasure to finally meet you. I've heard so much."

"All good things, I'm sure," he joked, his eyes shifting to Angelita. "When I met her, she was nothing but a street artist. Look at her now."

"I often do," Victor said.

Angelita blushed.

"I must admit I'm new to the art scene and have a million questions." What Victor really wanted to know was why Dr. Epson used so much cologne.

"Victor's a doctor too," Angelita bragged, as if she gained something from having educated friends. "He has a Ph.D."

"Clinical Psychology," Victor added to save Epson the trouble, "and you?"

He laughed. "Art history, although my interests lie in politics. Please. Call me Winslow."

Winslow then beckoned everyone to follow him into the museum. Victor checked his raincoat, and together the group entered the gallery, their shoes clattering upon the hardwood. Rounding a corner, Winslow pointed to the far wall.

"There's our masterpiece," he explained with *amour-propre*, "a work of living art."

A large flat case hung against the wall, roughly seven feet wide by six feet tall. Constructed from glass, it framed a black, red and green flag with a white crest in the center.

"It's made entirely of sand," Winslow proudly explained.

Angelita chimed in, "It was hard to make. It took nearly five weeks."

"I can't imagine how you did that," Victor said, hoping to engage her.

But Winslow interrupted. "First we built the case. It's interspersed with glass pilings to support the weight of the sand."

Victor stroked Angelita's arm. "But *you* made the sand painting, right? How did you do it?"

She became uncharacteristically shy, batting her eyelashes at Winslow as if to ask permission. "I hung a flag of Afghanistan on the back of the case. Then I poured sand down a funnel. It was Winslow's idea."

"It was grueling work," Winslow interrupted. He put his arm around her waist, which made Victor sick. "She's my star student. I don't think she left my studio for a week at the end."

Angelita looked at him, fawning.

"Wow, I bet," Victor responded, his mind chewing on what Winslow had just said. "I can't imagine how you did the Arabic writing."

"It's *Pashto*," Winslow corrected. "It's more akin to Persian."

Angelita childishly added her two cents, as if trying indignation on for size. "The situation in Afghanistan is unconscionable," she decried, muddling her way through the five-syllable word. "No country has suffered so much."

"Foreign interference," Winslow added.

"Yeah, like from America," she explained. "We're just using them like the Russians did."

Rubin was surprisingly quiet through it all, which meant he was drunk. Victor was grateful. This was just the kind of smug posturing that pulled the string on Rubin's back.

Angelita concluded her exposition, looking at Winslow the whole time. "In fact, when we originally planned the project, the flag was black, white and green. The colors changed again after we bombed their country."

Rubin interrupted. "We bombed the Taliban. Remember ... The people who attacked us on 9/11?"

Victor put his fingers to his lips and made a zipping motion. Then he shrugged at Angelita. "You were saying."

"It's a protest against U.S. involvement," Winslow stated. "We've released ten thousand ants into the chamber—*lasius fuliginosi*. They're great diggers, and are taking the flag apart as we speak."

"Can they multiply?" Victor asked, his mind never resting.

"Not without a queen."

"That's my dilemma," Rubin blurted, extemporaneously. "Where's the food? I paid twenty clams and I'm not leaving hungry."

"There you go again, thinking with your stomach, heh, heh," Angelita said. She looked at Winslow. "That's my roommate. The one I told you about."

"Oh."

Victor took Rubin by the arm. "Why don't you go find the buffet?"

Rubin complied, lumbering toward the banquet—a lavish oblation of caviar, cheeses and spreads; all surrounding a tinkling fruit punch fountain. He began to build a sandwich for himself despite being clearly drunk. A rich woman with a jewel-encrusted dragonfly brooch stared at him with conceit, pursing her *Botoxed* lips like a snapping turtle. Incapable of embarrassment, Rubin seductively licked goose liver pâté from a cracker, which drove her off in disgust.

He resumed his sandwich art—overloading his plate until it sagged. Sucking his digits, he ogled the sheet cake. But as he was cutting a piece, he noticed a peculiar trail of crumbs. It led from a stack of fudge brownies into the floral display. He tried to brush it from the table cloth, but it scampered instead. Low and behold, the entire buffet was infested with ants!

"Mary Mother of God!" Rubin shouted, drawing stares from social-ites. He threw his plate and began whacking the table with his cane.

The din of breaking glassware drew bystanders, and a museum guard confirmed Rubin's assessment. "Ants everywhere! Somebody get help!"

Pandemonium erupted. Checking their plates, many discovered that they, too, were crawling with ants. Shrieking, stiffly mannered lords and ladies now danced about, brushing their silk blouses and Italian suits.

Victor, who had been monitoring Rubin's shenanigans from afar, could see that it was a nightmare come true for Angelita. She left his side and ran to the scene.

"This can't be happening," she gasped, lifting the corner of the exhibit from the wall. Somehow an entire seam had cracked; and when she moved it, nearly a quarter of the sand poured onto the floor. Panicking, she moved a ficus tree which revealed a teeming throng of ants on the floor.

"Oh my God," she mumbled, pressing her cheeks. Falling into a dissociative state, she realized that months of work had come to nothing.

Within moments, the museum curator arrived with several men and a large trash bin on wheels. Throwing food into the dumpster, he scowled at Angelita and shouted as kindly as he could, "Miss, please take your artwork to the street! Hello? MISS!?!"

Her face awash with despair, she watched Victor and Winslow fling the exhibit from the wall. Hitting the floor, the frame broke and the entire flag disintegrated. The crowd gave them a wide berth as they lifted the wreck through the front doors. They carried it down the steps and set it heavily in the gutter, where it fell into shards.

"Oh honey, what happened?" came a voice from behind Victor. He turned and saw a dowdy-looking, middle-aged woman descending the stairs.

"She didn't use enough glue," Winslow complained. "I told her!"

"I'm so sorry I missed it, darling. Your son didn't bring the car back until eight thirty." The diminutive woman slipped beneath Winslow's arm and hugged him. He returned the embrace, shaking his head at the pile of sand. It felt like a funeral.

"I'll be inside if you need anything," Victor said. Winslow nodded.

Victor returned to the museum to look for Angelita, but no one knew where she was. He began searching, but the richly stocked museum lured him into a different state of mind. Eventually he found himself on the second floor, enjoying a collection of Native American blankets. He was tired of caring.

Rubin stormed into the chamber, his boots sliding on the polished floor. "Victor! There you are! I've been looking all over for you!"

"This place is amazing," Victor interrupted. "Did you know that they have over twenty thousand pieces here?"

Rubin was out of breath. "No, I didn't. Have you seen the sarong-wearing hippie hanging all over that Epson guy?"

"Yeah."

"She's Epson's wife! I'm not sure why, but Angelita's all in a tiff about it!"

"Where is she?"

"She's crying in the ladies room!"

"What were you doing in the girl's bathroom?"

"*The point is* that she's totally having a breakdown, and needs us to rescue her!"

Minutes later Victor stood at the cloakroom. He put his coat over Angelita's drooping shoulders and walked her outside in the hope of finding privacy. Standing at the ruined pile of sand, Victor tried his best to comfort her.

"At least you weren't using bees," he said playfully.

"You're not being helpful," she retorted. "The biggest night of my life and it's over. I hate him. If I ever hear the name Winslow Epson again I'll throw up!"

"I felt that way the minute I heard it," Victor said.

"I can't believe he had the nerve to bring *her* here!"

"I don't get why that made you so upset. Who is she?"

"His wife! Well, his second wife. He told me they were getting a divorce. It's a long story, Victor."

"It always is." Victor put his arm around her.

"I'm cold." Angelita snuggled closer.

"Girls are always cold."

Victor looked down at her, and when their eyes met he kissed her—for a while. Finally he pulled away and stared into the night sky, his head reeling. The clouds had dissipated, and the moon was a horn of silver.

"Look up," he bid her. "It's beautiful. When I saw you in your dress tonight you looked like that to me. Like the starry sky."

She raised her head and flashed her eyes, her pupils darting as she took in the heavens. "When I look up I think about all the people I know. I wonder if my friends are looking at the same moon. It helps me when I'm feeling alone."

Victor took her face into his hands. "I've felt alone since Thanksgiving. I miss the way we were—you, me, and Rubin. For a while, it felt like I finally had a family. Then it vanished. I wish things could stay the same."

"No you don't. If things never changed we'd all still be listening to Glenn Miller."

"You don't let me get away with anything, even feeling sorry for myself."

"That's a woman's job. We bring out the very best in men," she whispered, resting her head on his shoulder.

Victor touched her face tenderly, brushing her cheek with the back of his fingers.

"What do I bring out in you?" he asked.

"You love me so completely. I've never experienced that before. It's intense. That's why I push you away."

"And now?"

"I'm still afraid of getting lost in you. You're a little overwhelming, Victor."

Victor cursed himself. He'd heard that before—from supervisors, girlfriends, even his parents.

Hedging, Angelita asked, "What should we do tonight?"

"People ask for advice when they're looking for an accomplice. What would *you like* to do tonight?"

She took his hand and kissed his fingers. "I want you to take me home, Victor."

"I thought you drove."

"That's not what I mean. I don't want to be alone tonight."

"And the night after that?"

"All we can do is take life one day at a time."

This irritated Victor. "Why? Why is that all we can do?"

"Because there's *never* a tomorrow," she whispered, her eyes glazing over.

170

"There is if we create one!"

She offered no reply, so Victor requested her car keys. "I live two blocks from here. I'll have Rubin drive your car home."

He kissed her again and left her outside, wrapped in his jacket. Taking the steps two at a time, he went back inside to search for Rubin. Eventually, he found him in the Gallery of Contemporary Art.

"Where were you?" Rubin asked. "Let's blow this pop stand before I kill again."

"Are you sober?"

"Frighteningly so," Rubin replied.

Victor handed the car keys to Rubin.

"What are these for?"

"Angelita wants you to take her car home. She's walking home with me."

Rubin's veneer peeled away. "She's what!?! What the fuck, Victor?"

"Look, she's had a hard night. I'm gonna take her to my apartment until she feels better."

"You're gonna smoke pot and bang her, that's what you're gonna do," Rubin said, pointing his finger like a gun.

"I don't smoke pot."

"Well Angelita does, and that means you do as well."

"Rubin. Please, you're being silly."

"What about Spike? I can't leave him here!"

"She's got a bike rack."

"Fine!" Rubin said, storming out of the gallery.

Victor chased him. "I'm just asking you to take one for the team!"

Rubin stopped and turned. "Some team!" he shouted.

Victor held his palms in the air. "Why are you trying to make me feel guilty for something that you would do in a heartbeat?"

"You know what? When I met you I wanted to be your friend because you say a lot of beautiful things," Rubin answered, sharply.

Turning to go, he added, "The problem is that you don't believe any of them."

Victor closed his eyes, uncertain of how he might have handled the situation differently. He held the pose for several minutes until awakened by the electricity of Angelita's fingers.

"What's wrong?" she purred, slipping her fingers into Victor's shirt.

"Rubin's mad at me."

She answered without concern. "He'll get over it. He always does."

"I think it's different this time. It breaks his heart to see us together."

"That's just stupid, Victor. It's not your problem, and it's certainly not mine. He has it set in his mind that he's gonna be my boyfriend, and if he doesn't get his way he acts like an asshole. What kind of friend is that?"

"He's just in pain."

Angelita tossed her hair back. "Aren't all rude people? I wish we could get him to move out of the house. I'm sick of his weird love letters—and especially tired of his Turkish ass hairs in my lavender soap."

"Rubin's Turkish?"

"I don't know where the fuck he's from! I'm just sayin', let's go. This place has bad energy."

When they got to Victor's apartment, he cracked open the patio door so the night air might invigorate the room. With the blinds gently dancing, he lit some scented candles, put *Portishead* on the CD player, and turned back the sheets. Angelita emerged from the bathroom wearing black panties and one of Victor's t-shirts.

"Convenient that you had your toothbrush," Victor said, scanning his CD collection.

"Yeah it is, isn't it?" she answered, airily.

Angelita then slung her backpack onto the bed. Crossing her slender legs, she began stuffing marijuana into a glass pipe. Victor joined her as the flame sparked, disappointing his conscience to satisfy his heart. They coughed and laughed together. Then, with his hand behind her head, he laid her down on the blanket.

With candles flickering on the dresser, they tumbled into a mutual, spellbinding freefall.

Chapter
16

VICTOR SAT AT THE *ARMOIRE* as Persephone transformed him into a vampire. He barely recognized the hollow-cheeked man reflected there—powder faced and swathed in eighteenth century finery. As she finished darkening his cheeks, Victor couldn't resist smiling. His burgundy lips parted to reveal a pair of newly cemented fangs.

Before joining Rubin in the basement, he bounded upstairs to show off his costume. He found Angelita sitting at her easel.

"You look hot," she said, rattling her paintbrush in a jar of water. Wiping it on a towel, she invited the King of Vampires to suck her blood. It was a cute gesture, although unnecessary. Their toothbrushes had shared a cup for the past three months. Victor kissed her hand, promising to gorge on her before sunrise.

Moments later he found himself in a wooden coffin framed in lace. Looking up, Victor saw polymer cobwebs hanging in festoons like 4th of July buntings. Of all the absurdity he'd endured under Rubin's untoward influence, this took the prize.

Finding it difficult to speak with sharp canines, he lisped, "Why do I have to wear fangs? Why can't I just have glittery skin or something?"

"Because that would be gay."

"Are you sure I can breathe in this casket?"

"For the last time, it's a coffin. Caskets have four sides."

"I don't think you heard my question. Can I *breathe?*"

"Of course. There are boards missing in the top. I took a nap in there yesterday—slept like a baby! Are you sure you've memorized your lines?"

"I think so. After you pry the lid off I'm supposed to climb out of the casket…"

"Coffin! Go on. We haven't much time," Rubin demanded, looking at his watch.

"After you pry off the lid I climb out, right?"

"Right."

"Do we HAVE to nail it shut? I mean, couldn't we just pretend?"

"We're going for realism, Victor."

Victor scoffed, "This coming from a guy with plastic fingernails for teeth!"

"Can you stick to the program for once?"

"Okay, once I'm out, I make the speech. Help me get in the mood. What's my motivation?"

Rubin became a film director, throwing his body across the coffin like a Sicilian widow. His voice drifted between solemnity and rapture as he explained, "You are the father of *all* Vampires, the sole progenitor of the most awesome race of beings that ever inhabited the earth!"

"Sole progenitor? Don't Vampires have mummies?"

"Shut up and listen!"

"Sorry."

Rubin resumed the oration, his poet shirt flapping at his elbows. "Burdened with immortality for a thousand years, you're plagued by a Procrustean dilemma."

Victor sat up. "What's a crusty dilemma?"

"*Procrustean*. It means difficult!"

"Gotcha," he said, lying back down.

"While you have an irresistible urge to kill, you hate yourself because you're actually empathic toward mankind."

"I can relate to this guy! Go on!"

"For hundreds of years you struggled with this unholy dichotomy until it drove you mad. Unwilling to kill your prey, you made vampires of them as well—so now there are hundreds who owe their existence to you. Some are grateful, some seek vengeance, but to all, you're nothing but a legend—until tonight!"

"Oh. So I've been sleeping for two hundred years."

"Yes, you've been asleep this *whole* time, only to be awakened by the beat of a young woman's heart!"

"How's that?"

"Your spirit summoned me, the evil Count Orlock, to track down three living women from the royal bloodline of your deceased wife. She died a thousand years ago, and it's your belief that one of them is your reincarnated soul mate. You're going to kiss each girl in the hope of rediscovering her!"

"Why would I go to the effort?"

"So the two of you can rule the world as husband and wife! But you'll never get the chance! I'm going to kill you by locking you in the crypt and burning it to the ground—symbolically, of course. Then I'm gonna steal your girl. It's all very exciting!"

Victor looked hurt. "You're gonna kill me?"

"It's not like you don't have it coming."

"How will I know which girl to pick?"

"Pick the third one. She's the blonde. Now listen carefully. In the story, the girls are mortals who have been kidnapped and placed under a trance. I'll bring them into the basement here, we'll pry the lid off your coffin and, *badabing badaboom*—out you come!"

"Like a drac-in-the-box!"

"Exactly!"

"So you want me to say something vampish and then kiss each girl—choosing the LAST one, right?" Victor inquired, wiping drool from the corner of his mouth where a fang rested.

"Yes. Kiss them from left to right; First Mina, then Lady Parillaud, and then Loreena. I'll line them up right here." As he spoke, Rubin walked to the basement wall behind a moldy couch.

"Remember, you don't bite them or anything," Rubin reminded. "You just give each of them the kiss of death."

"Wouldn't I be ravenously hungry after two hundred years? I can barely make it past lunch."

Rubin was growing tired of Victor's inane questions. "Because, it's sexier this way. Besides, after two centuries you'd probably drink 'em to death."

"Whatever. As long as they're over eighteen."

"Who cares how old they are?"

Lying supine in his death bed, Victor annunciated his words, "I care, and I'm telling you I'm not kissing a girl, dead or alive, if she's under eighteen."

Rubin looked at his watch. "Five minutes to ten and you're suddenly a SAG member? It's not like you're tadpoling, Victor. It's just a kiss."

"Over eighteen or I'm not doing it!" Victor asserted, sitting up.

"RELAX. Do you have to use the bathroom? You're gonna be in there for a couple hours."

"I already went," Victor answered as the doorbell rang. "WAIT, one more question!"

"What?"

"Do vampires use the toilet? If so, do they have blood in their stool?"

"Fuck off. We're out of time."

Victor crossed his hands over his chest as Rubin lifted the heavy lid from the floor.

"Are you positively sure those girls are gonna stand there and let me molest them? I don't wanna get hit."

"Dead girls are easy," Rubin finished, dropping the lid over Victor's face and nailing the coffin shut.

Rubin was right about the accommodations. With the lid nailed down it quickly became warm, its diamond shape embracing him like a womb. Engulfed in all encompassing darkness, Victor's thoughts wandered.

As a psychologist, he'd often told his patients to model other people. He knew that by donning archetypes, one could be imbued with their powers—be they heroism, self-sacrifice or courage. But he couldn't imagine the merits of pretending to be a bloodsucker—a dealer of death who lived off of others.

Perhaps the outsider status of such a creature drew upon heart-strings of goths. Marginalized by their parents and misunderstood by society, vampire role-players could relate to a superhero who lived off the grid. No doubt these were the same isolated kids in school, now all grown up—well, sort of.

When Rubin came down the stairs an hour later with his hack-neyed theater group in tow, all Victor could hear was mumbling—first a man's voice, then the voices of women. With the approaching grand performance, Victor felt a tinge of stage fright. The stereo began to play organ music as he frantically reviewed what few character details he had. When he finally heard a crowbar wrench loose the nails, he knew that a symposium on bad acting was commencing.

Showtime!

The candlelight was blinding. As Rubin lifted the lid, Victor's damp skin chilled to the sudden draft. He played dead, waiting for his cue.

"What doest mine eyes behold?" Rubin asked aloud, painting on drama with a roller. "Could it be that yon legend is true? The signs that abound in this crypt tell but one, indisputable tale."

"What tale is that, my Lord?" wheezed someone in the corner. Victor immediately recognized Snake, the chubby kid from the rat hunting fiasco.

"Tis a tale of the king of vampires—the one who sired my sire, and the sire of his sire's sire."

Oh brother! Victor thought.

Rubin continued. "Behold, daughters of the Coven of the Black Tulip, the one whose seduction no mortal can resist."

From the flowery zephyr and the swishing of chiffon, Victor concluded that women were crowding around his coffin. Rubin gave more insipid gobbledygook about a magic amulet, and Victor heard the stiff hinges of a jewelry box squeak as it gave up its prize. The next thing he felt was an ice-cold medallion pressed against his forehead.

"GIVER OF IMMORTALITY! THY CHILDREN SUMMON THEE!" Rubin intoned.

Victor fluttered his eyes like he had a torn contact lens. Groaning in a dark voice, he asked, "Who dares to wake me from my dream?"

Rubin lurched from the coffin's side, bellowing, "He is risen! The one who first spat upon the circle of life!"

Victor dangled his fingers over the splintered edge of the coffin—slowly rising to a sitting position. He wisely skirted a Transylvanian accent, opting instead to emulate an insane German person. In other words, he channeled his mother.

"Do not shpeak so flippantly of defying ze vay of nature…" Victor warned, leaning on Rubin's arm as he stepped from the coffin. He caught his foot on the edge of the box and nearly embedded his teeth into a table, but recovered like a cat.

"…for ze fruit of nature's defiance is wrack and ruin," he finished.

"Good job!" Rubin mouthed, winking. Then he took Victor by the hand and knelt, smothering it with kisses. "Long have I dreamt of you, my Lord. I live in shame of my secret hunger."

"We welcome you, Sire," added Snake, reverently stepping from the shadows, his trench coat unfurling from the chair. "We have many questions about what we are, and how we got this way."

"SILENCE!" Victor rebuked, taking strange pleasure in yelling at these people. "Do not venerate me, you idiot! Can you not see zat I am a cold-blooded killer?"

Rubin grew obsequious. "But why were we chosen? Why did we receive the dark gift, Master?"

Victor pointed a gnarled finger. "Another feeble-minded question from you and I shall have you chained in ze blistering sun! You sink zere is a reason for everysing zat happens to you? In ancient times vampires did not make such pointless invuiries!"

A different actor then spoke. It was the other kid from the rat safari, Jim. "Master, we ask these questions to find the strength to go on."

Victor would gladly have obliged if he knew what to tell them. He had no choice but to remain obtrusive.

"Zen ask no longer!" he said. "Vat more do you need zan ze gift of time everlasting? It has *never* mattered vat happened to you. What matters is how you proceed!"

In the corner of the basement, Victor saw Rubin lining up the three girls—a procession of hooded ghosts, each holding a candle in a paper cup. Rubin whispered somberly, "Come, my brides, do not shy from destiny."

"I smell blood, living blood," Victor hissed, sniffing the air like a llama. He glided to where they stood.

They wore black dresses and Victorian funerary veils. The first girl, a waif calling herself Mina, trembled as Victor drew near. She was either a great actress, or was taking this vampire shit *far* too seriously. Victor took her fragile chin into his hand.

"A-h-h-h, ze sanguine visage of ze living," he said in as hypnotic a voice as he could muster. "Don't take your life so seriously, my dear, you von't make it out alive," he cautioned, bending to her face. Victor lifted the veil and kissed her on the lips. They were hot and sweet.

Not a bad kisser. I'd do her, he mused. "I can tell zat you hold back your desire." It was a fair guess. From the palpitations of her heart, this girl was clearly acting out some kind of fetish.

"Yes, my Lord," she admitted in barely audible voice.

"You have ze voice of a mouse! Shpeak like a lion, my child, or I shall kill you myself."

"Yes, my Lord," she squeaked.

"Live vith passion or not at all! Do you understand me?" he demanded, releasing her face roughly. Then he sidestepped to the next girl. "And you are?"

"I am Lady Parillaud, my Lord," the girl answered boldly. She stood like a game pheasant, with her back straight and her chest bursting from an Elizabethan gown.

A Ren-Faire nut job, to be sure.

Noticing a silver pentacle around her neck, he said, "I sense zat you are a priestess, my Lady. Ze blood in your veins tells me your secrets."

Then he circled her, pausing like a good sadist—slowly running his nails across her heaving bosom.

"Vith zis kiss, I condemn you to a life of everlasting Hell," he foretold, lifting Lady Parillaud's veil. Against her pale skin, he could see licorice lips quivering. He canted his head and kissed her; gently at first, then more passionately as she drew him in. There was a spark there, and her mouth was delicious.

Parting from him, the girl squinted in the light. She raised a candle to Victor's face and whooped, "VICTOR, is that you?"

Victor froze in shock, his mouth agape. "VIOLET? OH MY GOD!" he shouted, stumbling backward. Covering his face, he glared at Rubin. Then he peered through his fingers like the bars of a cage. "Who the Hell invited you, Violet?"

"The invitation said, 'The Vampire King summons you.' That would be *you*, right?"

Rubin looked confused. Abandoning his avatar, he cried out, "God dammit, Victor! What the fuck is going on?"

"I'm ad-libbing," Victor answered. Then he leered at Violet. "I can't believe this is happening."

"Hey everyone, this is my shrink!" Violet shouted. Her smile seemed to brighten the room.

"No I'm not," Victor said, unconvincingly. He pointed at her like a bird dog. "She left four months ago. She's not my patient anymore!"

One of the other girls protested. "We don't care. Are you guys gonna play the game or not?"

"No. We're not," Victor answered discourteously.

"Now if you'll excuse us," he added, seizing Violet by the arm. She followed him with an innocent grin, dreamily shuffling her feet as he pulled her up the creaky staircase. They emerged into the real world of the upstairs kitchen.

Violet saw liquor on the counter. "Pour me a drink."

Bracing himself against the sink, Victor's hand noisily bowled over the bottles. Righting the mess, he shouted over the din of glass. "Look, I'm not sure what you think just happened, but it's not cool!"

"What's not cool?"

"The kiss! All of this!"

"You're missing a fang, Victor."

"I'm what?" Victor's voice was filled with exasperation.

"Slow down Victor, this isn't *Gilmore Girls*," she teased.

"Violet, this isn't funny. It's grave."

"Of course it's grave," she repeated, giggling. "You just climbed out of a casket."

"It's a coffin, and I'm not laughing," he insisted. Catching his reflection in the kitchen window he pulled off the remaining fang. "See my mouth? I'm not smiling."

"Yes you are," she teased in a sing-song voice, drawing near to tickle him.

Victor slapped her hands away and charged into the living room. He paced the floor, raking his fingers through his hair as he worked out the ethical horrors of the evening. Yet as the wanton ridiculousness of the circumstances set in, he found it difficult not to smirk.

Looking at Violet, his professional facade melted. "Lady Parillaud, huh?"

"I told you, you were laughing! Yah gotta admit, Victor, this is some fucked up co-inki-dink."

"It makes it a little difficult to be your psychologist," he answered, looking as red as a beet.

Violet threw her arms. "So give it a rest for one night. What harm could it do to play a different hand? I'm not gonna boil your bunny. Like you said, I'm not your patient anymore."

"Once a patient, always a patient!" Victor insisted, pointing. "As long as you understand—that kiss never happened!"

"If you say so. I know *I* got tummy tingles," she said, grinning mischievously.

"Please, stop that. I'm happy to see you, but I have professional and ethical boundaries. I need you to respect them."

"It's cool, Victor. Relax."

Victor sat on the loveseat, and Violet plopped next to him with her hands folded. A few awkward minutes later, she scooted closer. There was a storm in Victor's heart. He peered at her askance before moving to the opposite chair.

"So how have you been?" Victor queried at last. "Asha was worried sick when you ran away."

Violet licked her lips to make them glisten. "How about you? Did you worry?"

"Of course I worried. I'm concerned about all my patients."

Violet's face bunched up.

"Look, I need to talk to you about something serious. You mentioned that you were close with your grandfather."

"Yeah."

"Was he in a nursing home here in Portland?"

"Yeah, Whispering Pines, why?" she wondered, her mouth ajar.

"What was his name?"

"Grampoppy to me, but his name was Efron."

Victor placed his elbows on his knees. Looking down, he folded his hands and took a deep breath.

"Are you gonna pray? Religion is like having a dick, Victor. It's great to have one, but it's rude to wave it around in public."

"No, Violet. I have something very important to tell you. But first I need to know that you're okay."

"I'm not suicidal anymore, if that's your concern. I mean, I have hard times like everyone else, but I'm not alone. I moved back in with Ashley."

"The angel girl?"

"Yeah, we're renting an attic. Life is good."

Victor looked at her skeptically. "Let me see your arms."

Violet sighed and turned up her wrists. "I told you that it was a one-time thing."

"Okay. I deliberated long and hard about telling you this, but I think you have a right to know."

"Telling me what?"

"That your grandfather was thinking about you on the day he died."

"It wouldn't surprise me. He loved me. It would make me happy to know that," Violet replied. She looked at the floor then lifted her eyes. "How do you know?"

"Because he wrote about you in his last diary entry. I stumbled across your last name in the records room at the nursing home. There was a page from his diary that referenced you directly. I took it but you left the hospital before I could give it to you..."

"There's something else, isn't there?"

"Yeah." Victor grinned. "You read me well."

"You shouldn't play poker."

"Apparently he was involved in the occult."

"I told you he was. For the last ten years of his life all he talked about were angels, and how a man could become one if he passed the right tests. It was more than a hobby, that's for sure."

"That's certainly the sense I got. But he wrote something else— something about failing you."

"He didn't fail me, we just lost touch. It wasn't his fault. He got sick..."

Victor listened intently.

"...Ashley and I ran away from home. We were gonna live with him, but when we got to Portland we learned that he was in a nursing home. The same week I had my abortion we were looking for a place to live. By the time I went to visit him he was already dead. I'd just missed him."

"I'm sorry."

"No shit. That same night I went crazy on drugs at the party. You met me the next day."

"Right."

"You don't have the diary with you, do you?"

"No. And it wasn't the whole thing, just one page. I shredded it."

"See? I told you I'm a world class fuck up. I'm so sorry about leaving, Victor. I just suck at goodbyes."

Victor smiled. "Normally we don't like therapy to end like that, but I'm glad we had this chance to wrap things up."

Just then, Rubin appeared in the kitchen. "Victor, are you gonna kiss Loreena, or should I just steal her from you? Everybody's waiting."

Victor pushed on the arms of his chair and turned to face Rubin. "There's been a change in plans. I'll explain it later."

This was not what Rubin wanted to hear. "That's two times you fucked me over. Third time's the charm," he snarled, flashing his fangs.

Violet aped Rubin as he left, which made Victor laugh. Then she noted, "You sound so official, Victor. I kinda wish you'd loosen up. I feel naked here, like I've bared my soul a thousand times and still I know nothing about you."

After the coffin and the kiss, any hope of a professional relationship is over. "Under the present circumstance I can't see what damage it could do. I'd like you to know that I'm not a hypocrite."

"Sounds cool. Why do you say that?"

"You said once that you wouldn't tell your secrets to a person who has none. Well, I have plenty of secrets."

"You do?" Violet grabbed a pillow from the loveseat. "Tell me about your life."

"It's a first generation immigrant story. It's like *The Joy Luck Club* with sauerkraut. What's important is that we share a secret. You once told me you feel stalked by the Grim Reaper."

"Oh yeah, my grandfather said that the angel of death has a name. He's called Azrael!"

"Violet, one of the reasons I'm helpful to you is because I can relate. I've always felt Azrael is stalking me as well," he said.

"Really?"

"Yeah. Since I was a kid, things just seem to die around me. That's why I hate geriatrics." Victor wasn't sure how far he wanted to go with his confession, so he let it bloom. "Remember Fritz the dog?"

"Yeah, you said he got run over."

"I kinda fibbed," Victor admitted, rising from the chair and walking to the kitchen.

"How so?"

"You want a soda?" he asked, leaning into the refrigerator.

"Sure."

He returned to the chair, placing the cans on the coffee table and popping their tops. "We lived in a rural area. Well, Fritz was killing the neighbor's chickens. So my dad came up with a cockamamie country remedy for renegade bird dogs. You tie the dead chicken to their neck. It's supposed to be so nasty that they stop doing it."

"You tied a dead bird to Fritz's neck?"

"I know it's crazy."

"And?" she said on the edge of laughter, looking cuter than ever.

"Well," Victor continued, grimacing apologetically, "I tied it a little tight."

"Oh Victor. That's harsh! I'm not laughing at you, but there's something funny about that in a fucked up way. It's not the end of the world, you know? Well, not *your* world."

Victor was lost in his memories. He stared through her. "There's more. A lot more."

"Go ahead, Victor. I think it's hella-cool that you're a normal person."

Victor felt encouraged, and in her words he found proof that she was not being harmed by the conversation.

"What I meant to say," he continued, "is that I can relate to the loss of your grandfather. My brother died when I was nine."

"What happened?"

"It was New Year's Eve. He got a bike for Christmas, and, well…"

"Well, what?"

"He rode it onto a frozen lake. I saw him fall through the ice. I tried to save him, but I couldn't. The ice was too broken up."

"Wow."

Victor lowered his head. "They didn't find him until spring. Everybody thought he was a swan, but it was his white sweater."

Violet sandwiched her face between her palms. "That's terrible. What was his name?"

"Kurt. He was named after my dad."

"That's creepy. In Judaism you never name your son after yourself."

"Why?"

"You don't want to confuse Azrael into taking the wrong person."

"Well, I guess he got confused that day."

"I'm so sorry," Violet said, placing her hand upon his.

Victor immediately regretted telling the story. Its purpose was to show her that he too had experienced loss—not to reverse their roles.

"I'm okay now. It was a long time ago," he quickly added, trying to reclaim his position as healer.

"Yeah, but a person *never* gets over something like that."

"That's true. I've always had empathy for people like you, who've lost family members. In fact, I wrote my dissertation on fratricide and family grief."

"It becomes a part of you, doesn't it? Although I was just a kid, my dad's suicide was a defining moment." This was followed by an uncomfortable silence, which Violet shattered by asking, "So, do you still think I'm insane?"

Victor crossed his arms and sat back in the chair. "It's a legal term, not a clinical one."

"Answer the question."

"Do you collect thimbles or spoons?"

"Nope."

"Have you ever purchased tiny ceramic figurines of German toddlers?"

"Nada."

"Last question. Do you now, or have you ever owned more than six cats?"

Violet set down her drink. "Damn. You got me."

"Well two out of three ain't bad," he said with affection. "Are you going back to the vampire game?"

"I don't really feel like playing dead anymore," Violet replied, retrieving her coat from the couch.

"I'm glad to hear that," Victor said. For a moment they stood across from one another, saying nothing.

"Well. I guess this is it," Victor finally said, wrestling with dangerous emotions.

Violet became dewy-eyed. "Right on. No escaping goodbye," she said with a sniffle. "Did you have any doubt we would meet again?"

"Well, I'm not big on destiny, but this one defies statistics," Victor agreed, tapping his thigh nervously.

He knew that he would miss her, but as he walked her to the door he felt relief. By chance, they had crossed lines that no therapist and patient should ever cross. But what's done was done. He hoped that he'd handled it well.

"Hey, good luck to you. I hope you have a good life," he offered from the door, shaking her hand.

"Same to you," Violet returned, looking like she was waiting for something. Kicking the floor mat demurely, she asked, "Can I have a hug?"

"Um, I don't think that would be a…"

While Victor struggled with propriety, she sprang like a kitten and embraced him, releasing him with a peck on the cheek. Then Violet stepped off the porch and skipped down the sidewalk. She whistled until reaching the curb, then turned around and shouted, "Thanks again, Victor. You're my guardian angel, you know?"

He waved back at her, with a broad smile masking an abysmal heartache. As she vanished into the darkness he couldn't help but wonder if any angels were looking over him.

Chapter
17

To avoid describing Angelita shallowly, it should be noted that she expended her energies in the service of an artful life. She knew enough about wine to be picky in an alluring way and yet was compassionate toward the poor. She promoted multiculturalism in hyperbole, rejecting drive-through burritos, and correcting anyone who called her Hispanic instead of Latina. But as Victor was soon to learn, she was best at self-righteous indignation.

Victor had been studying for months in preparation for the national *Examination for Professional Practice in Psychology*. This important test, the bar exam for clinical psychologists, represented his final hurdle toward licensure. Despite having better things to do than worry about Angelita, he went out of his way to be emotionally available.

So far, she seemed to enjoy her freedom. Their bohemian relationship was what she purportedly wanted. Although Victor never pried, she'd volunteered that she had 'important things' to do at the university, so it came as a surprise to discover that she was unhappy. It started out innocently enough, with a simple question.

"What did you work on tonight?"

Looking dog-tired, Angelita shed her jacket and dropped the tote containing her art supplies. With considerable effort, she answered, "A study of Frida Kahlo."

"Who's that?" Victor asked from behind a psychology book.

"Oh, Victor..." she answered, shaking her head in the darkness. "...if I have to tell you, then you can't understand."

Victor peered over the top of his book. "What's that supposed to mean?"

"It means that sometimes I wonder what we're doing together, that's all."

"Please tell me we're not gonna have this conversation right now. The most important exam of my life is in two days!"

Whether he knew it or not, this dynamic was central to his obsession with her. Sometimes, she rewarded his attention with tender kisses and talk of having beautiful children with him. But just as often, Angelita came home in a bad mood feeling smothered, or outshined by Victor's intellect. This caused him the deepest despair, for no matter how good it had been between them, such times were a cold reminder that their relationship was not moving forward at all.

As a child from a dysfunctional family, Victor was vigilant to the warning signs. There was that dizzy look in her eyes, an odd posture, or a certain way she would hold her wrists. On those occasions, Angelita became reptilian. So bizarre was the transformation that he suspected neurological problems from her methamphetamine abuse.

"Please don't get angry at me," Victor pled. "Just tell me who Frida Kahlo was. I want to understand."

Angelita switched on the light, unzipped her case, and set the canvas onto an easel. It was a glum affair—a stiff-backed self-portrait framed with roses. In the painting, Angelita was sitting with her hands folded in her lap, as if watching a string quartet. The flesh was peeled away from her torso, like paint chips, revealing a birdcage made of bones. An empty canary swing hung where her heart should have been.

Looking at the work, Angelita spoke with a level of adoration that Victor had not heard before. "Frida Kahlo was a communist revolutionary in the 1930s, a feminist, and probably the most famous Mexican artist that ever lived."

Glancing over her shoulder, Victor tried to sound like an art lover. "It's clearly not American in style."

"Could you be any more ethnocentric? Mexico is part of The Americas…"

Shit. Here we go.

"…it's typical of the *retablos* in a Mexican church. Her work was influenced by her health problems. It's a story about overcoming obstacles—kind of like my life."

"It's neat," Victor declared, trying to recover his standing. "I just prefer realism."

"Realism is a lower form of art. Anyone can paint what they see. Surrealism is about painting what you feel!"

Victor gave up. He grabbed a tube of red paint and handed it to her. "You forgot to paint yourself a heart."

She hung her head and took the tube.

"See? That wasn't so hard," Victor said, resolutely. "You taught me about Frida Kahlo." He was hoping that she would smile, but she didn't. There was something on her mind. "Okay, what is it?"

"I can't live with Rubin anymore," she announced, unflinchingly.

"What do you want to do about it?"

"I want you to tell him to leave."

"Shouldn't we close your door before we talk like this?" Victor asked, rising from the bed.

"He's at work right now. Besides, I really don't care what he thinks," Angelita said coldly, covering the painting with a towel.

"What did he do now?"

"He's a freak, Victor. He leaves me little love notes, and if I'm not mistaken, yesterday he came in here wearing your cologne."

"Maybe he ran out."

Angelita's shoulders fell. "Your best friend was bringing *your girlfriend* flowers while wearing *your* cologne! Am I getting through to you?"

"Is that where this bouquet came from?"

"Exactly. I'm sure they came from a graveyard."

"No, those are fresh daffodils. He's friends with that chick at the farmer's market."

"It gets worse, Victor, much worse," she said, "and I'm getting pretty tired of having to explain this to you. I'm a woman and I have instincts, and I'm telling you he's dangerous. To hear you makes me wonder if you love *him* more than me!"

Victor gave her a hug. "There's no danger of that. I'm just in a bad position. You guys might hate each other, but I'm still his BFF."

"That's what pisses me off!" Angelita turned around. "I can't believe you're not angry. He's treating me like a sex object!

"Oh, come on…"

"I've told him to knock it off a dozen times, and he sure as Hell doesn't respect you if he's in here behind your back giving me presents. He's obsessed with me."

"The Rubin I know is a sappy romantic, I'll grant you that. I'll even admit that he's immature, and very possibly delusional. But he's not dangerous."

"Then maybe you don't know him as well as you think!"

"He's never told me that he wants to harm you."

"That doesn't mean he isn't planning it."

"Show me proof!" Victor dropped his hands to his hips. "I'm not trying to be a dick, but this is over the top."

Angelita looked at her feet. She seemed guilty about something. Suddenly she turned and bounded into the hall. "I found something in his room."

"You were in his room?" Victor asked as he trailed behind.

Moments later they stood at Rubin's nightstand. Snatching a book that rested there, she thrust it into Victor's hands. "There's your proof!"

He turned it over, looking thoroughly confused. "*Wuthering Heights?* The only thing this proves is that he's depressed."

"Open it," she said, tapping her foot impatiently.

Victor complied. He discovered page after page of handwritten prose, cleverly glued between the leather-bound covers of a novel. Victor slapped it shut. "These are his private thoughts!"

"Uh huh. I thought you might find it interesting what he thinks about you and me."

Victor's forehead wrinkled.

"Open it anywhere, it doesn't matter."

Victor did just that, his eyes still fixed on hers. Without lowering his chin, his eyes fell upon the words—his lips moving as he read. Angelita watched his face for a reaction. Both stood there, quietly breathing, until Victor finally closed the book on his finger.

"It's vulgar. I'll give you that. He's got quite a flair for erotic fantasy."

"That's easy for you to say. You're not being raped by a herd of centaurs on page twenty-three."

Victor resumed reading, flipping through the dog-eared pages to the passage in question. The book opened easily—the binding cracked from repeated viewings. Victor read for a while longer then closed it with a thud.

"It's clearly fiction. There's no way a person could throat a penis that size."

Angelita gruffly stole the book from Victor's hands and poked him in the chest with it. "I hope you're not making a joke. In case

195

I need to remind you, your friend is writing sick shit about sexually assaulting me."

Victor shrugged. "It's inadmissible."

"What good are you? There's a guy stalking me, and planning what he's gonna do to me, and you don't care. Do you know what a turnoff that is?"

"Okay, I get your point. What is it you want me to do? He's *you're* housemate, not mine."

"I told you already. Tell him to pack up his shit and move," she demanded, pointing at the window. "I lived here for two years before he arrived. I shouldn't have to be the one to go."

"I don't see why he has to leave. Why can't we just ask him to cut it out?"

"He *listens to us having sex*, Victor!" She walked to the dresser and snatched a stethoscope that hung from the vanity. "Since when is Rubin studying medicine? Do you know what's on the other side of this wall? I'll remind you. Our bed!"

She was starting to make sense, although Victor found the whole thing ridiculous. He secretly thought it would be fun to give Rubin an extra good show tonight.

"What else do I have to prove before you show an ounce of outrage?" Angelita asked, sulking.

Victor put his arms around her and they stood quietly for a moment, sharing their reflection in the mirror.

"Nothing. I get your point," Victor said, lifting her hair to kiss her neck. "I'll go to *The Sentient Bean* and talk to him right now."

"I want him out of this house, Victor. I need you to be a man and take care of this."

"I will," he assured her. "You know I'll do anything for you."

Angelita walked him to the door. "I know. That's why I'm asking."

Victor drove down Burnside, thankful for the time it gave him to think up a strategy. But as he neared the South Park Blocks, he began to feel as if he was coming to shoot Old Yeller. This was a no-win scenario, with no respectable way to proceed.

Jenn stood behind the register with a bottle of spray cleaner. Making tiny circles on the counter with a rag, she acknowledged Victor.

The spring-loaded butterflies on her banana clip wobbled spritefully. "Hi, Victor. Haven't seen you in a while."

"Yeah, it's been a month at least. Is Rubin here?"

"He's in the stockroom. I'm making him work for a change."

"That's good. Idle hands are the devil's workshop." Looking up at the menu on the wall, he covered his mouth in thought. "I'll have a soy latte."

Rubin emerged from the stockroom, bitching like a teenager on trash day. Slouching, he swung a gallon jug of milk from each emaciated arm as if it weighed twenty times what it actually did.

"Hey Egor, make your friend a soy latte!" Jenn ordered, giving him her best alpha female look.

Rubin jumped to the counter. "Victor, what brings you here? Is Angelita not in heat this week?"

"Cute. My apartment's right across the park, remember?"

"Well, I'm glad to see you."

Victor's ears perked up. "You are?"

"Yes. Your friendship is important to me. Granted we've seen some rough times, but on average you bring more pleasure than pain."

Victor breathed freely. "Wow. I feel like we can pretty much speak our minds."

"Yeah. It's cool that we can say whatever we're thinking, without the other person getting their feelings hurt."

This is going smashingly! "I'm glad you feel that way 'cause I need to talk to you about something. Are you busy right now?"

"No, he's not." Jenn interrupted. She flashed her eyes at Victor, then scowled at Rubin. "I'll do the stockroom since you didn't finish. Just know that I'm tired of doing the shit that I ask you to do."

"Yes, Mistress," Rubin said, bowing. When she left he made a sour face. "Ignore her. Bros before hoes, right?"

"Right. Anyway, I came to talk to you about…"

"Say no more. I know why you're here, Victor."

"You do?"

"You need help with a patient. Granted, I'm not Lord Faustus, but I'll give it my best."

This is going better than I'd hoped. I'll deliver Angelita's eviction notice subliminally, Victor thought.

"I have a patient who's obsessed with a girl. The problem is, she doesn't like him. She's even told him as much. Of course that doesn't stop him from acting like a dork."

Rubin looked confused, so Victor continued. "Despite her disapproval, he leaves her unwanted gifts."

"Like what?"

"Like flowers. He can't stop."

"You mean to tell me that if I gave this loser a million bucks to wake up and smell the coffee, he wouldn't?"

"I'm not sure, Rubin. A person has to *buy* the coffee before they can *smell* the coffee." Victor sipped the foam on his latte. "I'm afraid he's still drinking tea."

"Maybe he's just in love."

"Doesn't matter. He's stalking her. That's not love."

"I'm all for stalkers rights! When someone tears your heart out and feeds it to you on a platter you're supposed to act like the Buddha and move on? I can't believe the murder rate isn't higher."

Victor frowned. "Nobody owes you love, especially when your affection is unsolicited. If you were the victim of a stalker, I think you'd have a different opinion."

"Okay." In a fabulous moment of clarity, Rubin put his elbows on the counter and knit his fingers. "Here's what you do. Tell your patient that the agony he feels will wear off, but that it's not all about him. He needs to show some pride, and stop cold turkey. It's no different than any other addiction!"

"I'll be sure and tell him that," Victor said, feeling much better. Rubin had shown remarkable insight into his problem, even if he didn't grasp the subtext. Victor sipped his coffee, deciding to simply pray for the best.

"I'm glad I could be helpful to you, Victor. Now, tell me, what are you doing at the end of August?"

"Um, let's see," Victor mumbled. "I'll be finishing my residency! That's cause for celebration. Why?"

Rubin clapped his hands. "Fabulous! Because I have a big surprise for you!"

"No vampires or rats…"

"Even better!"

"You're scaring me."

Rubin splayed his teeth like piano keys. He produced a gift box with a ribbon tied around it. Handing it to Victor he implored, "Go on. Open it!"

"You shouldn't have."

"Fuck off! Now open it."

Victor held it to his ear and shook it. Hearing no sound, he placed the box on the counter and untied the ribbon. Inside, he found a golden ticket.

Rubin blurted, "I bought us tickets to Burning Man!"

"Burning Man?"

"It's an art festival in the desert."

Victor must have looked frightened. Framing the air with his fingers, Rubin continued. "Picture thirty-thousand artists working together to create the most intense tribal experience the world has ever known."

"In the desert? With you?"

"Fucking Burning Man, dude! This year's art theme is about spirituality. It's called 'Beyond Belief.'" Rubin waited a few seconds, then tilted his head. "You look unhappy."

"I'm in shock. I didn't know you cared about spirituality." Victor looked at his ticket.

"Of course I do. I just don't care to define it. How can anyone know for certain if God loves them or not?"

"I think if we're created in God's image, then God loves us to the degree that we love one another."

Rubin shook his head in amazement. "Can I write that down? That makes me want to suck your cock."

Victor left *The Sentient Bean*, secure in his belief that while Rubin was nuts, he had no intention of hurting Angelita. Apparently Rubin's diary gave him a healthy outlet for his fantasies. With this in mind, Victor wondered if he should start a journal of his own.

Chapter 18

RIDING ON THE SWELL of tourism that was the Portland Rose Festival, the punk rock concert attracted enough interest to fill the *Roseville Theater*. It wasn't Victor's style of music, and it was WAY too loud, but for Angelita's sake he pretended to like it. The way she'd explained it, some friends of hers from Santa Cruz had a band. They had done well enough to obtain financial backing and were touring the western seaboard to promote their first CD. Her attendance was mandatory.

There is something about old friends that brings out dormant parts of our personalities. While Victor dug out his ear plugs, Angelita insisted on attending the after party at a nearby hotel. Strangely effusive, she began dancing around some naughty topic that no doubt involved drugs. Insisting that Victor needed to expand his horizons, she squeezed and groped at his conscience like a tomato at the supermarket.

As they walked to the hotel, Victor played dumb while she vacillated between condemning narcotics, certainly for his edification, and raising the virtues of trying new things. Victor inferred that she wanted him to snort cocaine. He'd already resolved to do it. Their relationship could not withstand another falling out.

So, when his pager went off on the promenade of the sumptuous *Columbia Regency Hotel,* he was relieved to let her walk on without him. Abandoning her in the elevator, Victor located a telephone in the mahogany ornamented lobby. He twisted his belt, but didn't recognize the number. Enjoying the mystery, Victor pushed a quarter into the payphone.

"This is Dr. Albrecht. I was paged."

"Victor! I'm glad I got a hold of you," came Dr. Lindsey's raspy voice. *"My sister died today."*

She sounded deflated, and was lacking her usual black-hearted confidence. In his most sympathetic voice, Victor tried to comfort her. "I'm so sorry. Is this the one who had cancer?"

She said something in reply, but Victor couldn't make it out.

Cupping his hands around the receiver, he implored her, "Could you speak up? I can barely hear you."

She tried to raise her voice, but coughed instead. Victor held the phone from his ear until she finished hacking. Clearing her throat she resumed, saying, *"Yes. Just last summer she was here on vacation. Now she's gone."*

"It was fast, then? The cancer?"

"Yes. As you can imagine, I've got a million things to do. Then, I have to settle some financial affairs. It's a big mess. The reason I'm calling is that I'll only be in the office until noon tomorrow, so I need you to cover all of my patients until I get back."

"But I work at the nursing home on Fridays."

"Not for a while you don't."

"Who will see my patients?"

"Come on, Victor. It's not like they'll miss you. Every day is goddamned Groundhog Day over there. You have two new intakes at Pioneer tomorrow. The first is at nine."

202

"Are you sure you're okay?" Victor asked, wrapping the phone cord around his hand.

"Listen. One of the intakes you already know. It's that girl from the locked unit six months ago. I want you to take her on as a solution-focused client. Meet with her every other week or so—six sessions maximum."

Victor nearly dropped the phone. "I'm sorry. I don't think I heard you correctly."

"You know that girl. What's her name?"

Dr. Lindsey had released a butterfly in his heart. "You mean Violet Cain?"

"Yeah. She asked for you, specifically."

Victor's eyes widened.

"She said she needed to tie up some loose ends. I thought you'd be happy to see her. Plus, it's a good opportunity to work on some of your boundary issues."

Victor toyed with sharing that he had French kissed this particular "intake" while indoctrinating her into a vampire cult. He balked. "I'm not sure that's a good idea."

"Why not?"

"I think it would be inappropriate for me to see her in therapy again."

"Nonsense! You only have three months left in your residency, so it's not like this can go on forever. Just set firm limits, and we'll talk about it in supervision when I return."

Fat chance! Victor thought. "Have a safe trip, then. I'm sure you have better things to do than talk to me."

"Right. I'll see you in two weeks," she said. The phone rattled in its cradle.

Victor sat on a couch and stared at the pattern on the floor, his mind whirling with the spiral mosaic. The prospect of seeing Violet again both thrilled and frightened him.

Why does that girl keep reappearing in my life?

Victor boarded the elevator, and soon arrived on the thirteenth floor. The noisy hotel room was packed with the same pathetic groupies he'd met before. Although it was a lavish suite, the crowd occupied it fully. Victor swam through a sea of people in search of Angelita. Not finding her, he came to rest on the narrow balcony outside. Clutching the iron rail, he found a moment of peace in the twinkling Portland skyline.

Eventually, he went back inside to find the beer keg, and was directed to the bathtub. Standing at the bathroom door he heard Angelita's voice. The door was ajar, and he could see her reflection in the mirrored wall. She was seated on the counter top with one foot in the sink. Victor could tell from her expression that she was beguiled by the lead guitarist. Neither of them were aware of Victor's presence, so he listened surreptitiously.

The tattooed rocker held one finger against his nostril and threw his head back. Snorting loudly, he pointed with a straw and asked, "Who's that loser you brought with you?"

"His name's Victor."

"That's a gay name. Can you get rid of him?"

Victor listened carefully for her reply. She answered, "No … He's kinda with me."

Kinda?

Victor was blindsided. Moreover he was mortified by his own behavior over the past year—unable to answer what the Hell he was doing there and why he followed Angelita like a shadow. The evening droned on for what seemed like an eternity. Profoundly laconic, he watched as she spun her web of deceit and wondered what his next step should be.

I'm going to break up with her.

By the end of the night, Angelita was so drunk that Victor had to drive. While she never admitted to snorting blow that night, her sexual appetite had been piqued. She mauled him in the car, feverishly clawing at his pants. Moving a tendril of hair from her eyes, she dove into his lap. What they didn't finish in the car, they carried into the bedroom. By the time she fell asleep on his chest, both had received the absolution they were looking for.

Victor stared at the ceiling, watching the shifting trapezoids of light. He convinced himself of all the ways their relationship was actually good for him. The more successful he was at re-inventing the truth, the guiltier he felt for failing to evict Rubin from the house. He decided that the best way to keep their relationship alive was get Rubin to leave.

But can I do this and keep my best friend?

Chapter
19

Victor found Violet in the waiting room with a backpack at her side. He smiled when he saw her—sitting there with one knee poking through torn jeans, and a t-shirt emblazoned with the logo 'You are all sheep.' Her obsidian hair was in pigtails, and her eyes were darkly rimmed. She didn't see Victor until he stood over her.

"Whatcha reading?"

"*Flying Magazine*," Violet answered, closing the glossy cover. "It was either that or *Sailboat Tycoon*," she said shrewdly, lifting a magazine with a yacht on its cover.

"Nice boat."

"How many of your patients do you think have these hobbies?" she asked precociously. "I mean, five minutes in your waiting room and I'm ready to kill myself for being such a loser."

"Oh? And which magazines would you recommend?"

"Something with trucks and taxidermy ads. At least you should have *The Portland Mercury*."

"We had the *Mercury* for a while. We got rid of it because of all the swear words."

"No fucking shit! That makes total sense," she replied, swinging the heavy backpack over her shoulder.

Victor eyed her with discernment as they walked. "I must admit, I'm a little concerned to see you again." He silently prayed that she wouldn't bring up the kissing incident. For once, it appeared that God was listening.

"A long time ago you told me that you wouldn't abandon me," Violet said, clarifying her motive. "I was kinda hoping you'd keep your promise."

When they reached the therapy room, Violet flopped into a recliner, raising a waft of perfume. She made herself comfy while Victor moved his chair. The Freudian behind-the-patient style was too impersonal; and to sit across from her, too confrontational. Victor found that he preferred to sit like two drivers at a four-way stop.

He crossed his legs, exhaled loudly, and inquired in his most official sounding voice, "So. What brings you back?"

Violet excavated her book bag, making a small heap of black and purple beauty supplies. Eventually she withdrew the bowed feather Victor had given her months ago. Flapping it at her shoulder, she answered, "My wings."

Victor's crow's feet deepened. "It looks like it has a lot of mileage on it. We need to get you a new one."

"Not on your life. This little feather and I have been through a lot together," she finished, safely wrapping it in a handkerchief.

"I love that you're sentimental."

"No, Victor. You love that I'm mental."

"Hmmm. If the feather is so effective, I'm wondering what you hope to get out of more work together."

"I wanna know if I'm crazy. I've been having the same dream, over and over again."

"You're not crazy, Violet. We've been over this."

"Certainty is a trap."

"Carl Jung said that dreams nag us until we receive their message," Victor posed, tapping the leather of his shoe. "What's it telling you?"

"Have you ever had a dream that makes no sense at all?"

"Sure."

"Like what?" Violet asked.

"Oh gosh. Lately I've been dreaming that it's raining. Except instead of water, bicycles are falling from the sky. It's the weirdest thing." Victor remembered with chagrin that it was his job to control the conversation. "Listen, Violet, if we're gonna work together we need to set some ground rules, especially after the vampire incident."

"Go ahead."

"I'm acquainted with the Violet that you *want* me to know. We have a rare opportunity here to move on to the one who cries in the shower when nobody's watching. Do you understand what I'm saying?"

"I think so," she answered, playing with her hair.

"I nearly refused to see you. Before we start working together again, you need to understand that I'm taking a vacation in August, and then I'm not gonna be employed here anymore."

Violet's face fell. "Where are you going?"

"Like I said, I won't be working at Pioneer Community Hospital after August. That means that we'll have maybe six sessions together before I leave, forever. I want us to have a goal and a treatment plan so we can see how we're doing each week. I'll do my best to keep us on course, but it'll be your job to do the paddling."

"Okay," she said, kicking her feet. "My flippers are ready."

"One more thing. If at any point I get the impression that you're here to play games, we'll have to stop. Do you understand?"

"Yes sir," she answered, like a little girl.

"So, what do you want to work on?"

Violet chewed her lip. "That's kind of where the dream comes in, Victor. Can I tell you about it?"

"Let's have it," Victor said, reclining tentatively.

As Violet spoke, her head danced on her neck. "Okay. These dreams started right after the vampire thing." She pointed her finger and drew circles in the air. "You know, the thing that happened between us that didn't really happen?"

"PLEASE! Go on."

"Sorry," she said contritely. "In the dream I'm much younger—a little girl, I think. I'm at a birthday party, you know, with balloons and all that junk. I know it's *my* party 'cause there's a birthday cake and I'm supposed to blow out the candles. My mom and brother are there. We've all got pointy hats on with the tinsel on top." Violet touched her scalp.

"Do you mind if I take some notes?" Victor asked, scrambling for a clipboard.

"Go ahead. Anyway, one of the chairs is empty. Obviously it's like a *dad's* chair. It's bigger than the others. I didn't have a father, but I imagine that he would have sat at the head of the table."

"Go on," Victor said, his pen scrawling.

"I'm about to blow out the candles when there's a loud knock at the door, so I run and open it. It's a package—a present from my grandfather, except…"

"Except what?"

"Except that *you're* the delivery guy."

Victor looked up and set down his pen. "I'm the guy at the door?"

"Yeah. There's one of those big trucks in the driveway, and you're wearing a uniform. It's definitely you and, if I might say, brown is not your color."

"What do you think it means?"

"It means that you'd make a terrible Jedi."

"No, retard," Victor said, "What does the *dream* mean? I'm sure you've thought about it."

Violet snickered. "My shrink just called me a retard."

"Go on."

"My grandfather wants *you* to deliver some kind of gift to me. That's why I'm here today. The dream's happened enough that I finally had to take it seriously."

"Hmmm. That's interesting," Victor said, resting his elbow on the arm of the chair. "I wonder how this ties in with his diary—that whole bit about unfinished business with you. Maybe we planted the idea in your head."

"It could be, but I'm a little more mystically inclined than that. My grandfather was a shaman of sorts who spoke with angels all his life. I think he's trying to contact me from the otherworld."

Victor squinted. "Do you have any idea what's in the box?"

"I can't imagine. I can see the box as if it was right here in my hand, but I always wake up before I open it."

"Let's try a different angle. How are things going with you right now?"

"Things have been great. For the first time in my life I can see the light at the end of the tunnel and I know it's not an oncoming train. You've helped me so much. I've even started to date again."

Victor felt the cruel heartburn of jealousy. Pointing at her with his pen, he said, "Tell me more about your grandfather. We've never really gotten into your relationship with him."

"You know most of it. He promised to move back to Victoria, but never did. I guess he had it in his mind to step in and play daddy. Let me tell you, I sure could have used it. My teenage years were especially hard."

Victor uncrossed his legs. "Sadly, you're not alone. A lot of dads get emotionally distant when their daughters become sexually mature."

"There were never any decent men in my life *to begin with*. I mean, my grandfather was the only one," she said, looking at Victor dreamily. "Until now."

"Tell me about your trouble with guys."

"Who said I have trouble with guys?"

Victor chortled.

"First, you need to know that I ran out of Celexa a while ago. I couldn't afford to keep taking it."

"Antidepressants?"

"Yeah. That stuff makes you fart. Great for your love life."

"Really? Nice visual."

"So anyway, it was Valentine's Day and I was all depressed because I had to buy myself a chocolate heart at Fred Meyer. Then I met him."

"Him?"

"Yeah. Have you ever been so in lust with someone that they can do no wrong?"

"I can imagine what that's like."

"Well, I met the *perfect* guy at the comic store on Hawthorne. He was hella-cool in all of the ways that I'll never be. He was a snow-boarding instructor with a bod to die for."

"Interesting choice of words," Victor said.

"We ended up in bed the first night."

"Your first mistake. Go on."

"What an asshole. I followed him around for weeks trying to guess what he wanted until he literally told me to leave him alone! It was so embarrassing. I've never stalked anyone before."

"It's curious that you described him as both 'perfect' and 'an asshole,' Victor said, doodling in his pad. "The beginning of mental health is learning to accept people for who they are *without* exaggeration."

"You're so right, Victor, you're like a demigod."

211

Victor leaned in. "I'm wondering what having a boyfriend does for you. What does it *mean* to Violet to be all alone?"

Violet squirmed. "I guess it means that I'm worthless."

"Is that true? *Are* you worthless?"

"My boyfriend Jake thought so."

Victor took a big risk. "Well, you *are* a waste of time when you think about it."

"I am not!" she replied, indignantly. "For your information I'm a *good* person. I care about people. I worked two jobs just to support my family. I can't believe you would say that!"

"Don't stop there, keep going," Victor said with a sparkle in his eye. "You see, nobody can make you feel inferior without your permission."

It took Violet a minute to realize what he was doing. Broadly smiling, she yapped, "You ass! How did you do that? You made me be nice to myself."

"Jedi mind trick," he said self-assuredly. "It's quite simple really. The kind of person who makes you cry is not worth crying over, and the kind of person worth crying over will never make you cry. Did you get all of that?"

"How do I do that?" she asked, throwing a shrug.

"By making sure that the bad decisions in your life are behind you."

Violet pulled on her earring, letting it all sink in.

Victor continued. "It's not enough to want to *find* the right person. You also have to *become* the right person."

"But how? I kept my journal like you said. I don't drink half as much as before. Hell, I even quit smoking pot."

Victor worried that maybe she had changed too fast. "Those are wonderful things. Who you are is never as important as who you're striving to become."

"I'm down with that."

"My suggestion for our remaining time is that we reinforce the gains you've made. Let's not start anything new."

Violet looked dissatisfied. "That's okay, but I'd kinda like to get rid of 'The Mark of Cain.'"

"Cain? The one who killed his brother?" Victor asked. He swallowed hard.

"Relax Victor, it's just something my mom says when she's joking about our bad relationship curse. Maybe you can teach me how to have better judgment."

Victor started writing again. "That's a great idea. Why don't we make that a treatment goal?"

"Where do I sign?"

When they were finished, Victor walked her to the front desk and scheduled a two-week follow-up. The secretary had some questions, so Victor waved goodbye and returned to his office. Along the way, he passed Dr. Lindsey's office. Her door was open and he heard voices inside.

Victor peeked around the doorframe, finding both her and Dr. Clifton. The two seemed unusually chummy. Sam had dragged a chair to the side of her desk, and was clearly counseling *her*, probably about the death of her sister.

Upon noticing Victor, Dr. Lindsey hoisted herself to a standing position. She looked in terrible health. Her hair was a mess, and her makeup was smudged from crying. Pulling down on her polyester skirt, she looked like a potato crammed into a gym sock, and for the first time, Victor felt pity for her.

"Dr. Clifton and I were just finishing up," she announced, as if to avert any hint of impropriety. She breathed into Victor's face, and it was clear that she had gone through a carton of cigarettes.

"What do you want to talk about?" she asked, slurring so that Victor wondered if she had been drinking as well.

"I saw Ms. Cain this morning."

"Good. I'm sure it went well." She sat down.

"Yes it did, although she brought up some interesting ideas. I'd like to throw an esoteric question at you, if you aren't too busy."

The springs on her chair protested as she leaned forward. "Go ahead."

"Ms. Cain told me her grandfather was some kind of scholar on angels. From what I gather he was kind of like a Jewish shaman."

"Shamanism? Isn't that where you put a bone through your nose? Honestly, Victor, I told you she was psychotic. That girl needs to be on medication."

"I was wondering if you could tell me the difference between shamanism and Schizophrenia."

"As far as I'm concerned, there *is* no difference."

"That's not quite accurate," interjected Dr. Clifton. He closed his briefcase. "A shaman is a tribal medium who goes into a psychotic trance, thereby enabling himself to move between worlds."

"Impressive..." Victor said, turning to face Dr. Clifton.

Not about to be outdone, Dr. Lindsey sharpened her minimalist viewpoint. "All hocus pocus aside, shamans eat mushrooms to *become* psychotic, whereas Schizophrenics have no choice in the matter."

"But why would you need to be psychotic to talk to spirits, especially those of dead people?" Victor asked, persisting.

"Maybe to suspend disbelief," Dr. Lindsey said, sadly. "So that you can say all the things you wish you'd said while the person was still alive."

Dr. Clifton interrupted. "Actually, in aboriginal cultures, the reason for contact with spirits can vary. The shaman may want to control the weather, divine the future, or conduct a spiritual healing. It's altogether different from the organic disease we call Schizophrenia.

The Koreans, for example, strictly differentiate between shamanism and run-of-the-mill insanity."

Victor was intrigued. "As a scientist, do you think it's possible that some people actually make contact with, say, angels?"

Dr. Lindsey scornfully opined. "There is no afterlife."

At that moment Victor shut Dr. Lindsey out of his heart. He turned to Dr. Clifton and said, "Maybe it's so great on the other side that nobody comes back to tell us about it. What about Joan of Arc, or the prophets? It seems reasonable that some people have mystical experiences."

Dr. Lindsey spun around in her chair and poured herself a cup of tea. "Really now. Keep talking like that and you'll end your career before it begins."

Dr. Clifton defended Victor. "I'm not so sure. We can only hear a fraction of the sonic scale, and we perceive only a narrow wavelength of light. We're practically deaf, blind and dumb compared to animals."

"Dumb is right," crowed Dr. Lindsey. "I hope you aren't telling your suicidal patients that the afterlife is a party."

Dr. Clifton crossed his legs. "I think we have to be careful when diagnosing people with beliefs different from our own. Take *amok*, for example, a Malaysian form of dissociation; or *Susto*, a disorder among Latinos, where it's believed that the soul has been displaced from the body."

Victor shoved his hands into his pockets. "Wow, Sam. I've known you for a whole year, and just now you blew me away."

Dr. Clifton's face contorted. "Why is that?"

"Don't take this wrong, but you don't seem like a very religious guy to me."

Dr. Clifton squeezed his palms together piously. "*Fronti nulla fides,* my friend. In appearances place no faith."

Victor explained himself. "I guess you're lacking a certain spiritual aesthetic."

"Aesthetics aren't everything," he said with a condescending chuckle. "They lead to perdition."

"Perdition? That's Holy Damnation!"

"I should know. I used to be a Catholic Priest."

"A-w-w-w, cut it out, Sam. Now you're yanking my chain."

"It's true," Dr. Lindsey confirmed. She opened the top drawer and retrieved his curriculum vita. Holding it by the staple she read aloud, "Blessed Apostles Seminary. Cleveland, Ohio. Graduated 1976."

Dr. Clifton finished for her, swaggering with a lisp, "For several years I was even pastor of my own church in North Carolina."

Victor's eyes shined like the full moon. "That's amazing, Sam … I mean, Father Clifton. I've been wondering where you learned to speak Latin. Why did you quit?"

Dr. Clifton browsed his memories. "Let's just say I had a problem with the seven deadly sins. Would you believe that housewives actually put their phone numbers into the offering basket?"

"*That* I believe. What's preposterous is that some priests *call* them!" Dr. Lindsey said, cackling.

"Psychology wasn't that big of a career jump. I still take confessions," Dr. Clifton joked, sharing a knowing glance with the woman he had counseled moments before.

Victor was beside himself. "Well I'll be damned."

"You may well be, my son," Dr. Clifton said with a knowing look.

Chapter 20

THE SUN SIZZLED like the yoke of an egg, scorching the five-hundred thousand spectators who lined the parade route. Rubin and Victor joined the crowd, stepping off the MAX train at Memorial Coliseum. Navigating the barricades, they walked down MLK Boulevard in search of their seats. There were vendors, stilted clowns and street performers frolicking on the hot pavement. When police announced the imminent start of the Rose Parade, the swarm of revelers only thickened.

Driving one hand across the other, Rubin posited, "Imagine the fun we could have with a snow plow."

"I've come to the conclusion that the Navy was right about you."

Rubin sneered. "This coming from a man who pretends to care for a living?"

Victor chortled and tied his windbreaker around his waist. "Why so grumpy?"

"One of us is getting laid, and it isn't me. God likes you better."

Victor frowned. "How can you be sure that the devil isn't responsible for the woman in my life?"

"Things not working out with you and the strumpet?" Rubin asked, his interest purely voyeuristic.

Victor walked in contemplation. "I'm not sure."

"How's that?"

"Did you know Angelita's mother is in town?"

"No. But then she rarely talks to me anymore," Rubin replied, stopping at the entry gate.

Producing his ticket, Victor added, "I found out last night, almost by accident. I asked her if she wanted to go to the carnival on the waterfront."

"And?"

"I got the feeling she didn't want me to meet her mom. Every time I made a suggestion she was like, 'no, no, that's not gonna work, blah, blah.' I just gave up."

"Chicks are a waste," Rubin vented. His feet clanked up the aluminum bleachers ahead of Victor.

"Not all chicks," Victor said with a thousand mile stare. He shook his head, knowing that nothing good could come from thinking about Violet that way.

"Misanthropy is my antidote for the blues. Ever read Jean Paul Sartre?"

"Can't say that I have," Victor answered, standing to buy a sack of kettle corn from a vendor.

"When asked, 'What is Hell?'" he answered, *'Hell is other people.'*"

Just as Rubin spoke, three Christian zealots crossed the street toting posters with messages about the imminent return of Christ. Rubin became agitated, squirming in his seat as if he had diaper rash. "You know what really gets me about those fuckers?"

"I can't imagine, Gandhi. Do tell."

"They think that God is so small that he needs them to do that."

"Please, don't say anything. Just once."

Ignorant of the peril in which he placed himself, one of the evangelists approached the bleachers. He may as well have marched into the coliseum of Marcus Aurelius when he held up a sign that read:

BEHOLD, I COMETH QUICKLY. REVELATION 3:11

Unable to contain himself, Rubin launched from his seat. "MAYBE YOU SHOULD SEE A SEX THERAPIST!"

Victor admonished him, yanking on his belt. "Will you shut the fuck up? Jesus effing Christ, dude. I work in this town!"

Rubin fell into his seat. "She's really got you down, huh? If you were an *Etch A Sketch* I'd shake yah."

"That might help. Rubin, when it comes to art, what's better— realism, or surrealism?"

Rubin looked at him blankly, so Victor rephrased the question. "Angelita and I had an argument about it, and I felt like an idiot because I gave the wrong answer."

"How can a question of *what you prefer* have a wrong answer?"

"Just tell me. What is the best form of art?"

"Hentai," Rubin answered.

Victor sighed.

Rubin placed his hand between Victor's shoulders. "Let me guess. She pulled her holier-than-thou *'I'm an artist and you're not'* routine."

"How'd you guess?"

"It's all she has going for her. She does that whenever she feels inferior. I hope you didn't play into it."

"Are you kidding? I gave her a piece of my mind."

Their conversation was interrupted by a cacophony of fire truck sirens. The boulevard cleared, making way for an endless train of marching bands, antique cars and flower-covered floats. As a team of cowgirls rode past, Victor forgot his concerns. He nudged Rubin, saying, "I'd let her brand my ass!"

"Then I've got just the thing to cheer you up," Rubin gushed. He pulled a flyer from his pocket. It had a picture of the fiery dominatrix, Sophia.

"Sharing your porn? I'm not sure I want to take our relationship to the next level."

"No, idiot. Read the back!"

"Demonic Submission, June 9th."

"You wanna go? It's tonight!"

Victor felt saddened. The flyer reminded him of Angelita, and he hated himself for caring. Surrendering to outrage, he replied, "Sure. Why not? If she's gonna go to the carnival with her mom, then I should be able to do whatever I want."

"Now you're talking like a man."

The more Victor thought about going to the club, the more excited he became. It would be the perfect opportunity to ask Lord Faustus about Efron Cain's obsession with becoming an angel.

The parade continued until the transmission fell out of a floral tribute to the Philippines. With little to do but wait for a tow truck, the gala ground to a halt. The disruption took so long that the marching bands set their Napoleonic hats on the concrete and sat down.

"It figures. Made in the Philippines!" Rubin growled. Rising to stretch his legs, he invited Victor to get some cotton candy.

"You just can't get enough red dye in your diet," Rubin joked, his tongue now cherry red. "Did you know it's made from ground up mealworms?"

"No I didn't," Victor answered, tearing a piece of the sugar cloud from Rubin's hand. "It looks like fiberglass insulation," he kidded, the sweet stickiness melting in his mouth. Deciding that no moment would ever be right, he blurted, "I need to ask you a favor."

"You name it."

"It's probably the biggest favor I've ever asked."

"Knock off the foreplay already!"

"As you know, Angelita's been in a strange place. It has to do with the tension between you two."

"She has a crush on me?"

"No. The opposite. She doesn't feel safe around you anymore. It's about the stuff you wrote in your diary."

"You read my *diary?*"

"No. I mean, yes. She showed me one page of it," Victor admitted, hoping to salvage some virtue.

"Finish what you were gonna say," Rubin uttered, expressionless.

"She was hoping that I could get you to move out of the house. It would mean a lot to me if you would."

It took a moment for the coin to fall through the machine. As it fell, so did Rubin's shoulders, until the cotton candy hung at his side. "What the fuck? I thought we were friends."

"Of course we are," Victor insisted.

"How can I tell?"

Victor said nothing, his tongue growing fat and clumsy. He knew this was not going swimmingly.

"Of all the cruel, treacherous deceit that I've known in my short, shitty life, this takes the gold."

"Rubin, please don't get mad. I just wanted your opinion," Victor said in full retreat.

"Don't placate me like one of your stupid patients. Morality is caught, not taught, and you're busted!"

"Relax. I didn't mean to hurt your feelings. If you don't want to do it you don't have to."

"That's mighty thoughtful!"

"Rubin, please," Victor begged, showing his palms in supplication. "There's no need to shout."

"I never imagined that you could be this whipped, man, but you are. She honestly has you by the balls *and* the brain."

"Rubin, it's not like there weren't problems in the house. Don't make me out to be the bad guy."

"No, *you* listen, mister psychologist! You *are* the bad guy. If you're looking for a friend who has no faults you'd better get used to being alone!"

"Rubin, wait. You have this all wrong…"

"How am I supposed to have it? You *used* me like you use everyone. And the sickening thing is that you think you're enlightened." Rubin punctuated the air with his fingers. "The word 'therapist' is spelled the-rapist for a reason."

Victor knotted his arms. "So I made a mistake. Why can't you forgive me?"

"I might begin to think about it if you were *truly* sorry, but after all the times you've let me down this year, I think you're incapable of remorse."

"Honest to God, I'm sorry. Rubin, please! I realize that what I just said was wrong."

"Don't worry about wronging *me*, Victor. As long as I've had the misfortune of knowing you, I've watched you wrong yourself repeatedly."

"But we're friends," Victor pled.

"No, we're not. I hate you the way a hippie hates soap!"

"But I thought we were gonna camp together at Burning Man— just you and me, like it was in the beginning."

"Why? So you can kick me out of the tent at the first sign of a fish taco? You can go to Hell, Victor. I was never anything but a path to Angelita."

"Wait! I'll make it up to you."

Rubin threw his cotton candy into the trashcan. "Not this time. I've had my fill of both of you. If you assholes want me to move out, then that's what I'll do."

Victor searched for a reply. He knew they were on the precipice of losing their friendship forever. "What about the Burning Man ticket? You paid a lot of money."

"Keep it," Rubin said venomously. "It was a gift from a friend!"

Victor watched, speechless, while Rubin vanished into the crowd. Crippled with regret, he stood in a catatonic state. Rubin's words were titanium, armor-piercing projectiles of veracity. They rendered him a smoldering, shell of a man. No longer in the mood for parades, he walked home. It was a funeral procession.

When he arrived at his apartment he tried to call Angelita, but no one answered. Unable to find comfort in her voice, or to reinvent his behavior into martyrdom, he slammed the receiver. Falling into bed, he formed a partner out of pillows—coming to terms with the fact that Angelita had never been there for him. He'd received everything he asked for since arriving in Portland, and yet he still felt cold and empty inside.

I'm the problem.

After an uneasy rest, he ambled downtown to find respite from his conscience. Like sirens, the screams of teenage girls drew him to the waterfront carnival. Night had fallen, transforming the bank of the Willamette into a mile-long amusement park. In the black water of the Willamette, Navy ships tugged on their moorings, their riggings made festive with holiday lights. Above the treetops, a blinking Ferris wheel slowly turned.

Drinking too much beer, Victor stumbled through the carnival with his eyes on the downtrodden grass. Someone had dropped a strip of tickets and, stooping to pick it up, Victor smiled for the first time in hours.

What luck! Perhaps my fortunes will change…

He raised his eyes to see a House of Horrors. So he pushed his way through the turnstile, summoned to the labyrinth by an enormous fiberglass devil, leering with eyes aglow. Inside, cackling clowns mocked him as he fell over uneven floors to catch his warped image in the mirrored wall. He had to close his eyes to survive the spinning tunnel, while strobe lights and ear-rupturing butt rock assaulted him from every angle. As soon as it began, it was over. Bouncing from a bungee spider web, Victor shuffled into the night air.

He opened his eyes to see Angelita and Winslow Epson, walking hand-in-hand as lovers do. The corners of his vision narrowed, and as the meaning of this scene coalesced, his heart convulsed as if filled with molten lead. He followed them for the better part of an hour, his vision warped by tears. Angelita giggled, tossing her foot back, as she climbed Winslow's chest to give him a kiss. Victor realized at last that their entire relationship had been a lie—an extravagant work of fiction that had simply run its course.

Drawing stares from passersby, Victor began to weep so hard that he nearly suffocated. Hiding behind a ticket booth, he pulled himself together enough to approach the couple—but when they stopped to kiss again, it was obvious that they were sexually intimate. Again, Victor lost his composure.

Eventually, he deadened himself enough to face her. He caught up with them, halting several strides behind.

"Angelita!" he shouted.

She glanced over her shoulder. Seeing Victor, she released Winslow's hand and let out a long, protracted sigh. Speaking to her art professor, she excused herself. "Baby, you'd better go on without me."

Winslow smiled like a cat at a bird show, placed his hands upon her waist and kissed her gratuitously. Once he was gone, Angelita faced Victor.

"What are you doing, Victor?" she asked, stupidly.

"I would have been good for you," he answered.

"That sounds like advice. I thought therapists don't give advice."

"I'm not your fucking therapist." Then there was silence. "You never loved me, did you?"

"That's not true. I loved you…" she insisted, adding with a coy shrug, "…in my own way."

That hurt like Hell, for Victor knew what it meant. She was a reptile. He looked away, unable to fathom how a person could be so cold. Fearing the imminent bursting of the dam, he pressed his eyes shut, but to no avail.

"You'll come back to me! You'll see," he predicted, his tears flowing in earnest.

Angelita slowly shook her head from side to side. "I'm sorry, Victor. It's just not gonna happen."

"Do you honestly think Winslow is *half* the man I am?"

"Twice the man," she said, smugly.

"I suppose you've been faking your orgasms then!"

"Why not, Victor? You've been faking foreplay." Then, perhaps with the mercy a cat shows a wounded mouse, she added, "The chemistry's just not there. Don't take it personally."

"Winslow is a pompous ass!"

"Et vous?" Angelita now snuffed any trace of empathy, uttering, "You're not the end-all, be-all of men."

Suddenly a light came on in Victor's head. He looked at her askance, the words slipping from his mouth. "You actually hate me."

"I wouldn't say that, Victor. Hate would be too strong an emotion," she said cruelly.

"You've broken my heart," Victor mumbled, his eyes focusing inwardly.

"Don't blame *me!* You made choices. I was as honest as a girl could be."

"Honest?" Victor's eyes popped. "What are you talking about? You were *cheating* on me."

"I don't see what the big deal is. As long as I've known you, you've been lying to both of us."

"What are you talking about?"

"Remember the Jeff Buckley/Eva Cassidy concert you wanted to go to? They're both famous for being dead, Victor. You were too busy pretending to have something in common with me to notice."

"My God."

"My God is right. You wanna know why I'm seeing Winslow? I'm seeing him because he has a backbone. Believe me Victor, I'm doing you a favor by telling you this."

Victor forced her back with the intensity of his conviction. "Well I curse you to be yourself! Do you hear me? I curse you."

"You're mean."

"I've only begun. You're a parasite. A hollow chocolate Easter bunny. You've never had an original thought. You're nothing but a moth looking for a flame, and everyone around you knows it. You flutter through life seeking the light of charismatic people so you can enjoy a moment by the fire."

"That's fucked up!"

"Shut up. I'm not finished with you. You've cheated your way through school. You're corrupt. You're a snob. You're anorexic. You have leather for skin. Your politics suck, and when you offer an opinion, people laugh behind your back because they know you understand nothing."

Angelita pouted. "Finally, we see the real meaning of Victor's love. When he doesn't get his way he becomes hurtful."

"Maybe I've taken off my rose-colored glasses."

"It's about time," she said with a tremulous lip. "When I was with you I was *truly* with you. That has to be good enough."

Victor looked down and spoke at his shoes, dejectedly. "Really? Then what color are my eyes?"

Angelita's jaw moved, but no sound came out. She kicked at the dirt and threw up her hands.

"They're green, Angelita," he emphasized with consternation.

"What else?" Angelita asked with her hands in her pockets, like she had so many times before.

"Is that what you do when your empty brain runs out of shit to say? You ask 'what else' and leave it up to other people to bare their souls, so you can imagine for a moment what it's like to have one? You're a bowl of wax fruit, Angelita. THERE IS NOTHING ELSE!"

Angelita's eyes glistened, and for the first time since the art show fiasco Victor had evidence that she actually cared. Or maybe she just cared about herself. She appeared to waver, and for a second his heart soared at the prospect that she might break down and finally profess her undying love. Instead, she turned to ice.

"Fuck you, Victor. I give you permission to move on," she said, flipping her hair as she walked off. He watched her shrink into the night, waiting for her to look back as before. But it was the last conversation they ever had.

Chapter 21

ICTOR FINALLY KNEW why they play music in elevators. Like most Americans, he had come to loath being with himself. Bursting into the parking garage, he stormed to his car. The tires spun, leaving a cloud of blue smoke. A river hop and a few turns later, he found the warehouse nightclub called *Hades*.

Propping up the bar, Victor drank whisky and water. When he felt it rise in his throat, he dove onto the crowded dance floor. Stumbling between shafts of light, he jumped to the beat until his hair ran with sweat. As the mirrored ball spun, Victor twirled beneath it. Losing his footing, he fell squarely at Mistress Sophia's sandaled feet.

"Whoa! Careful there, dude. Hey, I remember you!"

"You do?"

"You're Angelita's friend," she shouted. The towering woman looked like a Greek goddess, framed in smoke and strobe light.

"I'm nobody's friend."

Sophia lent her hand. Her lips formed a sinister crescent. "Man, you're fucked up!"

"Don't I know it," Victor mumbled, shakily rising to his feet. He swung his face in her direction, overshooting as if his head was too heavy.

"Beat the fuck out of me," he slurred. "Make me doubt what I believe."

"Do what?" she asked, eyeing him obliquely.

"I wun-na feel the pain on my skin," he explained, clumsily pounding on his chest. "I don't want it inside anymore. Fuck me up."

His behavior was so bizarre that it took a moment for Sophia to realize what he was asking.

"Don't look at me like an idiot. That's what you do, right?" Victor slurred. "You punish people?"

Taking his hand with surprising kindness, Sophia led him up the platform. Standing at the cross, she commanded Victor to remove his shirt. He fumbled, so she tore it from his shoulders, scattering the buttons. Then, choking him with her whip, she drove his bare chest against the splintery mast.

A crowd gathered as she buckled Victor's outstretched wrists to the arms of the crucifix. With grating musical accompaniment, her searing lash commenced to raising his skin. Each white hot lick brought Victor closer to the truth. With his life-long pattern of self-abuse now scarring his ravaged back, it could never covertly influence him again. By the end, he'd begged her to stop.

Meanwhile, in the corner of the club, Lord Faustus gathered his entourage in an abandoned cocktail lounge. Wherever Faustus went, a dozen followers accompanied him. At twenty dollars a head, it made good business sense to give him his own space.

At one end of the discarded lounge, a pair of saloon doors marked the entrance. At the opposite side, a shallow stage was built from shipping pallets. There, like a cherry atop a fudge sundae, Lord

Faustus held court. An altar to his ego, Faustus' throne was outfitted with plastic skull finials. Behind it, an ominous flag hung from the cinderblock wall. The standard was emblazoned with arcane symbols from the eighteenth century *Hellfire Club*—a white circle on black, crossed by lightning bolts with devils tails.

Victor appeared in the doorframe of the lounge, disheveled and broken. He limped into Faustus' parlor, the saloon doors fanning behind him.

"A-a-a-h, the good doctor returns from his expedition," Faustus announced, floating from his chair. He was dressed in a Franciscan monk's robe, his face concealed by a baggy hood. Reaching up with both hands, he uncovered his bald head. A single flask of wine rested on the bar next to a candelabrum. Scattered throughout the room, his impish followers lurked and listened.

Faustus opened the flask. Offering the drink, he gestured for Victor to sit. "I trust that God is in Heaven, and all is well with the universe?"

"There is no God," Victor answered, lifelessly.

"That's what you've discovered?" Faustus asked with a wry smile. "Regale us, won't you?"

Victor closed his eyes. "I've nothing to report but heartache and disaster."

Victor's shirt hung open, and Faustus delighted in the blood stains where Sophia's lash had left their mark. "All healers get crucified. It's their lot."

"Tell me about fallen angels. I need to understand and I'm running out of time," Victor demanded.

Lord Faustus placed his hands upon Victor's raw shoulders. "A little tender, I see," Faustus whispered with a perverse smile. "God speaks to us through suffering."

Victor turned his head. "Go on…"

"God will never tell you *what* you need to know. Instead he flogs you, repeatedly, with some unfortunate theme, waiting for you to get it."

"Well, I get it already."

"Good. The fool deafens himself with pain killers—love, wine, work. The master, on the other hand..."

Victor grew introspective. He hung his head.

Faustus passed his hand through the candle flame. "Fallen from grace, have you?"

"To put it mildly." Victor cut to the chase. "Who was Enoch?"

"A man like you, except that he became an angel."

"So it's theoretically possible?"

"Theoretically."

Victor strummed the air with his fingers. "I thought *everyone* got a harp when they died."

Faustus' eyebrows plunged like serrated knives. "Oh no. Angels are *not* deceased people. That's Hollywood. Real angels are monstrous and magnificent!"

"Monstrous?"

"Victor, these are not the angels of *It's a Wonderful Life*. They're awesome creatures, superior to us in every way. They're a different branch on the tree of creation, somewhere between God and man. The book of Psalms warns us that as man is superior to animals, angels are superior to man."

"I'm not intimidated," Victor said with undue bravado.

As Faustus continued to toy with the candle, the steel rings in his eyebrow glistened in the flickering light. He suddenly withdrew his hand, the stench of burnt hair up borne on a wisp of smoke. "Then you're a fool. Angels are not to be trifled with."

Seating himself on the barstool, he searched Victor's eyes. "They appear in all the world's religions. It was Gabriel who dictated the Koran to Mohammed. Even Hinduism and Buddhism speak of demigods, devas and asparas. The Greek gods Nike and Hermes were angels. Oh, they're real. No doubt they're here right now."

The candle sputtered. Victor asked, "Tell me more about Enoch. What did he have to do to become an angel?"

"His story is told in the Ethiopian *Book of Enoch*. Because the information found there was heretical, it was rejected from the Bible."

"What made it so offensive?"

Lord Faustus pressed his lips together. "You might say that certain details clashed with Catholic doctrine."

"Like...?"

Faustus made Victor wait while he poured himself a glass of wine. The candle glowed through the jostling liquid, casting a blood-red pall upon his fingers.

"Like angels having genitalia," Faustus replied at last. "This did not fly with the church's distain for all things earthly."

Victor straightened. "If angels had genitals, they were capable of lust!"

"I'm sure the so called *Virgin* Mary would agree."

"Go on."

"In Greek, the word *angelos* means 'messenger.' Angels are supposed to be guardians. It's a big responsibility, requiring self-denial. Above all, their duty was never to harm or exploit humankind."

"You said they were *supposed to be guardians*. They screwed up, didn't they?"

"Under the leadership of an angel named Semyaza, two hundred angels fell in love with human women. These women were mortals who had been placed under their protection."

Victor circled the rim of his glass with a finger, making it sing. "I suppose the women consented."

"How is a woman supposed to make a rational choice in the presence of such a creature—handsome, iridescent, without flaw?"

"What happened?" Victor asked, gulping the last of his wine.

Lord Faustus leaned into Victor's face. "Abomination the likes of which we cannot speak!"

"Let's not, then. You still haven't told me how Enoch earned his wings."

"First, you must break the glass," Faustus said, pointing behind the bar.

"Do what?" Victor asked.

The dark figure continued to point, now shaking his finger. "Break the glass. We never wash a glass here. It's tradition."

"Where?"

"The wall behind the bar."

Victor threw it. The glass pulverized in the shadows.

Lord Faustus continued, "The idea that a person can be upgraded from human to angel is found in other books as well. A man named Elijah became an angel, but with more fanfare—taken to Heaven in a 'chariot of fire.' Even Jesus refers to our becoming like angels if we behave accordingly."

"So how is it done?"

"The 'Rite of Abramelin' permits you to meet your guardian angel face to face. If that goes well, you move to the next stage."

"Which is?"

"The archangel Metatron holds the keys to their world. He alone would be the arbiter of such a request. You would have to formally request an audience. But remember, to these beings we are insects!"

"Metatron! I've heard that name before," Victor said aloud, chewing on his thumbnail.

"Metatron is Enoch. He's the angel who stopped Abraham from sacrificing his son, and it's believed that any who would approach God must first get through him. Magicians throughout history have paid for impudence with their souls."

"Suppose some old guy in a nursing home did the ritual…"

"It's not that easy to do. He'd have to follow a year-long ceremony including fasting, ritual bathing and close adherence to Kabbalism. Then it gets complicated."

"It already sounds complicated."

"You must also have a 'boundary occurrence' for angels to appear."

"What's that?"

"Something life-altering must happen to you. It has to tear the fabric of your beliefs. It could be anything that changes the way you think—a death, a loss or traumatic event. Angels come to us in moments like this."

"Like an old man finding out he has cancer?"

"Perhaps, if it affected him emotionally. If he lived a worthy life, he'd enter into a trance and receive instruction. This would involve a checklist of responsibilities he would have to perform."

"Like what?" Victor asked, teetering on the edge of his seat.

Lord Faustus climbed the platform. Speaking with his back to Victor he answered, "You know, good deeds. Live right and fulfill your heavenly ordained duty on earth."

"Then what?"

"You're paid in feathers."

"Feathers?"

Pinching the wool of his robe, Lord Faustus sat upon his throne. He raised the hood from his shoulders and hung it over his brow. "Be the first on your block to collect them all, and you free yourself from the endless cycle of death."

"Holy shit! It's a token economy!" Victor effused.

Faustus looked at Victor, nefariously.

"It's a behaviorist term. Collect enough poker chips and you get off the psych ward!"

Victor must have looked like he was scheming, for Lord Faustus quickly appended, "Of course, it's all metaphor."

"Yeah. Of course," Victor agreed. "Metaphorically speaking, what happens if you come up one feather short?"

"I suppose you don't get to become an angel. It's an all-or-none proposition."

"As are most things in life."

As Victor left the goth club, he toyed with the possibility of it all. Feeling the sting of his shirt, he found much needed comfort in the idea of a universe that was bigger than he had imagined. Something was unfolding. He didn't know what, but for the first time in his life he understood what it meant to have faith.

Chapter
22

VICTOR SPENT HIS LUNCH HOUR gathering blackberries in the parking lot. He sacrificed his dress shirt, reaching into leafy brambles for that one black orb that promised to be better than all the rest. He liked that the seeds wedged between his teeth, reminding him all day that there was still pleasure left in life.

Despite it being his last week at the hospital, Victor felt sad. With nothing but time on his hands after the loss of Angelita and Rubin, Violet became his personal mission. She kept having the same dream, yet the two of them were no closer to figuring out its meaning.

She had been the perfect patient—relapsing here, gaining ground there, but always evolving. Like two archaeologists, they used every precious minute to excavate her motives, thereby baring the subconscious origins of her destructive behaviors.

When she was not in therapy, Violet wrote fanatically in her journal. To this end, she came to each session toting dozens of questions—unwilling to leave with anything but answers. Sometimes serious, other times irreverent, they cried, laughed and labored their way to a deeper understanding.

Violet's life was more interesting than Victor's, and at times he got more out of her stories than she did. Her exuberance bordered on boasting—like the time the members of Jake's band covered her in sandwich meat and "ate her" for lunch. Such accounts not only gave evidence of her chronic lack of self-respect, but provided visuals for Victor's fantasies as well.

He was in danger as a clinician. With no one to talk to, he was slipping. For months he had thought about Violet every day, agonizing over the cruel twist of fate that introduced them as therapist and patient, rather than lovers.

With his residency coming to an end, he gained no peace from the idea of becoming an independently functioning doctor. Without Dr. Lindsey to steady his keel, he would have to rely upon his own integrity to stay out of trouble. Yet he no longer believed in his ability to make responsible choices. For Victor, the use of reason only provided stepping stones to immoral desires.

No loyal friend had been there for him, including his colleagues. This especially befuddled him, for in the depths of his obvious despair, no one at the office even noticed that he was depressed. The whole field of psychology seemed like a massive joke. He decided that it was his turn to enjoy life, so he pulled out his fountain pen and procured a sheet of paper:

> Dear Violet,
>
> I've always believed that without love there can be no healing. For this reason, I allowed myself to fully experience you. Much to my surprise, an extraordinary thing has happened. My heart has staged a coup.
>
> I simply cannot bear the thought of never seeing you again. The 'imperfections' you so desperately want

to shed are the very things that make you irresistible to me.

Still, I must leave this up to you, for it would kill me if I ever hurt you. So, at the bottom of this letter, you'll find my cell phone number. If you call me, I promise to tell you everything you ever wanted to know. Then there will be no difference between us, and we can be together at last!

Your friend and confidant,

~ Victor

Glancing over his shoulder, Victor grew acutely paranoid. The note seemed like it was written by someone else—one of those evil people he'd learned about in his ethics classes. His stomach tied into knots as he imagined his entire career swirling down a drain of litigation. He pictured the disappointment of his parents, and the insurmountable student loans for a degree he could never use.

Violet was late for her session, which was odd, since the bus usually dropped her off fifteen minutes early. Suddenly the telephone rang loudly, waking him from his funk. He stuffed the letter into his pocket and fumbled with the phone. Finding the cord twisted into an unserviceable clump, he stooped so it could reach his ear.

"Hello. This is Dr. Albrecht."

"Dr. Albrecht, your one o'clock patient just cancelled."

"You've got to be joking. It's our last session."

The secretary seemed annoyed, as usual. She answered flatly, *"Ms. Cain said she didn't have enough bus fare."*

"Okay. I'll take care of it," Victor snapped. Now lucid, he waited for a dial tone then punched in Violet's number from memory. After four rings she picked up.

"Hello?"

Victor spoke as politely as he could. "Hi, may I please speak with Violet Cain?"

"This is Violet," came a weak voice, as if she was just waking.

"Violet. This is Victor. In eight weeks you've never been late. Is something wrong?"

"No. Just the usual pity party."

"I was kind of hoping you'd come in today so we could say good-bye. My last day at work is Friday."

There was a pause on the other end of the line. Finally, Violet answered, *"I wanna come in, but I don't have the money."*

"You don't have two bucks for the bus? You wouldn't happen to be avoiding this, would you?"

"To be honest, Victor, I can't afford the co-pay."

"How much is it?"

"Twenty bucks."

"I'll be darned. Isn't that a weird coincidence?" Victor dumped the contents of his wallet on the desk.

"What's a coincidence?"

"The last time you were here you left twenty bucks in the chair. I have it right here."

"You asshole."

"I've been called worse by worse people."

Violet exhaled, and Victor could tell she had a cigarette in her hand. *"I'll be there in an hour. Are you free at two?"*

"Of course."

"See you then, dork," she voiced with an audible grin.

Victor immediately dialed the secretary. "Do I have anyone scheduled for two o'clock?"

"Yes. You're seeing Mr. Cortez."

"Jesus?"

"Yes. He's back, and wants to see you."

"Tell him I'm not available!"

When Violet finally arrived, she wore a headband with furry cat ears. Her face was impeccably detailed in the gothic flapper style, with a tiny spiral drawn below the corner of one eye. Her mouth sported a new piercing—a silver ring in the center of her lower lip. In her hands she carried a milkshake and a knapsack.

Never short on words, she loosed a torrent of expository. "I adore this time of year," she announced, holding the drink aloft. "The best part of autumn is Burgerville blackberry milkshakes!"

"You don't say," Victor replied, absentmindedly flipping through her chart. "Interesting that you had money for the shake," he threw in, sardonically.

Violet shrugged. "My bad. I hate this shit, Victor. I got really upset when I realized that I was never gonna see you again."

Victor looked at her unblinkingly. "There will always be pain. Suffering is an option."

"I just figured you're tired of seeing me cry. I gotta warn you, I cried all night about this. This sucks hella bad. I decided it would be better just to write you a letter."

"Great minds think alike," Victor said, jeering from his desk. "I wrote you a letter, too."

He pulled the letter from his pocket and tore it into a hundred pieces.

"Don't tear it! I wanna read it," Violet complained, leaving her chair.

"It's better this way. Why read something when you can say it?"

"Because, if you're anything like me, you're a far better writer than talker. I'm a blubbering idiot, Victor. Half the time I'm afraid of what I might say," she said, tonguing the ring in her lip. Dropping her backpack, she flopped into the chair. "So what are we gonna talk about today, Doc? I guess there's no point in bringing up anything new."

Victor loosened his tie. "Let's go over what you've learned this year."

"That could take hours!"

"Brevity is a virtue…"

"…and virtue is its own reward."

"Remember our talk on your tendency for histrionics? Less is more," Victor reminded her, rubbing his knees with nervous hands.

"Okay. I've done a lot of growing, and I feel pretty good about my future. I'm a dopeless hopefiend and I'm even talking to my mom again! I'd say *that's* pretty impressive."

"Absolutely. You not only have initiative, you have *finishiative*. You said what you meant, did what you said, and finished what you began," Victor explained, counting on his fingers.

"I'm not a quitter, you know. If I want something I always get it."

"I still smell cigarettes on your clothing. Nursing homes are filled with people who never got around to quitting."

Violet held up her finger. "Don't forget the puking! I've stopped hoarking up my food, although I think I've gained some weight," she added, poking at her belly ruefully.

"That used to be a serious problem. How do you deal with the self-loathing?"

"Whenever we feel fat, Ashley and I go to *The Pancake House* on Sandy. It was her idea."

Victor looked concerned. Chewing his pen, he said, "So you're still binging, then."

"No, no! We order iced tea and watch people. No matter how fat we think we are, there's always someone fatter at *The Pancake House*. Ashley even saw one guy have a heart attack. She tried to revive him."

"Did he die?"

"I think so. Right there in the parking lot."

"You and your crazy stories. You know, I feel good about our work together except for that dream you keep having."

Violet shook her head. "Don't sweat it, Victor. It's pretty obvious what it means. My grandpa promised to be part of my life. I don't know why he did. It really wasn't his job."

"But still, it bothers you."

"Like you said, every girl needs *one* special guy in her life—the prototype for all men to come. I suppose it never happened for me, so I still have a hollow place inside."

"Uh huh." Victor nodded, thoughtfully.

"It's a gift I'm never gonna get. I have to deal with it and move on."

"Does it still affect you?" Victor asked, weaving his fingers behind his head.

"I'm sure it does. I'm attracted to older men who are out of my reach." Her eyes sparkled.

"I understand," Victor said, watching her intently.

Her lips looked fuller and more luscious than before, stained as they were with blackberries. Saying nothing, she closed her eyes and opened them again in slow motion. Victor's breath grew shallow.

"You know me, Victor. I like kind, intelligent men like you." Violet rearranged her legs, wiping the creases from her barber pole stockings. Then she said, as if to taunt him, "There's nothing wrong with setting our sights high. We could get lucky."

Victor looked away and answered, coldly, "There's nothing wrong with that, except you're setting yourself up to be frustrated." When he felt he could mask his longing for her he caught her eyes again. "You really should thank God for unanswered prayers."

"Victor, there's something I need to say to you."

Victor swallowed hard. "You're sweating."

"Southern girls don't sweat. We glisten…" Violet tarried, staring at her boots, pensively. "I'm kinda embarrassed…"

Victor put down his pen. "You weren't embarrassed to tell me the hotdog story from the 10th grade, but you're embarrassed to tell me this? It must be pretty dicey."

Violet giggled. "It's different. More dangerous, I guess. I'm taking a risk…"

Victor was aware that patients often save the worst detail for the last session, when there's no more time to work on things. It's thought to be a passive-aggressive act—a combined wish to avoid a problem, and prolong therapy.

Victor licked his lips. "Just say it, Violet."

"I'm madly in love with you."

Victor was overcome with anguish. At last he heard the words he couldn't get Angelita to say in a year. Coming from Violet, it was beautiful poetry. He cleared his throat. "Don't be embarrassed. That's one of the most wonderful gifts a person can give."

"You knew it, didn't you?" she wondered aloud.

"I was pretty sure you *liked* me after the vampire incident." Victor's face assumed a devilish grin as he added, "But we psychologists have other ways of knowing."

"Do tell!"

"You come to the clinic with makeup on, even though you know it's just gonna get messed up when you cry."

"Suddenly I feel silly. I'm such an idiot. I always want something I can't have. This is my Edgar Allan Poe existence."

Victor spoke softly, cradling her with his words. "Never be down on yourself for loving someone. There's not enough love in the world."

"So how do you feel about me?" Violet probed, putting on the clinical air that all women possess when eviscerating the topic of love.

"It doesn't matter how I feel about you. What matters is how YOU feel about you."

"That's a cop out, Sigmund," she insisted, lifting her feet to the chair and hugging her knees. Then she spread her legs and flashed her underwear. *"Basic Instinct!"*

"STOP IT!" Victor dug his nails into his palms. "Okay, okay. I've had a lot of patients this year. Each one holds a special place in my heart. Some more than others."

"...and?"

"There *is* no 'and.' I've enjoyed knowing you a great deal. I feel blessed that you've shared my life with me."

Violet smirked.

Pressing his eyes shut, he corrected himself. "I mean *your* life. I'm happy that YOU shared YOUR life with me!"

Violet's face fell like a Jack-o'-lantern in November. Her lip quivered. Victor touched her knee. She instantly placed her hand upon his. They sat in silence together, their eyes promising a love that neither could fulfill.

Victor broke the silence. "It's perfectly normal to have intense feelings for your therapist. I'm caring. I listen. I never judge you. But believe me, whatever you think you know about me is not reality, Violet. It's a fantasy."

Violet sniffled. "What's so wrong with having a fantasy?"

"Nothing kills love like having an agenda, Violet," he said, furrowing his brow. "A dream is one thing, but a fantasy implies self-delusion. It's dangerous, and it's part of the problem that brought you to this hospital."

"I know more about you than you think, Victor Albrecht. I might be crazy, but we can smell our own. You're dark inside like me. Something terrible happened to you when you were younger. I also know that your heart's been broken."

"You do?"

Violet pointed to his desk. "You used to have a picture of some bitch on your desk and now it's not there. There's more to your story than you let on."

"You can tell all that from a picture?"

"No. I can tell because you talk about pain with authority. It's not book knowledge you've been sharing with me—it's experience."

Victor pulled on his knee. "I'm impressed."

"You talk a lot of shit about our professional relationship. What's up with you calling me at home and offering to cough up my co-pay?"

"We have a therapeutic relationship, Violet," he said, condescendingly.

"What do you think a relationship is? It's a two-way street. You've read into me, and I've been reading into you the whole time. Except that this time you've met your match."

"But you've done all the talking."

"As if talking was how people communicate," she countered, deftly.

"It's getting kind of hot in here don't you think?" Victor said. He rose from his chair and cranked open the window.

Violet looked at the trashcan. It was overflowing with paper coffee cups. Any conversation would suffice, as long as it prolonged their time together.

"Drink enough coffee, Victor?"

"I didn't know a person *could* drink enough coffee," he replied, pleased to have ended her inquisition. "I can't imagine a morning without it."

"I'm that way about making love. The sleepy smell when you roll over. Having breakfast. There's nothing better."

Victor raised his eyes and looked at his watch. It was time for them to stop. He had another patient scheduled in fifteen minutes.

With surgical coldness he announced, "Well, it looks like our time is up. We have to say goodbye now."

"Forever?"

"Forever."

"Does that mean I'm cured?"

"There are no cures. Be a student of life—a scientist."

"Can I be a mad scientist?"

"From now on, you can see your life as a series of screw-ups or experiments. It's up to you."

Violet had nothing to say, so Victor focused on the kitty ears on her headband. "Those headaches you've been having are not related to nicotine withdrawal."

"They're not?"

"No. There are two brawling cats in your head."

Violet's eyes grew wide. "There are?"

"Yes. One cat fears abandonment and scratches itself. The other cat has self-respect and ambitions. They're fighting tooth and claw!" Victor explained, swiping at the air with his hands.

"Oh no," she exclaimed, demurely placing her hands on her cheeks. "Which kitty wins?"

"The one you feed."

Violet seemed to finally understand, so Victor quickly opened the door. "Although I'm sorry to say, it's time for us to part."

"The End!" she sighed, yanking a fistful of tissues.

"Good luck to you, Violet. You're one of the most wonderful people I've ever known, in or outside of therapy."

"Please..." she said, crying in earnest. "...can I have a hug? A *real* one this time?"

"I suppose it couldn't hurt," Victor said, pretending to hesitate. He knew that she would tackle him no matter what, so he closed the door so no one could see.

Violet looked up with bottomless, dark eyes. "My grandpa once told me, 'when someone gives you a hug, you should never be the first to let go.'" Then she wrapped her arms around him so tightly that he couldn't breathe.

With his head on her shoulder, his arms found the small of her back. Feeling soft hair on his face, he filled his lungs with her scent. He drank of her as if she was a fountain in the desert, feeling her gentle heartbeat beneath soft, warm breasts as they held onto each other for dear life. When his desire became unmanageable, he pried loose.

"I thought it was up to *me* to stop!" she protested.

"I seem to recall that your grandpa was a bit of a troublemaker."

Victor opened the door and slipped into the hall, leaving her no choice but to follow. When they reached the reception area she took hold of Victor's hand.

"I left my backpack in your office."

Swooning, Victor freed his fingers. He didn't want to be alone with her for one second longer. "Go and get it," he said, exhaustedly. "I'll give the secretary your co-pay."

Violet jogged down the hallway, sniffling as she went. As sad as she was, there was an ember of joy in her heart—a spark of hope in a nest of kindling. She lifted her backpack from the floor, but stopped in her tracks. Paralyzed from disbelief, her eyes focused on a box on Victor's shelf.

It was the exact package from her dream—a gift box with a knotted ribbon! She peeked down the hall to see if anyone was coming. Finding herself alone, she returned to the shelf. She lifted the box, held it to her ear and shook it. Hearing no sound, she placed the box on the desk and untied the ribbon. Inside, she found a golden ticket.

Chapter
23

AT THE FIRST SIGN OF A CAR laboring beneath a papoose of camping gear, the God-fearing people of Gerlach, Nevada raise the gas prices. Snatching their children from the dusty road, the good folks bear reluctant witness to a convoy of aliens who make an annual pilgrimage to the Black Rock Desert.

To those who turn a blind eye to the inner child, Burning Man is a Woodstock wannabe. To those who get it, it's *Mardi Gras* on acid, an art show, a techno-trance orgy, an experiment in modern tribalism, a spiritual renewal, and a hedonistic Bacchanalia where drugs and sex are as free as the people in attendance. It's a haven for those who believe that if they beat on drums, or expose their genitals to the desert air, they will somehow reconnect with a culture that their ancestors lost.

Above all, it's a Rorschach test.

What Victor needed most was quietude, and at some point during his ten hour drive to Nevada, his journey was kissed by the divine. An hour from Gerlach, in the lunar landscape of Nevada, he began seeing other vehicles encumbered with camping gear. As night fell, the caravan became a phosphorescent serpent of taillights, slithering through the valley.

With stars in evidence such as he had never seen, the planet Mars was uncommonly bright. Orange among the Hosts of Heaven, it hung momentously in the center of his vision. The scene so eerily mimicked the star of Bethlehem that Victor turned off his music in deference to the moment. It was an archetypal trek, an ancient rite of gathering, and Victor felt himself part of the human family.

He arrived at the entrance at midnight, where he was greeted with a stranger's hug and a hearty "welcome home!" He was told to follow a plume of dust from the car ahead. The billowing silt roiled in his headlights as he faithfully pursued the taillights of the other car. By the time Victor reached his campsite, demarked only by wire flags in the broken clay, he didn't have the energy to pitch a tent. Instead, he reclined in the seat of his Geo Metro and fell asleep.

Victor woke in an oven. Dripping with sweat, he crawled from the 150 degree car and pitched his tent on the flat surface of the playa. Laying out a sleeping bag, he tried to nap, but it was like sleeping on a frying pan. So he walked to Center Camp, a large circus tent where Burners lounged away the sweltering day. Plopping onto a couch, Victor drank coffee, played with Legos and watched a marionette dance to a Cole Porter song.

Then he heard a familiar laugh. Searching a forest of dusty heads, he spied Rubin lying on a pile of pillows. Victor's heart jumped. *It's not absurd to think that Rubin might forgive me under the present circumstances. He's wearing nothing but a shirt and shoes, for Christ sake!*

When Rubin finally left the big top, Victor tracked him on the busy road—a flat band of desert silt demarked only by convention. Rubin walked into a cluster of motor homes then vanished from sight.

Victor paced the road before a sudden dust storm forced him to make a decision. Pulling a scarf over his mouth, he followed Rubin's path, and ducked into a group of tents beneath a tarpaulin shade structure. The whole thing was decorated with Tibetan prayer flags, which flapped loudly in the tempest. With no Rubin in sight, Victor walked from tent to tent, searching in the powdery torrent.

Further toward the rear of the compound, a geodesic dome came into view. Thirty feet in height, it was made from steel pipe, and covered with a parachute. It was the perfect desert home, with a Persian rug that led to a doorway. Victor heard music over the howling wind—the violin solo from Camille Saint-Saens *Danse Macabre*. Drawn by the melody, he lifted the flap and looked inside.

Rubin stood in the center of the dome, now with pants, one foot upon a case of beer. The violin was pressed between his chin and collarbone. The bow, daintily pinched between his fingers, rocked from side-to-side as he sawed the strings. His eyes were pressed closed as if the notes came at great effort.

His campmates on the carpet applauded. Victor joined in, shouting over the din. "BRAVO!"

Rubin opened his eyes and lowered the instrument. "Hello Victor," he said guardedly. "You came."

"That's a very nice violin you have."

"It's a fiddle," he said, rapping his knuckles against the soundboard. Rubin knelt and placed the instrument into its felt-lined case.

"I never knew there was a difference," Victor said, praying for the conversation to continue.

Rubin walked to where Victor stood, halting inches from his face. He looked at Victor with discernment, as if to drink him in.

Victor returned the gaze, trying to look penitent. "So what *is* the difference between a violin and a fiddle?"

"Lessons!" Rubin asserted, his façade melting into an ivory smile. He hugged Victor tightly, patting him like a dusty rug. Victor cried, so acute was his relief at Rubin's magnanimity. His tears drew lines in the silt on his face.

"Everyone! This is my *best* friend, Victor," he announced, his arm around Victor's neck. Then he turned and asked, "Where's your tent?"

"Out in no man's land, on the perimeter."

"Well, then. I guess you'll just have to bring your shit here. As you can see, we have plenty of room in our shade structure."

"Are you sure? I'd love to," Victor said, reservedly. He knew that Rubin was being very kind.

"I'm sorry we fought, Victor. Let's not do that again."

"Oh God, I agree," Victor said, zealously. He hugged Rubin again. "I'm probably the world's biggest jerk."

"No. You ARE the world's biggest jerk. But resentment is kinda like drinking poison and hoping the other person dies. I'd rather not."

By this time the dust storm had blown over, so Rubin led Victor on a walkabout. "To be honest, Victor, you're breaking up with Angelita was the smartest thing you ever did. She and I got into a huge fight after you left, and I kicked that bitch to the curb."

"Wow. You made her *move out?*"

"Not exactly. I left that dump. I got an apartment on the east side with Red and Creep. You remember the guys from the rat hunt?"

Victor scratched his head. "I thought *you* were Creep."

"Ah fuck it … whatever their names are, they're both camping with us!"

Rubin led Victor to an ice chest. He pulled out two bottles of home-brew with flip tops. Popping the cap, he offered. "Hard cider. I make it myself. Golden Delicious and a pinch of bread yeast. The last batch exploded, nearly putting out my eye."

"Here's the shower," Rubin said, pointing to a ramshackle frame on a shipping pallet. He seemed especially proud of the shower curtain—a torn bed sheet. Pointing to a ditch lined with garbage bags, he added, "This is our gray water collection facility. When the water evaporates it will be your job to scoop out the pubic hairs."

"I've noticed a lot of camps are following the spiritual theme. Does your camp have a name?" Victor wondered.

"Yeah. We're *Camp Asshole!*"

Victor smirked. "You've been drinking *a lot,* haven't you? I don't mean water."

"We've pretty much blown off that whole 'piss clear' nonsense." Then Rubin hooked his arm around Victor, unburdening himself of too much weight. "Have you ever done shrooms?"

"Shrooms?"

"Yeah, psilocybin. Magic mushrooms. Red brought a whole jar. We're gonna eat 'em Saturday before The Man burns."

Victor thought of the good times with Rubin and Angelita, and how he'd ruined it. He felt self-destructive. "Count me in!"

"Great. Let's get your tent."

Boarding a bus-sized shark whose body contained a working bar and discotheque, they rode to the edge of the playa where Victor had set up his lonely bivouac. They pulled up stakes and threw the tent over Victor's car. Once settled back at Rubin's camp, the two left for a walk.

"From space, the layout looks like a phoenix rising from the ashes!" Rubin declared. "As the days roll on this entire desert will be taken over by campers."

"Wow." Victor nodded, stepping aside so that a golf cart masquerading as a pink bunny slipper could pass.

"Once the porta-potties get here, the city rises out of the sand like a pop-up book."

Walking farther, they came across a life-sized crucifix with a living man hanging in the sun. From the silt covering the man's skin and hair, it was clear that he had been up there for awhile.

"This guy is paying for our sins," Rubin said, crossing his arms at the base of the cross.

"Why would someone do that? It looks painful."

"Books aren't the only way to learn, Victor. Burning Man is participatory."

Several minutes later they came across eight vinyl reindeer and a sleigh, fastened to the dry ground with steel rebar. A sign beckoned:

Welcome to the North Pole!

They gleefully ascended the candy cane promenade to the dome. As they lifted the flap, Victor saw three diesel cooling units on trailers. Inside, a winter wonderland had been erected, complete with real evergreens, icicles and snow! They were greeted by Santa, who served them spiked eggnog and sugar cookies. They hung out, talking to dwarves in elf costumes until they were both so drunk they could barely stand.

Eventually, their wandering took them to the base of an enormous pyramid. With the clouds tinted orange, Victor raised his chin to behold the namesake of the event—The Man himself. A seventy foot tall scarecrow with arteries and veins of neon tubing, The Man evoked an aboriginal sense of awe. Built to burn, the androgynous form was packed with paraffin bundles and fireworks.

"His head looks like a sushi restaurant!" Victor joked, referring to its tissue paper and wood lattice design.

Rubin explained, "If the playa's a church, then The Man is the altar. He's a monument to impermanence. A sacrificial goat to some, a Dionysian god to others, he watches our celebration from his mountain. Of course, some people are just here to fuck and do drugs."

He had, for once, not exaggerated. There were so many naked people that, after a while, clothing seemed out of place. With The

Man standing upon his pyre in the hazy distance, he and Rubin jumped on trampolines, rode gasoline powered horses, and tore up their knees sand skiing behind a four-wheeled yacht.

Thirsty, and with their shoe leather worn thin, they arrived at a Bedouin tent. Complete with carpet, hookah, pillows and half a dozen nude belly dancers, it was the perfect ending to the day. Before long, he and Rubin were naked on the rug, staring up at the orange and purple sky. Liberated from their inhibitions, their bodies were massaged, oiled and painted with henna. They were sent into the evening with a kiss and a gift necklace.

His body refreshed and his feet now feeling as if he was walking on clouds, Victor bent to look at the curious amulet around his neck.

"That stick figure is the symbol of Burning Man," Rubin explained.

"I feel like we're witnessing the beginning of a new religion."

"Maybe we are. Think of the dinosaurs. We know that God's changed his mind before."

Chapter
24

I F THE DAY WAS FOR SOCIALIZING, then the night was for magic. The art exhibits, camps, and floats—impressive enough in the daylight—exploded into phantasmagoric carnivals of light. While the sun slept, hundreds of fire spinners took to the open desert, soaking their *poi* in lamp oil to paint the air with flaming spirals. This occurred every night, all night, to the redundant boom-boom-boom of techno-trance nightclubs and art cars towing generators to power their colossal sound systems.

Victor had spent the week with Rubin, dancing himself to lassitude between the sun and the compacted silt. He felt he was at last coming out of a long period of depression. He was sick to death of his own thoughts and opinions, so he lingered in a state of openness. He was willing to listen to anyone who might show him how to re-ignite his soul.

So on the Saturday night of the burn, when Rubin, Snake and Red appeared with a jar of mushrooms, Victor followed them without hesitation. Burning Man had been good to him, and he had no reason to doubt his continued fortune. Reaching its climax, the city now rivaled Las Vegas in spectacle. As the entire municipality prepared for the burning of The Man, the collective anticipation became electrifying.

Bristling with excitement, Victor borrowed a torn kilt and long-sleeve top. Once they had achieved a sufficiently barbarous look with their tribal make-up, they assembled on the rug in the center of the dome. Red leaned back and dragged a haggard looking book-bag into their circle. Reaching inside, he produced a pickle jar full of psychedelic mushrooms, to which the entire company reacted as if it was the Emerald Buddha.

Staring at it for a while, they made small talk, until Rubin pulled the golden urn into his lap. He struggled to unscrew the lid. "Did you guys know that a severed head remains conscious for eight seconds?"

"Hurry up," Snake wheezed.

"Yeah, give it here," Red complained, reaching across the circle and tearing it from Rubin's arms. "I got these in Seattle. They're supposed to be really good."

Victor took a sip of beer and watched the lid come loose. "Is that honey?"

Red eyed him suspiciously. He never forgave Victor for letting the rat go, and considered him irretrievably un-hip. "It covers the taste of the mushrooms. They're pretty rancid."

Rubin then held up four spoons, warning, "One spoonful aught to be enough. So be careful."

Victor wiped the sweat from his palms as he imagined the damage that poison mushrooms could do to his liver. "You sure these are safe?"

"Why are you at Burning Man?" Red asked, petulantly.

What Victor really wanted was for Red to go first in case death was instantaneous. He got his wish.

Red swallowed, but it offered little consolation. If they were toxic it would take a while before his internal organs were destroyed.

Victor watched with trepidation as each man twisted their spoon in the amber liquid.

"Bottoms up!" Rubin mouthed with a grin. He placed the gooey spoon into his mouth and licked it clean. "Your turn," he said, sliding the jar to Victor.

With three sets of eyes fixed upon him, Victor lifted the sticky jar. *I shouldn't do this,* he thought.

"Shrink's gonna wimp out again!" Snake teased.

"Shut your pie hole, Arbuckle," Rubin parried.

"No. I want to try it," Victor asserted, driving his spoon into the mix and withdrawing a heap of mushrooms. Victor held the spoon over the opening, allowing the excess to trickle into the jar. He could see tiny chunks of the baneful fungus through the golden syrup.

Rubin cautioned, "That's kind of a lot, Victor. You sure you want that much? It's your first time."

"No, this is fine," he answered, shoving the utensil into his mouth. Victor swiped his tongue across the spoon's cold depression, curling it back and swallowing the sugary lump. Then he patted his belly. "What happens now?"

"We sit and wait," came Rubin's reply. "There's still an hour-and-a-half before the burn. Let's just hang out here."

The group sat together a while longer, discussing past psilocybin trips. Eventually Snake struggled to get up, farting as always. He'd gained weight since Victor saw him last, and rose with a kick of his foot like an elephant. "I wanna get a good spot before the Friday fucknuts get there. We should go now."

"Just wait, skinny," Rubin complained. "What if we get out there and it's not working?"

"I'm feeling it," Red proclaimed, opening and closing his fist in front of his face.

Rubin shook his head. "Already? There's no way."

"I'm telling you, I'm feeling it," Red insisted. He began slapping his own face.

Rubin looked up from the floor, his face wrinkled in annoyance. "Well, I'm not. This sucks."

"Then eat some more. Shit, man, you don't need to ask for my permission," Red vented. He tipped the jar with his foot and rolled it.

Rubin turned toward Victor. "Do you want some more?"

"Sure, why not. I'm not really sure what I'm supposed to be feeling."

Each had another spoonful and, after arguing with Red and Snake about the importance of getting to the burn early, Rubin asked them to leave. As they exited the dome he shouted after them, "Be sure you guys are at the six o'clock position or we'll never find you!"

Victor began to feel lightheaded. His thoughts took on a tingly, meditative quality, as if separated from his body by physical distance. "Something's happening to me."

"Me too. Close your eyes and tell me what you see."

Victor followed Rubin's request, but his eyelids were no longer curtains. They were movie screens! He bellowed, "I see fireworks!"

"You do?"

"Blue, green, red, yellow. Amazing!"

Rubin followed suit, and the two of them o-o-o-d and a-h-h-h-d like it was Independence Day on the waterfront.

Check this out, it's really weird." Rubin scooted himself closer so that he and Victor sat knee to knee. He took Victor's hands and massaged the palms.

"That feels incredible," Victor said. Then he burst out laughing.

"What's so funny?"

Victor pointed at Rubin's face. "Your nose is stretching. It's like an inch longer. I always knew you were a fucking liar."

Rubin clutched his face. "I'm a REAL BOY!"

They sat for a while longer, laughing and losing track of the time. As the chemicals severed the tethers holding Victor to earth, he felt his flesh melt away. He began to feel an intimacy with Rubin that he had never felt for another human being. They were two liberated spirits, mixing and melding in the ether.

"Oh yeah. It's coming on strong now," Rubin whispered. He closed his eyes and began rocking. Victor did the same, but with their boundaries obliterated, they rammed their heads together.

Both yelped, and Rubin touched Victor's forehead. "I'm sorry!"

"Don't be sorry. I'm the one who's sorry."

"No. I'm sorrier," Rubin insisted. Both of them laughed stupidly.

"Who has time for sorrow?" Victor mumbled, his voice echoing from somewhere else. Enraptured by the palate of his imagination, he massaged Rubin's forearms. His fingertips were singing.

Rubin lifted his arms to Victor's neck and began to massage him as well. "You're tense," he whispered into his lap as his head rolled from side to side. "You're always so serious, Victor."

"I never meant to hurt you, Rubin."

"It's okay. I'm an idiot."

Victor experienced an overwhelming sensation of love. A sudden appreciation for humanity exploded his heart, and the sparks fell into every part of his body. Leaning forward, he put his arms around Rubin. "I love you, man."

"I love you, too, Victor," Rubin answered, his mind awash in dopamine.

"I've never been able to say that to a guy," Victor added, sheepishly. "My dad never said it to me."

"It never was about Angelita," Rubin mumbled.

"No, it never was," Victor rejoined. "I should have respected what we had."

"I know you're confused, Victor. I'm confused too," Rubin said, short of breath. He trained his brown eyes on Victor's face.

"That's good," Victor answered. His eyes were still closed, and his torso swayed from the yaw of his befuddled nervous system.

Then Rubin took Victor by the face and kissed him.

Chapter 25

VICTOR BURST FROM THE DOME with his mouth on his sleeve. He ran faster than was safe in the dark, bounding down the silt road for several blocks. Finally winded, he stopped and bent at the waist, his elbows resting on his knees. Eventually Rubin caught up, his feet slapping at the dust.

"Motherfucker," Victor cursed, spitting on the ground.

Rubin's hands were quaking. He shouted, and his voice broke between sadness and anger. "You said you *loved* me. You're so fucking impossible, Victor."

"You're a homosexual!"

"I'm a homosapien!" Rubin said with outstretched hands.

"Stay the fuck away from me," Victor yelled. Stumbling backward, he demanded, "What the Hell is wrong with you? That's so fucked up."

"What is? That I love you? You've said it a dozen times, Victor!"

"Sssh! People will hear you!" Victor cried, scanning the street with eyes like golf balls.

"We're at Burning Man for fuck's sake! Why does an experience have to change how you view yourself?"

"Because I'm not gay!" Victor insisted, churlishly.

Rubin kicked the ground. "You say that like your relationships are healthier for it!"

"Are you for real?"

"At great cost, it seems. I'm not gay or straight, Victor, I'm just a critter."

Victor's hallucinogens kicked into high gear. With faerie bells tinkling in his ears, Victor surveyed the people on the road. They were wildly costumed with rabbit ears, butterfly wings and other outlandish accessories. When it all became too threatening, Victor closed his eyes, but could take no respite in the kaleidoscope he saw.

"Victor! Are you listening to me?" Rubin plead, unaware of his friend's unraveling grip. When Victor clutched his stomach, Rubin leapt to his aid. "Are you okay? You look terrible!"

Victor moaned, "I'm about to lose my mind. Please forgive me!"

"It's okay, friend. Should I get a Ranger?"

"No! No! I just have to get away," Victor answered, pushing Rubin. Victor fell into the undulating stream of bodies flowing onto the playa. Heading for the open desert, he yelled, "I have to go!"

Drawn by steel cables, The Man raised his arms to the sky, accompanied by the cheers of forty thousand people. When the dynamite charges detonated, fireworks rocketed to the heavens, blossoming like peacock feathers over the desert. Victor spun in shock, his face warmed by the explosion. Brilliant flames abruptly climbed the wooden structure, leaping from rib to rib until The Man was engulfed by the ferocious, crackling inferno.

Driven by the feverish blaze that consumed the bone-dry structure, the crowd went mad. The Man staged one last defiant pose— one arm thrust into the air, the other broken limply at his side. Eventually the guide wires snapped and his white-hot skeleton listed—dropping face first into the roaring pyre. A volcanic shower of sparks catapulted into the heavens, enveloping the night sky with a million orange comets.

With this spectacle, the cast of thousands ran amok. Frenzied people pushed on the tottery fire barricade until it broke. Firemen abandoned their posts. As the line breeched, a tsunami of people rushed toward the inferno, which burned with such intensity that it seemed the very sun had fallen there.

A surge of scorching heat pushed the crowd back, causing a reverse stampede. Struggling not to catch fire, Victor averted a spiraling column of dust and ash. Fueled by the updraft, the dervish spun along its erratic course. Dancing through the yellow arena cast by the dazzling flames, it finally dispersed over the crowd, releasing a barrage of scalding glitter.

Eventually, the structure beneath The Man followed him into oblivion—its grid work crashing into the embers. By this time the pagan drumming, which had been a constant backdrop, reached a manic tempo. Mesmerized, with his shoes in one hand, and his eyes clamped shut, Victor danced in time with a thousand unknown friends.

One pair of feet, diminutive and ornamented with bobby socks and plastic Mary Janes, had managed to follow Victor all day. The young woman skulked and shimmied through the crowd, jumping at times to see, but patiently waiting to make her move. When the time was right, she stepped into the clearing. From there, she giggled as Victor shook his dirty, windblown hair to the rhythm of goat-skin drums.

Victor opened his eyes and saw her—a rag doll in a four-pleat skirt with blueberry Popsicle streaks in her hair. "VIOLET?"

She held her hand to her mouth. "Victor! What a small world!"

Victor seized her by the hand and roughly led her to the dark edge of the ecstatic throng. It was cold and dark away from the fire. "What on earth are you doing here!?!"

Violet's Catholic schoolgirl outfit made a mockery of her guilt. She pinched and twisted her fingers. "I've been a bad girl."

"Yes you have!"

"I saw the coffee cups in your office trash can. If there's one thing I understand, it's addiction, so I waited at the Center Camp coffee bar."

Victor found it difficult to be angry. He tried to sound serious. "In other words you followed me!"

"Stop being a sour puss," she said. "I always wanted to come to Burning Man. Knowing you were here was an added bonus!"

"Are you stalking me?"

"Oh, please, Victor, if I'm not mistaken your definition of love and insanity are surprisingly alike."

"They *are* alike!"

"That's what makes it so exciting!" she said, clasping her hands between her knees.

Victor hesitated too long, so Violet filled the void. "Listen. It's obvious that we need to fuck, and what better place to have a romance than here?"

Victor was about to retort, but began shaking instead. With a cadaverous pallor, he folded his arms across his stomach. Then he fell to one knee in agony.

Violet squinted. "Dude, are you tweaking?"

"No, I'm fine..."

"Tell me the truth. Are you high?" she inquired, placing her hand on his forehead. With concern, she added, "You're sweating."

"I had mushrooms. It was a big mistake. I'm okay if I keep dancing."

"There's a metaphor for life. Wait. You did shrooms?" she asked, pointing with her lollypop. "That's rad!"

Victor moaned. "I'm seeing shit, big time. Whenever you move, I see streaks of color."

"Holy cow, my therapist is trippin'!"

"When you put it that way I feel so much better."

Violet put her hand on his neck. "I think you've overdosed. You have goose bumps. Can you walk?"

"Where are we going?"

"Back to my camp. I've seen this before," she claimed, lifting him to his feet. "Here, put your arm around me."

Victor leaned on her, heavily.

"You shouldn't have this kind of reaction." Walking toward the Esplanade, Violet explained, "Some people put LSD on pizza mushrooms. I think you got gypped. Where'd you get 'em?"

"Seattle."

"You did Puddle City fungus? Oh Victor," she teased, squeezing his hand. "You have so much to learn. This time I get to take care of you, okay?"

Victor tried to speak, but retched instead. Then his world turned black.

Regaining consciousness, he found himself in Violet's bed. It was a cot, covered with blankets. From the lack of music he deduced that it was early morning. Violet had undressed him, and judging from the freshness of his skin, given him a sponge bath as well. Pretending to sleep, he watched her through his eyelashes. She moved about the tent in the lantern's glow, folding her things as she sang to herself.

His heart jumped when she raised her hands to untie the bows in her hair. For a precious moment, he imagined what it would be like to be her husband. She shook out her braids and, kneeling before her duffle bag, removed her blouse. As the last button popped on her cotton shirt, a black bra appeared. She reached behind and unhooked the clasp. Victor's breath hitched as the lace fell away—her nipples standing in the chill.

"You slept three hours," she said, softly. Violet unscrewed the cap on a bottle of water. "Drink. You're dehydrated."

Victor drank liberally. "I've had the strangest dreams," he said, speaking to the roof of the tent. "I'm still seeing stuff."

"Like what?"

"Things moving in the corners. Colorful sparkles." Turning on the pillow so that he could see her better, he added, "angels."

Violet blushed.

"What have you been up to?" he asked.

"Watching you sleep," she admitted, her eyes smoldering. Turning her back toward him she casually threw in, "You shouldn't do drugs. They're bad for you."

Victor watched in awe as she slid her fingers into the waist of her skirt. When she pushed it to the floor, her panties went with it. Her denuded figure turned in the shadows, and Victor noticed a jewel in her bellybutton.

"You take my breath away," he said, weakly. "All I ever wanted was a woman who cared for me, and here you are."

"I feel the same," she echoed, drawing the sheet. "Can you make room for me in there?"

Victor closed his eyes. It had been so long, and she so perfect. He sat up and rested on his elbows. It was the hardest thing he'd ever done.

Turning down the lamp's flame, Violet insisted, "PLEASE lay down, Victor. It's my turn to give YOU something. All I have is me."

Victor ignored her plea. Exhaling, he swung his feet to the floor of the tent. He twiddled with his hair then let out a sigh of exasperation.

"No, Violet," he said, standing. Then he draped a blanket around her body. "I work for you, remember?"

"Well you're fired! Please, Victor…"

"It's time for bed," Victor said, forcing her to sit. The cot connected with the back of her calf, and she fell into bed. Once supine, he tucked her in. Using his hand as a wedge he reached around her body, shoving the fleece beneath her until she was tightly wrapped in a loving cocoon. Sitting on the edge of the cot, he stroked her cheek.

Violet protested, meekly. "What happens at Burning Man stays at Burning Man. I swear!"

Victor's eyes reflected the lantern's flame. "I'm not saying that I don't *want* you. Oh Lord, that's not it. It's just that I love you *too much*."

"Oh Victor," she said with resignation.

Victor searched in the shadows for his clothes. Then he sat again. Touching her hair, he whispered, "I want to tell you a bedtime story."

Violet understood where this was going. She sank into her pillow as the tension left her body.

Wiping the creases from the blanket, Victor began. "Once upon a time there was a beautiful fairy princess. Her father was a brave king, but the battles he'd fought left him with many injuries. Not wanting to be a burden, he kept his wounds to himself until, one day, he died from them."

"That's sad," she said, shrinking beneath the blanket until it rested on the bridge of her nose.

"Yes, it is," he said, nodding. "Especially since he wanted more than anything to be worthy of so wonderful a daughter. But sometimes bad things happen, so the queen was left to care for her family alone."

Victor paused to take a drink of water. "It's very hard to be a queen, and she made a lot of mistakes. You see, the queen knew that if her daughter was to rule someday in a dangerous world, she would have to be strong. I'm sure she did the best she could."

Violet cooed.

"Anyway, as all children do, the princess felt responsible for her father's death. This made her so sad that she lost the will to live."

"What did she do?"

"Well, the court wizard, being a kind old man, taught her magic!"

"Magic?"

"Yes. And she used that magic to summon an angel. It was her hope that the angel could teach her how to live again, and the two of them became close friends. Luckily for her, the angel knew of a spell that could give her the power she'd lost! But for the spell to work, the angel had to vanish, for if he stayed, the princess would never know if the power was her own."

"Did she live happily ever after?"

"I've no doubt."

"You're that angel, Victor," she said, blinking tears.

"And you are truly that princess. But it's time for me to do my last trick. You need to pay attention, because I can only do it once."

"Why?"

"Because it's a *disappearing* spell. The way it works is that you must close your eyes and count to ten. When you open your eyes again I'll have vanished from your world forever, but not from your heart."

The blanket rose at Violet's neck then fell again. "I love you so much."

Leaning over her, he kissed her on the forehead. "Good. Then the spell will work. Keep pure your highest ideal, and strive ever toward it. If you meet a man who can't appreciate those things that I find so irresistible, know that he's not worth your time, and move on."

"Okay. I promise."

"I will always believe in you, Violet Cain. Now believe in yourself." He waited for a minute, listening for the voice of his muse, and when there was nothing more to say, he added, "I suppose now would be a good time to start counting."

Violet covered her head with the blanket and counted aloud, each number floating down a sweet river of tears. And when she pulled the covers from her face, Victor was gone.

Chapter

26

HUFFLING PAST THE GLOWING MOUNTAIN of embers in that darkest time before the dawn, Victor forgot even his own name. The drumming by the fire had long since given way to a more sublime enchantment. Now folk singers, lotus sitters and guitar strummers tended the dying ashes. Silhouettes only, they hugged one another and spoke in hushed tones. Victor thought they were ghosts, beckoning him to walk into the brimstone. He could no longer carry the pain, and for the first time in his life he understood why people take their own lives. Running into the fire would be a perfect act of self-denial.

Victor clenched his fists and stepped toward the searing heat. Then he panicked and bolted for the open desert, recklessly throwing his body headlong into the pitch black emptiness. He ignored the pain of his blistered feet until self-immolation became a distant possibility. Winded, he fell down, tearing his knee on the crust of the playa. His feet were destroyed from a week of walking, and his socks stuck to the open blisters. With nothing left to give, Victor rolled onto his back and cursed the heavens.

"Come and get me, you bastard! I give up!" he swore at the dappled rim of the Milky Way. Laying there by the trash fence, disavowing the instinct to live, he saw a luminous mirage on the horizon. Thinking it another hallucination, he rubbed his eyes. The blue incandescence remained.

What's that rattling sound?

Eventually the object emerged from the darkness in glowing neon. It was a person on a rickety bicycle, wearing a pair of cardboard angel wings. Covered with strips of toilet tissue and electroluminescent wire, the wings were strapped to the back of a vivacious, young, blonde woman. When she finally reached him, the blue-eyed seraphim gripped the handlebars, squealing to a stop.

"Hay-lo," she said cheerfully, dropping her foot from the pedal. It crunched the gravel near Victor's face, and he smirked at seeing a slender ankle in a stripper's pump. Above her painted toenails, a tuft of white feathers shimmied in the breeze. Victor said nothing.

"I said Hay-lo! It's a pun, get it?" Her eyebrows drooped in the light of a cockeyed halo. "Someone's forgotten how to laugh. Looks like I got here just in time!"

"Get lost!" Victor mouthed, "I'm trying to kill myself."

"That's silly, you could die doing that."

Straining to sit up, Victor looked her over. She was wearing a white bathrobe. It fell open, revealing white lingerie. She wore stockings and garters with tiny bows.

"You're an unusual angel," he said, from the corner of his mouth.

"That I am," she answered, placing her hands together. Flapping her fingers, she added, "No two are the same. We're like snowflakes."

"Did you make those wings?" he asked, out of politeness. He pulled off his boot and cradled a foot.

"Heck no, they were a gift. Although it's funny how gifts can feel like burdens."

"If you say so," Victor mumbled.

The girl continued. "I don't normally pick up people I don't know, but you called. Do you want a ride or not?"

"No. I didn't call anyone. I want to be alone."

"You seem like the kind of guy who's alone in a crowd."

Victor's forehead bunched up. "To be perfectly explicit, I don't feel like explaining myself to you."

The girl smiled. "You're pretty smart, huh?"

"So I'm told."

"You need to be careful. To be more explicit, all that brainy stuff isn't going to save you. *You* wanna lose your mind and come to your senses!"

"Who the fuck are you?"

"That's a silly question. I'm an angel, see?" She rocked her body so that the cardboard wings flapped.

"Well I'm a devil, so get lost!"

"Heavens to Betsy! Reality check on isle six, six, six!" she quipped, speaking into her hand like a microphone.

"Why are you mocking me?"

"I do things just for the *heaven* of it."

"Cute."

"I tried to stop myself," she said glibly, touching her lips.

"Look, you're a pretty girl, but you're starting to irritate me."

"That's good. True words are rarely pleasing, and pleasing words are rarely true." Dropping her hand from her mouth she pointed at Victor. "I know! Maybe you need someone to talk to."

"It's doubtful."

"What makes you so sure?"

"Because I'm the world's biggest liar!" Victor blurted.

"Nah. I know an angel who lies *way* more than you."

"That's nice. But unless you're a *real* angel I have no use for you."

Resting her chin on her knuckles, she offered, "I have an idea. Why don't you *pretend* that I'm a real angel? I mean, a person doesn't have to be a shrink to be helpful. All they need to do is listen with love."

"What?" Victor said. "I just want to die! I want to go into the light and be done with it."

"You don't have to die to do that." Her luminous blue eyes locked with his. "Look, Victor, whatever you did, it's not your fault."

"Fuck off!" Victor cried, now weeping into his hands. "You're making me crazy!"

"Don't fight it. Some people need to be sane. Guys like you *need* to get crazy. It's not your fault."

"Stop it!"

This time she sang it. *"It's not your fault!"*

Victor began to shake as his façade of rationalism crumbled. He bawled for several minutes before threading together four horrible words.

"I murdered my brother," he finally confessed, hiding his face. "Oh God! I killed my little brother!"

"My goodness!" the girl exclaimed, lowering her kickstand to join him on the ground. Her bike fell over anyway. She shrugged, then put her arm around him.

"I didn't want him to die! I just wanted him to fall through the ice!"

"I'm trying to understand, but you're talking too fast. Your brother fell through the ice?"

Victor clutched her terrycloth sleeve. "I *told him* to ride his bike on a frozen lake. He didn't want to, but I made him feel bad. He looked up to me. I *knew* there was thin ice. I wanted him to break through, but I thought I could rescue him!"

"Why would you do that?" she asked, batting her eyelashes.

"I wanted my dad to think I was a hero!"

"A hero?"

"Dad didn't love me. Do you understand what that does to a boy?"

"You don't think he loved you at all?" she asked, lifting his hand. She folded his fingers and kissed his knuckles.

"If he loved me I had no way to know." Victor stopped to catch his breath. His face grew dark—his eyes darting. "My little brother was some kind of super genius—talking by six months, doing math by age three. My father forgot I existed!"

"You didn't remind him?"

"It wasn't my job! We weren't alike. I wanted to create beauty and art. I wanted to dream—all the shit he was too small-minded to encourage. I wasn't gonna be a blue-collar slave like him! I knew back then I was destined to become a philosopher—a GOD!"

"Careful there," she said, raising her finger. "It's a big job. You don't want it."

"I just wanted him to be proud of me. I've spent my entire life trying to prove myself to that son-of-a-bitch, and all they talk about is Kurt. I have a Ph.D. for crying out loud and STILL they have *his* fucking picture on the mantle! He's been dead for over twenty years now, and they keep his room like a shrine!"

"A-h-h-h-h, so it wasn't an accident. You actually *hated* your brother."

Victor looked at her with terror in his eyes. "Oh yeah, I hated him. I plotted against him. But I planned to save him that night, I swear. I even put a sled next to the boathouse so I could pull him out of the water!"

"So what happened?" she asked, watching as he re-traumatized himself.

"He was gone..." Victor said with crazy eyes, as if his own life had followed his brother to the bottom of the lake. Then he chewed his thumbnail. "He must have gotten tangled with his bike."

"Are you sorry?"

"Haven't you been listening!?!"

"What I mean is, are you sorry for *him*, or just yourself?"

Victor cried again, his hands trembling. "I'm just a human being, right? I can make a mistake can't I? It was a FUCKING MISTAKE—a horrible god-awful mistake that's cursed my entire life!"

"You still feel that guilty," she said.

Victor lowered his voice. "It's worse than that! I know it sounds crazy, but I'm chased by the Grim Reaper! He's behind me everywhere I go. Everything I touch turns to shit. Everything I love dies, passes away, or is forbidden from me. He's always on my heels!"

"Then stop running."

"Look at my feet. The race is over."

"I think I can help," she said, standing to dust off her palms.

Victor watched her dig through the basket of her bike. When she turned around with a tube of red lipstick in her hand, his anguish gave way to curiosity.

"Kneel right here," she said, pointing at the ground.

Victor complied, resigning himself to her whimsy. He crawled to where she stood and kneeled on the balls of his feet. Then he looked up at her, as if waiting for communion.

"Are you sorry for hating your brother?" she demanded, lording over him.

"I'm sorry I killed him."

"A-h-h-h, that doesn't matter," she said, dismissing him with a wave. "Six in one, half-a-dozen in the other, it all evens out in the end." Repeating herself, she said, "I asked if you were sorry for *hating* him."

"Yes, of course," Victor answered, sniffling. "I'm sorry about so much I don't know where to start. I've been a judgmental ass my whole life. I KNOW the world is amazing. There's so much beauty. I want to see it all, share it all, and for the first time I'm open to it!"

"There you go! So you don't wanna die anymore?"

"No!"

"You sure? I want you to say it like you mean it!"

"Hell no! I WANT TO LIVE!"

"Good enough," she said matter-of-factly, pulling the cap from the lipstick. Victor watched her with crossed eyes as she drew a bright red 'x' on his forehead. Admiring her artwork, she licked her finger and fixed a smudge with her pinkie. Then, with surprising authority for a girl of her stature, she bellowed, "THE ANGEL OF DEATH SHALL PASS OVER YOU!"

"Thank God!" Victor shouted exuberantly, falling backward onto the playa. "I never want to see that ugly face again!"

"UGLY? Careful buddy," she said, fixing her hair.

Victor didn't answer, but instead looked into the diamond sky. There were things to work out with his parents, but he was proud of his treatment of Violet. He loved Rubin, and knew that they would be friends again. The dread that had been his companion for decades had vanished. At last his heart knew the meaning of peace.

"Now don't wash your face till you get back to Portland," she warned.

"Don't worry, I won't," he promised, cheerfully. "You know, you're really good at helping people. I should know. I'm a great psychologist!"

Kneeling down in front of his face, she pinched his cheek. "No, Victor. You're a great *person!*"

She watched him for a minute then got up and zipped her pack.

"And you're a great person too, um, I forgot your name," he said, sitting.

"It doesn't matter what we call ourselves. It only matters how we act," she said. Then she tossed her purse into the wire basket and straddled the bike. With a portentous wink and a ring of her bell, she straightened her halo and rode off.

Remembering that he was stranded with blisters on his feet, Victor shouted, "Hey, i thought you were gonna take me with you!"

She didn't stop, or even slow down. Instead, she pedaled her bike in a wide circle. As the clay crunched beneath her tires, Victor heard her say, "I just promised not to!"

He smiled over her nonsensical ways, and those ridiculous tissue wings. Eventually she vanished among the twinkling lights of the nomadic city, which was domed by a purple morning sky. And as she slipped into obscurity, Victor thought about all the things she'd said. Taking her words to heart, he dusted himself off and began the long walk home.

"I want to be an angel,
And with the angels stand,
A crown upon my forehead,
A harp within my hand."
URANIA BAILEY

Chapter 27

"YOU MIGHT AS WELL SHUT OFF YOUR ENGINE. You're gonna be here a while. There's been an accident about a mile up the road," said a man in dreadlocks, pointing toward the hills.

"What happened?" Violet asked, her arm resting against hot steel. Ashley leaned into her lap from the passenger seat, anxious to hear the news.

"I'm not sure. From what I heard a bunch of bikes untied from the roof of an RV and crushed the car behind it."

"Oh no! Did anyone get hurt?"

"My friend called me on her cell. She said the driver made it, although his head was all bloody." Dropping a hacky sack on his toes, he began kicking the tiny bag of sand.

"Heavens to Betsy! He must have good karma," Ashley said, twiddling her blonde hair.

Thus the narrow road to Oregon was rendered unusable for the better part of an hour. This left Violet, Ashley and several hundred Burners stuck in the desert with nothing to do but smoke cigarettes and make sculptures out of rocks.

Violet bent the rearview mirror, capturing her face. For the first time since breaking up with Jake, she actually *liked* the person she saw. Putting her hands to her necklace, she gently stroked the feather that Victor had given her.

When the traffic finally moved again, they lurched past the accident scene. A white Geo Metro sat upon a swath of broken glass. Behind the policeman waving them on, orange-vested men surveyed the wreck—a pile of bicycles stuffed through a sagging windshield. Violet wondered how the driver could have survived, but was happy he did.

When she arrived in Portland, she made some heady decisions about her life. Among these was the conviction to return to college to study psychology. Her grandfather had left her a small trust, and by winter semester she'd moved back home to enroll in classes at the community college. Of course, she still fought with her mother, but with her sights set on bigger dreams, she'd lost interest in winning.

One day, Violet's mother strolled into the kitchen and handed her a year's worth of mail—a stack several inches thick, bound with a rubber band. Dropping her book bag on the kitchen table, Violet poured a glass of iced tea. Reaching the bottom of the pile, she found a letter from her grandfather, dated from a year before. She grabbed her purse and snatched the car keys from the junk drawer.

"Mom, I'm going to the graveyard!" she shouted as the the screen door slammed.

Violet was already in the car when her mother appeared on the porch. "I made you peanut butter and jelly!"

"I'm not hungry."

"Are you sure you know where the headstone is, honey?"

"Yeah. It's where daddy's buried," Violet yelled. Her tires spit gravel.

It wasn't far—less than a couple miles down Red River. With her windows rolled down, Violet coasted over the crushed rock until she reached the back of the graveyard. It was a pretty day, sunny and hot, so she parked in the shade of a gargantuan oak tree. After locating a row of tombstones with Stars of David, she found one for Efron Cain.

Sitting on the grass, she pulled the pedals from a wildflower. Tears came easily. When she finished weeping, she opened the letter:

My Precious Violet,   23 October 2002

For the first time words don't come easily. I know that this letter will be scrutinized for some sign that I'd grown feeble-minded. The nursing home staff already thinks I'm crazy.

By the time you get this letter I will have taken my life. I can see no reason to go on living like this, if living is what you'd call it. I'm in too much pain, and the medicine they give me no longer works. But that's not why I'm writing.

When you were a little girl, you were afraid that I would abandon you in the same way your father did. My work took me away from you, but I remember telling you not to worry, for if I died I would become an angel and watch over you. I've discovered that it's not such an easy thing to accomplish. To be honest, I've come up one feather short.

What if my blood failed to fulfill its cosmic design? The result would be leukemia, the very thing that threatens my life. How is this different from an artist who won't paint, a gifted child who refuses school, or a grandfather who doesn't show up for his granddaughter? All of these things are forms of cancer.

I'm sorry. I know you could have used my guidance over the years. As with all those who face their final hour, tonight I stand closer to God than ever before. So I've used this opportunity to pray that you'll someday know the unconditional love of a man. Have faith that, in the battle between this request and the falling axe of time, my love for you will be the victor.

Forever Yours,

Grampoppy

When she finished reading, she rolled the letter into a taper and produced a clove cigarette from her purse.

Holding it to her nose, she deeply inhaled its saccharin aroma before pinching it between her lips. She found a lighter, lit the taper and touched it to the cigarette. As it burned, the letter folded toward the fire—curling and breaking away in tiny shards of ash. When the flames licked at her fingers she let it go.

Rising to leave, she stopped. Her face beaming, she returned to the grave. Her fingers found the feather necklace at her throat. She tugged, and as it snapped, her prayer beads scattered over the marble headstone.

"This should make for a full set of wings."

www.ingramcontent.com/pod-product-compliance
Lightning Source LLC
Chambersburg PA
CBHW071309170626
46809CB00001B/390